Praise for

# A TOWN CALLED SOLACE

National Bestseller
Longlisted for the Booker Prize
Shortlisted for the OLA Evergreen Book Prize
Named a Best Book of the Year by
*The Globe and Mail* and *The Daily Telegraph*

"This deftly-structured novel draws together the stories of three people at three different stages in life, each of whom is grappling with loss. We were captivated by *A Town Called Solace*'s beautifully paced, compassionate, sometimes wry examination of small-town lives." —2021 Booker Prize Judges

"A lovely, gentle novel with edge." —*Saga Magazine* (UK)

"Lawson's writing is clear and emotive. . . . [A] poignant novel." —*The Telegraph* (UK)

"Lawson's books are a pleasure to read—they conjure a space where quiet reflection and owning your past mistakes bring gentle rewards; they feel kind and wise and brimful of empathy." —*The Times* (UK)

"*A Town Called Solace* keeps you breathless with anxiety, then relief and finally even joy." —Ferdinand Mount, author of *Kiss Myself Goodbye: The Many Lives of Aunt Munca, The Observer* (UK)

# A TOWN CALLED SOLACE

## MARY LAWSON

Vintage Canada

Published by Vintage Canada, a division of Penguin Random
House Canada Limited, Toronto, 2022. Previously published in
hardcover in Canada by Alfred A. Knopf Canada, a division
of Penguin Random House Canada Limited, Toronto, 2021.
Distributed in Canada and the United States of America by
Penguin Random House Canada Limited, Toronto.

Vintage Canada and colophon are registered trademarks.

www.penguinrandomhouse.ca

LIBRARY AND ARCHIVES CANADA CATALOGUING IN PUBLICATION
Title: A town called Solace / Mary Lawson.
Names: Lawson, Mary, 1946- author.
Description: Previously published: Toronto: Knopf Canada, 2021.
Identifiers: Canadiana 20200273957 |
ISBN 9780735281295 (softcover)
Classification: LCC PS8573.A9425 T69 2022 | DDC C813/.6—dc23

Cover design by Kelly Hill
Cover art by Jeremy Miranda
Back cover texture by Isla Fraser

Printed in Canada

2 4 6 8 9 7 5 3 1

Penguin
Random House
VINTAGE CANADA

For Alex and Fraser

# One

# CLARA

There were four boxes. Big ones. They must have lots of things in them because they were heavy, you could tell by the way the man walked when he carried them in, stooped over, knees bent. He brought them right into Mrs. Orchard's house, next door to Clara's, that first evening and put them on the floor in the living room and just left them there. That meant the boxes didn't have necessary things in them, things he needed straight away like pyjamas, or he'd have unpacked them.

The boxes were in the middle of the floor, which made Clara fidgety. Every time the man came into the living room he had to walk around them. If he'd put them against a wall he wouldn't have to do that and it would have looked much neater. And why would he bring them in from his car and then not unpack them? At first Clara had thought it meant that he was delivering them for Mrs. Orchard and she would unpack them herself when she got home. But she hadn't come home and the boxes were still there and so was the man, who didn't belong.

1

He'd driven up in a big blue car just as the light was starting to fade, exactly twelve days after Rose ran away. Twelve days was a week and five days. Clara had been standing in her usual place at the living-room window, trying not to listen to her mother, who was talking on the phone to Sergeant Barnes. The phone was in the hall, which meant you could hear people talking on it no matter what room you were in.

Clara's mother was shouting at the policeman. "Sixteen! Rose is sixteen years old, in case you've forgotten! She's a child!" Her voice was cracking. Clara put her hands over her ears and hummed loudly to herself, pressing her face against the window until her nose was squashed flat. Her humming kept breaking up into short bursts because she had trouble breathing when her mother was upset and she kept having to stop and gasp. But humming helped. When you hummed you could feel the sound inside you as well as hearing it. It felt like a bumblebee buzzing. If you concentrated on the feel and the sound you could manage not to think about anything else.

Then there was a scrunching noise, louder than the hum, the noise made by wheels on gravel, and the big blue car rolled into Mrs. Orchard's driveway. Clara had never seen the car before. It was fancy and had what looked like wings at the back and it was light blue. At another time, a safe time, Clara might have liked it, but this wasn't a safe time and she wanted everything to be exactly as it had always been. No unfamiliar cars in driveways.

The engine stopped and a strange man got out. He closed the car door and stood staring at Mrs. Orchard's house. It looked just like it always had; it was painted dark green with white window- and doorframes and there was a big wide porch with a grey-painted floor and white railings. Clara hadn't given much thought to how the house looked before, but now she realized that it matched Mrs. Orchard perfectly. Old but nice.

The man walked over to the porch, climbed the steps, crossed to the front door, took some keys out of his trouser pocket, unlocked the door and went inside.

Clara was shocked. Where had he got the keys? He shouldn't have them. Mrs. Orchard had told her there were three sets of two keys (one for the front door and one for the back) and Mrs. Orchard had one, Mrs. Joyce (who came in to clean once a week) had another and Clara had the third. Clara wanted to tell her mother, who was no longer on the phone, but her mother sometimes cried after speaking to the policeman and her face got all red and blotchy and it frightened Clara. And anyway, she couldn't leave her place at the window. If she failed to keep watch for her, Rose might not come home.

A light came on in Mrs. Orchard's hall—the glow of it spilled out onto the porch for a moment before the man closed the door. It was getting quite dark inside the house. The living room of Mrs. Orchard's house was right next to the living room of Clara's house and both had windows at the side, facing each other, as well as at the front, facing the road. Clara scooted across to the side window (so long as she was at one of the windows, Rose wouldn't mind which one), arriving just as Mrs. Orchard's living-room light came on and the man walked in. Clara could see everything that happened and the first thing was that Moses, who'd been hiding under the sofa (he always hid there if anyone but Mrs. Orchard or Clara came into the house), shot across the room and out of the open door at the other end so fast that he'd disappeared before the man was fully through the doorway, so the man couldn't have seen him. He would have gone into the mud room, Clara knew, and from there out into the garden. The mud room had three doors, one to the living room, one to the kitchen and one to the garden, and the garden door had a cat flap at the bottom. "He skedaddled," Mrs. Orchard would have said. She was the only person Clara had ever heard use the word "skedaddle."

Clara herself had been in the mud room an hour or so earlier to give Moses his dinner. She allowed herself to leave her place by the window for a little while morning and night because she had promised Mrs. Orchard she would look after Moses while she was in the hospital. Rose would understand.

"He'll be happy with you here," Mrs. Orchard had said. "He trusts you, don't you, Moses?" She'd been showing Clara the mysteries of the new can opener. It was electric. You had to hold the can in the right place to begin with but it did everything else itself, it even turned the can around, slowly and smoothly, as it cut off the lid.

"A gadget," Mrs. Orchard had said. "Mostly I don't hold with gadgets but that old can opener isn't safe and I don't want you cutting yourself." Moses was winding himself around their legs, desperate for his dinner.

"You'd think we starved him," Mrs. Orchard said. "Now then, the can opener leaves the lid behind—do you see? It's magnetic. Be careful not to touch the edges of the lid when you pull it off the magnet. You have to pull quite hard and the edges are very sharp. Keep the can in the fridge until it's empty and then give it a rinse and put it in the garbage outside, not in here or it'll smell. Mrs. Joyce will deal with the garbage when she comes to clean. I've spoken to your mother and she's happy for you to come in and feed him twice a day for the duration. I won't be away long."

But she had been away long, she'd been away weeks and weeks. Clara had run out of cat food several times and had to ask her mother for money so that she could go and buy some more. (This was before Rose disappeared, when everything was normal and Clara could go wherever she liked.) She'd expected Mrs. Orchard to be more reliable, and was disappointed in her. Adults in general were less reliable than they should be, in Clara's opinion, but she'd thought Mrs. Orchard was an exception.

She could hear her mother moving about in the kitchen. Maybe she was feeling better now.

"Mommy?" Clara called.

After a minute her mother said, "Yes?" but her voice sounded choked up.

"Nothing," Clara called quickly. "It's OK."

The man was moving around the house, switching lights on—Clara saw their pale shadows outside on the lawn. He didn't bother to switch them off when he left a room. If Clara or Rose had done that, their father would call, "Turn off the light!" But now Rose wasn't here. Nobody knew where she was. Clara's mother kept telling Clara that Rose was in Sudbury or maybe North Bay and she was fine, they just wanted her to come home or phone or send them a postcard because it would be nice to know she was OK. Which meant that her mother didn't actually know if Rose was fine. And which was why she shouted at the policeman because he hadn't found Rose yet.

With so many lights on in Mrs. Orchard's house it was getting hard to see anything outside. You couldn't see much in Clara's own living room either, but she didn't switch on the light because then the man would have been able to see her. If you're in the light you can't see people who are in the dark, but if you're in the dark you can see people who are in the light. Rose had told her that. "You can stand a foot from the window," Rose had said, "and they'll never know. I watched Mrs. Adams getting undressed the other night. Completely undressed! Naked! Her panties and her bra and everything! She has great big rolls of fat all over and her breasts are like enormous flabby balloons! It's gross!"

The man was back in the living room, looking at the photographs on Mrs. Orchard's sideboard. There were lots of them, all in frames. Some of the frames were silver and others were plain wood. Two of the photos were of Mrs. Orchard and her husband when he was still alive, one with them sitting side by side on a sofa and the other of them standing on some steps, and in both of them Mr. Orchard had his arm around Mrs. Orchard. There also used to be a photo of him on his own, leaning against the door frame of a house (not this house) with his hands in his pockets and smiling at the camera. It must have been a beautiful house because there were flowers climbing all over the wall beside him. Mrs. Orchard talked to that photo as if it was Mr. Orchard himself, still alive and in the room, Clara had heard her many times. She didn't sound sad, just ordinary.

There had also been a photograph of Mr. Orchard standing beside a little boy. The boy was sitting at a table eating his breakfast; you could tell it was breakfast because there was a jar of Shirriff's marmalade on the table—Clara could just make out the label. Mr. Orchard had a tea towel folded neatly over his arm and a platter heaped with food (Clara had studied it closely and decided it was sausages and bacon, which would fit with it being breakfast) rested on the tea towel. Mr. Orchard was standing very upright and stiff, looking down at the little boy, who was looking up at him and grinning a huge grin. Clara had asked Mrs. Orchard if the boy was her son and Mrs. Orchard had said no, they hadn't had any children, he was a neighbour's son, but she and Mr. Orchard had loved him very much. Is it your favourite photo? Clara had asked, and Mrs. Orchard smiled at her and said they were all her favourites. But Clara suspected that wasn't true because Mrs. Orchard had taken that photo plus the one of Mr. Orchard in the flowery doorway with her when she went into hospital, Clara had noticed they were missing straight away. If you were only going to take two photos you'd take your favourites.

The strange man had stooped over now and was examining the photos. "Don't touch any of them," Clara whispered fiercely, but as if he had heard her and was being deliberately disobedient he immediately picked one up. Clara's fingers clenched tight. "It's not yours!" she said out loud. He was studying one in a wooden frame. From its location Clara thought it might be the one of Mr. and Mrs. Orchard together but she wasn't sure—it might have been the one of Mrs. Orchard's sister, Miss Godwin, who had lived alone in the house before Mrs. Orchard had come to live with her, and who had died a few years ago.

The man put the photograph back on the sideboard with the others. He stood for a minute more, looking at them, then turned and went out of the room and out of the house.

Clara ran back to the front window—you could see Mrs. Orchard's driveway more clearly from there. For a moment she thought he was leaving but then he went around to the back of the car, opened the trunk and lifted out one of the boxes. One after another he unloaded them, two from the trunk and two from the back seat, and took them into Mrs. Orchard's living room and put them on the floor. At first Clara had the encouraging thought that they might be full of things for Mrs. Orchard (though what would she want that was so heavy and took up so much room?) and having delivered them he would now get back into his car and drive away. But instead he did something that wasn't encouraging at all: he took out a suitcase.

She ate her dinner standing at the window. She hoped her father would come home before her bedtime so that she could tell him about the man next door, but then she remembered: he was at a teachers' meeting at the school and wouldn't be back until late. So she finished her meal, said a silent goodnight to Rose, wherever she might be, and a real goodnight to her mother, and went upstairs. She'd rather have stayed at her post all night but going to bed was part of the bargain her father had worked out when Clara had started her window vigil ("vigil" was what her father called it), a week after Rose disappeared.

That second week was when Clara started feeling the cold, dark shadow of fear stealing over her. Fear that something had happened to her sister. "I can look after myself," Rose had said to her up in their room before she left. "You know that, right?" Clara had nodded miserably, watching Rose as she whirled around, grabbing bits of clothing from the floor and the cupboard and stuffing them into her school bag. It was true: Rose was smart and she was tough. Clara did know that, just like she knew that Rose was beautiful and funny and always in trouble with either their parents or the teachers (to their father's shame, because he was the history teacher at the school) because she really, really hated being told what to do. Clara also knew that when Rose was angry with their mother she said things she didn't mean, such as that she was leaving home and not coming back. She had left home at least twice before and each time she'd come back after a couple of days when she decided she'd scared their mother enough. That had always been her goal, something else Clara knew. Rose ran away to punish their mother.

But this time felt different; Rose had never before said to their mother, "You will not see me again. Ever. That is a promise." Rose took promises seriously. And she'd always screamed her threats before, whereas this time she spoke quietly, almost softly, which frightened Clara more than the screaming. The kitchen had seemed to smoke with her rage.

It hadn't even started out all that big a row—Rose had merely broken her curfew again—but the argument grew into a fight about whether or not their mother could tell Rose what to do, which Rose said she couldn't. Their voices went back and forth, getting madder and madder, until finally their mother said, "While you live in this house, young lady, you will do as you are told." Which turned out to be the wrong thing to say.

"You mustn't worry about me," Rose had said to Clara, up in their room, pausing with her favourite T-shirt scrunched up in her hand. "Promise you won't worry," she said sternly. She had tons of eyeliner on. Rose always wore loads and loads of makeup—the palest foundation she could find, almost white, with thick black eyeliner, black mascara, green or blue eyeshadow (this time it was green) and lipstick so pale it made her lips disappear. One time she'd drawn a black tear on her cheek. She dyed her hair pitch black and then peroxided the tips till they were like yellow straw and backcombed it all into a huge beehive. "I look like death," she'd said once, sounding pleased, examining herself in the bathroom mirror. "Don't you think I look like death?"

"I think you look beautiful," Clara had said, which she did. Rose was the most beautiful person in the world.

"But where are you *going*?" Clara asked now, watching her sister pack. "Where will you *sleep*?" Her throat was aching with the effort not to cry. Rose hated it when she cried. "When will I see you again? How will I know you're OK?"

Rose had hesitated. "I don't know the answers to those questions yet," she said finally. "But I'll get a message to you somehow. I don't know how and I don't know when, but I will. So look out for it. But you mustn't tell Mom and Dad about it when you get it, OK?"

She studied Clara for a moment, chewing a fingernail—the fact that she chewed her nails was the one thing about herself that Rose hated. "Don't ever start," she'd said to Clara once. "If you start biting your nails I'll kill you. Promise you won't."

Then she brought her hand down from her mouth and added, more gently, which was unusual because Rose wasn't the gentle sort, "When I've found a place of my own you can come and stay with me. We'll have the best time ever! We'll go out every night until really late and I'll show you *everything*!"

She smiled and Clara tried to smile back but her mouth was quivering too hard and she couldn't, and Rose suddenly looked stricken. She stuffed the T-shirt into her bag, tossed the bag down on the bed, came and wrapped her arms around Clara and rocked her gently from side to side. "I love you to pieces," she said into the top of Clara's head. "I love you to bits. Promise me you'll never forget that I love you to bits."

"I promise," Clara said, almost choking, because she'd lost the battle with tears. But Rose didn't get impatient with her like she usually did, just hugged her harder for a long minute. And then she left.

It was true that Rose could look after herself. Once, Ron Taylor had come up behind her and reached around and put his big fat hands on her small breasts and Rose had broken free and hit him in the face so hard with her school bag that she gave him a nosebleed. Clara had seen it with her own eyes. If Rose said she'd be OK, she'd be OK. So, at first Clara didn't worry about her safety, she just worried about when she'd come home. But after a week, worry stole up on her. It wasn't just that a week was more than twice as long as Rose had ever stayed away before; it was her mother's increasingly frantic state and her father's awful pretense that everything was all right. What if there were dangerous things out there that Rose didn't know about? Obviously her parents thought there were or they wouldn't be so worried.

Clara kept imagining she saw Rose. Eight days after Rose left Clara was walking home from school, counting steps (she had to count a hundred footsteps in a row as many times as she could all the way to school and all the way home again or Rose might not come back) and just as she was about to turn in to her own driveway she thought she saw her sister in the woods across the road. The land over there had never been cleared, it was just bush and it went on being bush for hundreds and thousands of miles. Sometimes deer appeared, grazing right up to the roadside, and from time to time a bear ambled out and wandered curiously through everyone's yards so that people were afraid to go outside. But on this day, just for a second, Clara thought she saw a splash of red—exactly the same red as Rose's jacket—within the darkness of the trees.

Sergeant Barnes and the townspeople had searched the woods already, of course; they'd searched everywhere for miles around. But Rose might have outsmarted them; she might have gone miles away to start with, and then when everyone had given up and gone home maybe she'd come back.

Clara waited, holding her breath, her eyes searching the trees. Nothing moved. Very quietly, as if Rose were a deer and might be frightened away, Clara crossed the road and stood at the very edge of the woods. "Rose?" she called softly. There was no sound. No movement. "Rosie?" she called again, and started walking, slowly, carefully, into the woods. Suddenly there was another flash and a red-winged blackbird flew out of a tree and disappeared.

So it hadn't been Rose in the woods. But Clara couldn't shake the feeling that it had been related to her. Maybe in some mysterious way it was a message.

That was the night she started her vigil at the window. When her mother came into the living room to say dinner was ready Clara informed her that she wouldn't be sitting at the dining table for meals anymore. Also, she wouldn't be going to school. Not until Rose came home.

Her mother didn't understand.

"Why can you leave the window to feed the cat but not to eat your own supper or go to school?" she'd asked, her hands against her cheeks as if she was holding her head together.

She sounded nearly desperate, which made Clara feel nearly desperate, because she couldn't think how to explain. She had to feed Moses and spend time with him because she'd told Mrs. Orchard she would; and she had to stay at the window the rest of the time or she might miss Rose, or a message from Rose. Who knew what form the message would take? At first Clara had expected that it would be a note, or perhaps a postcard that was supposed to be from someone else and only Clara would realize that it wasn't. But maybe it wouldn't be anything like that. If Rose *had* come back and was hiding nearby, she might want to speak to Clara and find out if this was a good time to come home, and if Clara wasn't watching she might miss her. But how could she say that to her mother without giving Rose away? Her mother would phone Sergeant Barnes and everyone would start searching the woods again, and Rose would run away for good and never be seen again.

"I'm waiting for Rose to come home," she said finally, not looking at her mother.

"Sweetheart," her mother said. "I know you're missing her, Daddy and I are too, but standing at the window won't bring her home. Please come and eat your dinner properly. I can't deal with this as well …" There was a catch in her voice, she was right on the edge of bursting into tears. Clara's body forgot how to breathe. She felt so dizzy she might have fallen down if her father hadn't come in.

"What seems to be the problem here?" he asked in the abnormally normal voice he'd used since Rose disappeared. Clara couldn't look at him because his face frightened her as much as her mother's. It wasn't blotchy with crying; instead, it had a cheerful look pasted on like a mask that didn't fit properly.

Her father couldn't stand arguments. If people were arguing he had to sort it out, he couldn't help himself. He'd wade right into the middle of it ("wade" was Rose's word). "Whoa there," he'd say, making soothing, patting motions with his hands. "Let's cool things down a bit, see if we can find a compromise." Or, "Let's see if we can strike a bargain. Who wants what, let's start with that." It drove both Rose and their mother crazy (according to Rose, being infuriated by him was the one and only thing she and her mother had in common). He waded in at school too,

Rose said, and it made people want to kill him. But in fact he was pretty good at it, at least in Clara's opinion. All problems had solutions, according to her father; it was just a question of finding them, and he always did seem to find them in the end.

The family rows were usually—in fact, always—between Rose and her mother. Clara hated arguments as much as her father did and anyway, up until now she'd never had anyone to argue with. Rose was never mean to her and Clara was so anxious not to upset her mother that she never did anything wrong. So this was the first time she'd been on the receiving end of one of her father's interventions. She was grateful for it.

Her mother was not. "Would you get out of here!" she said to him furiously. "Would you keep out of it for once!"

But he wouldn't. Or couldn't. And he did sort things out, though it took a while. The bargain he came up with was that if Clara went to school as usual and went to bed at the normal time, then for now she could have her meals in the living room or anywhere else she liked, standing at a window.

"How will she eat?" her mother had asked, her voice shrill. "There's no space for a table."

"We'll put the plate on the window sill," her father said gently.

"It will fall off! Look at the sill. It's too narrow! The plates are too wide! There will be food all over the floor, do you want her to eat off the floor? Why are you making such ridiculous suggestions?"

"We'll put the food in a small bowl," her father said, more gently still. "Let's try it at least, Di, see if it works."

"Would you stop patronizing me, please? I am your wife, not your child! And would you just stop *pretending* ..." Clara's mother stopped in the middle of the sentence and left the room.

But putting Clara's supper in a bowl worked just fine, and from then on—apart from night time, school time and feeding/keeping-Moses-company-time—Clara spent every minute of the day at one window or the other, watching for Rose.

Clara had a bedroom of her own but she only used it to store her clothes. Ever since she was tiny she'd wanted to sleep in Rose's room (it had two beds), and Rose had let her. Sometimes Rose even let Clara sleep in her bed with her, though Clara was nearly eight now and it was a bit crowded. It was the best thing ever. Clara tried to stay awake so she could enjoy the feel of Rose beside her, feel Rose's warm breath on the back of her neck, but she always fell asleep too soon.

At bedtime on the day the man arrived next door, after cleaning her teeth, getting into her pyjamas, folding her clothes and placing them neatly on the chair in her own room in the right order for putting them on again in the morning, Clara went back to the room she and Rose slept in, gathered up Rose's clothes from the floor, and hung them in the cupboard where they belonged. Then she got out some different clothes, dropped them on the floor beside Rose's bed, and messed them up as thoroughly as she could with her feet.

The contrast between their sides of the room was a kind of joke between them: Rose, in her own words, was "a natural-born slob," whereas Clara was a natural-born neat-freak. She'd been born tidy. "*Extremely* tidy," Rose used to say, teasing her. "*Worryingly* tidy." Rose's side of the room was always a complete dump. Their mother had given up shouting at her about it. If she wanted to live in a pigsty that was up to her, their mother said, and she certainly wasn't going to tidy up for her. Rose had considered it a major victory.

The night that Rose left, Clara had put all her sister's things away, thinking it would be nice for Rose to walk into a tidy bedroom when she came home so she could mess it up again. It had been a mistake. The room had looked so wrong Clara couldn't sleep, so after a while she got up and took some of Rose's things out of the cupboard, and scattered them on the floor. After that she changed the jumble every night so that if Rose crept back under the cover of darkness everything would be the way she liked it.

Now Clara climbed into bed and curled up on her side, thinking about Rose and wishing she'd come home, and thinking about the man next door and wishing he'd go away, until the two things somehow became one and she fell asleep.

In her sleep, she saw Rose wandering alone through the dark. She was moving very slowly and her feet were bare. At first she had her back to Clara but then she turned around and looked at her, and smiled. It wasn't her normal smile, though. It was the smile of someone who was trying very hard to pretend she wasn't afraid.

# Two

# ELIZABETH

Martha's holding forth again. I can't figure out what she's talking about but whatever it is she thinks it's disgraceful. She was ranting this morning when Nurse Roberts was doing the rounds, taking our pulses and temperatures. Nurse Roberts said (winking at me across the gap between our beds), "I agree. It's an absolute outrage. Shouldn't be allowed. Just stick this under your tongue for a sec, OK?"

She's very patient with us—most of the nurses are, but Nurse Roberts in particular. A lovely girl.

Martha shouted, "Show a little sense!" at whoever was inside her head and the thermometer shot out of her mouth and onto the coverlet. Nurse Roberts picked it up and wiped it with a tissue and said, "I'll try. Tell you what: you keep this under your tongue for two minutes and I'll try to show a little sense. How's that?"

You'd have fallen in love with her on the spot, dear one. (Nurse Roberts I mean, not Martha. Definitely not Martha!) You were always falling in love with pretty young women, particularly if they had something between the ears. I didn't mind in the least.

Actually I don't mind Martha as much as I did to start with. For the first few days I was here her babbling and shouting nearly drove me crazy but you get used to things. Now I find it kind of interesting, trying to figure out when she's completely out of her mind and when she's not. Sometimes she's quite lucid.

No one ever comes to see her. But then, no one comes to see me either. My few surviving friends no longer drive. When Diane heard I had to go into hospital she said she would bring little Clara to visit but I told her not to. It's a fearfully long drive and the roads are shocking, I didn't want anyone to feel they had to do it. Though to be honest I regret it a bit now. I didn't think I'd be in here so long and I didn't realize how endless the days can be.

But I have you, my love, so I'm not complaining. You and Moses.

A visit from Moses would be diverting. Everyone on the ward would be leaping out of bed, trying to cuddle him.

I've been worrying about him. The cat food must have run out weeks ago. Diane will have bought more if Clara alerted her (which she will have), but what will happen to Moses if the worst comes to pass and I die here? Clara will want to adopt him but Diane is allergic to cats so she just plain can't. I spent half the night worrying about it. Silly.

I can't tell you how I long for home. Just the normal routines of the day; they're what I miss most. Putting the kettle on. Perhaps having a little chat with Clara

21

if she pops over after school. I enjoy our conversations very much, you never know where they're going to end up. She doesn't make my heart lift the way Liam did, but no other child has ever done that.

Clara is one of two: her older sister is going through the rebel stage and leading their parents quite a dance, but Clara herself is a sweet child. No, sweet isn't the right word. Interesting, occasionally endearing, but not sweet. For a start she was born skeptical. I've known her from day one and virtually as soon as she was old enough to ask a question, she doubted the answer. She'd say, "What's that?," pointing at the toaster, and when you replied that it was a toaster and its job was to crisp up a slice of bread she'd look at you sideways, as if to say, "Pull the other one." From a three-year-old it was really very funny, but now she's nearly eight and it has grown with her, sometimes it's almost alarming. When I told her I had to go into hospital, she said, "What for?," as if she suspected me of malingering. I said my heart wasn't behaving quite as it should but it was nothing serious and I wouldn't be away long. She said flatly, "How many days?" I said I wasn't sure, maybe a week or two, which she thought about and then said, "Will your heart be fixed then?" I said I hoped so. That was clearly not a satisfactory answer; she wanted a yes or a no, none of this prevarication. I swiftly moved the conversation on to forestall questions about death. I asked if she would feed Moses for me and spend a little time with him each day so that he wouldn't be lonely, and she nodded firmly, once, and said, "Yes."

Then she said, "Will you be lonely?" which surprised me. I hadn't credited her with much empathy or imagination. I said probably not, because in hospitals there are lots of people around. She considered this and eventually decided it passed muster, though to be honest, my love, it made me suddenly fearful in a way I hadn't been before. Having lots of people around doesn't mean you aren't lonely. I decided to take the picture of you and Liam with me as well as the one of you in Charleston—those two photos in particular always cheer me up. They are standing side by side, slightly angled, on the little cabinet beside my bed here. I can reach them just by stretching out an arm.

Nurse Roberts thinks you're very handsome. I told her she had good taste.

Back to Clara: I'm not the reason she spends so much time at my house, of course. I don't fool myself on that score. It's Moses she comes to see. He likes her (which is rare, he's a suspicious cat) and even lets her stroke him from time to time. She doesn't try to pick him up, which is wise, he wouldn't like that. Mostly she just squats on her haunches and watches him, while he squats on his haunches and watches the hole in the baseboard behind which lives The Mouse. Moses has a long-standing thing going with the mouse. He'll sit watching the hole by the hour, his demeanour one of casual unconcern, the only giveaway being the occasional impatient twitch of his tail. Every now and again there will be a small movement behind the hole, the suggestion of a whisker. I've wondered if it could be deliberate

23

provocation on the part of the mouse—perhaps he has subverted the natural order of things and is playing "mouse and cat"? Moses will go rigid with hope and then crouch, flattening himself, tensed for takeoff. Clara crouches too, head and neck forward, determined not to miss a second of the drama. I don't know what outcome she is hoping for. I daren't ask.

I miss her. If I had to choose one visitor, she is the one I'd choose.

Liver for lunch. I hate liver. And I don't think it's tactful serving offal to patients whose own innards might be causing them distress. But there was apple pie and ice cream for dessert, which was some consolation. Not enough apple, of course, but the cook is good at pastry and it was beautifully sweet. You know they say that the elderly develop a taste for sweet things? It turns out to be true.

Meals are the only thing we have to look forward to in here. They must know that, so why don't they make a little more effort?

I had a nap after lunch and woke up to the realization that if I could only have one visitor, it would not be Clara I would choose, much as I enjoy her company. It would, of course, be Liam. You would be here already so it would be the three of us, just as it used to be.

*

Another day. Tuesday, I think, not that it makes any difference. I had a fall this morning. I imagine you would say it serves me right. They told me not to get out of bed on my own, just to call for one of them, but I needed to visit the toilet and there was no one around and things were getting urgent, so I decided to try. And straight away my legs collapsed under me and I was on the floor. Martha must have been having a lucid moment because she said, "Oh goodness!" and threw back her blankets and started scrambling to get out of bed herself. I suppose she thought she was coming to rescue me, which was nice of her, but silly, she's in much worse shape than I am. In two shakes she was on the floor as well. Then someone across the ward started shouting and the nurses came flying in and there was a great commotion for a few minutes until the two of us were safely back in bed. I whispered to Nurse Roberts that I still had my business to do and she whispered back that she'd get me a bed pan, and I said crossly, not whispering, that I didn't want a bed pan, I hated bed pans, I wanted to use the toilet like a civilized human being, and she sat on the edge of the bed and took my hand and said gently, "Not today, Mrs. Orchard dear. Not today, when you've had a fall. Let's wait until we've got you a little steadier on your feet."

It's hard to be furious with someone so nice, but I was.

I'm an old nuisance. I hate it. There's no point to life when you're nothing but a nuisance to people.

*

Martha was raving again in the night. Shouting, possibly at the same person as last time. Telling him or her to grow up. I wondered who it was, so this morning I decided to ask her. Nosy of me, I know, but the days are so endlessly the same you have to exploit every possible diversion. Otherwise, regardless of the ailment that brought you here in the first place you'd end up dying of boredom.

It was breakfast time and we were all propped up on our pillows. Martha was eating Shredded Wheat. The nurses cut it up for her but not small enough, there are always bits of it sticking out of her mouth like a horse eating hay, except that horses don't have milk dribbling down their chins. In fairness, it's hard not to dribble when you're in bed. You can't sit properly upright, something to do with your legs being out straight. Also, Martha's teeth don't fit. They wander around her mouth, I'm sure that doesn't help. The nurses tuck a towel round her neck to act as a bib and it's always soaking wet.

"Who are you so mad at?" I asked.

She turned her head and looked at me. "Wha"?" she said, through her mouthful. You can tell a lot about people by the way they eat and I can tell you Martha's mother was no great shakes when it came to table manners. My manners are beyond reproach, I'm glad to say. As were yours; yours were absolutely impeccable. You seldom spoke about yourself, my love—in fact never, unless you were really pushed—so I know very little about your childhood, but I do know that you were exceedingly well brought up. (Is that true of the English generally, I wonder, or is

26

it a matter of "class"? I've never worked out how your class system works or where you fit into it. Though you went to boarding school so I suspect there was money somewhere. In my opinion the practice of sending young children off to boarding school is absolutely barbaric, but we'll leave that for another day.)

"You were shouting at someone in your sleep," I said to Martha. "I wondered who it was, that's all."

She chewed some more. Seemed to be thinking about it. Swallowed two or three times, her skinny old neck making elaborate contractions like a snake swallowing a golf ball.

"Janet," she said at last.

"Who's Janet?"

"My sister."

"What did she do that made you so mad?"

"Threw herself at men, one after another. Finally ran off with a sleazy, lying ..."

After a minute or two, when she added nothing more, I said, "Did she sort herself out, eventually? Was there a happy ending?"

"No," she said. "There was not."


A child born out of wedlock—that will be what happened to Janet of course. A disgrace, a stain on the family name. A bastard. An unwanted child.

An "unwanted child." The words, the very thought, seems to me a blasphemy.

*

Bedtime. The nurses on night shift have arrived. There are just two of them at nights. They sit at a desk in the middle of the ward with the light they use for reading shielded with a towel so that it doesn't disturb us. Judging by the snores, some of the patients seem able to sleep the night through, which I find astonishing. I seldom get more than a couple of hours.

But you keep me company, my love. I go back to a particular day, or a particular moment, generally not a dramatic one, just something normal. Our "normal," during the brief period when Liam was part of our lives, was the greatest joy I have ever known. Last night, for example, I dredged out a very simple memory from that time: I was in the kitchen preparing a late-night snack for the two of us (we had eaten supper very early with Liam, who was now asleep on the old camp cot at the foot of our bed). I was unable to open a jar so I took it into the living room to ask for your assistance and found you so deeply absorbed in your book (something thrilling to do with parasites or a new blight affecting wheat, no doubt) that it seemed wrong to drag you out of it.

That was the miraculous thing. Having that glorious child asleep in our room felt so natural, so right, that you could lose yourself in a book and I could make a snack.

Anyway, I didn't want to interrupt you so instead I held the jar down low enough that you would be able to see it out of the corner of your eye, and waited; and sure enough, after a long, long moment, your left hand slowly rose to take it from me, and your right hand let go of the book, your elbow dipping down to prevent it from closing, and then—still reading—you twisted off the lid of the jar, leaving it sitting loosely on top, and slowly, slowly passed it back up to me. I said, "Thank you, dear one," and after such a long time that I had given up and headed back towards the kitchen, I heard you say vaguely, from an entirely separate segment of your brain, "It's a pleasure."

That memory kept me happy all night long. "It's a pleasure."

# Three

# LIAM

After he'd brought in the boxes and taken his suitcase upstairs there was still a bit of light in the sky so he decided to walk into the centre of town and see what it had to offer. The answer was not much. There were two streets at right angles to each other, one running north-south, parallel to the lake, the other running east from the lake for a couple of blocks before petering out altogether at the edge of the woods. Apart from some small farms, a new-ish secondary school all on its own in the middle of a field, a sawmill and a lumber camp a couple of miles out of town, that was it: Solace, Northern Ontario, as of September 1972.

Liam had driven through forest for six hours that day. He was city-born and -bred, and in his opinion there were just too many trees up here. The reds and golds were blazing their way across the hills but beneath the gaudy colours, when you got close up, the forest floor looked ominously dark. If for some reason you managed to fight your way a couple of yards into it you'd be swallowed up and never see daylight again.

The stores, ranged along the two main streets, consisted of the basics plus a couple of extras aimed at the tourists. There was a small grocery store with a liquor store tacked on the back as if hiding from the authorities, a post office, a bank, a fire station, a Hudson's Bay store with parkas and snow boots in the window already. A sports outfitter with a window full of fishing tackle stood next to a squat little blue-painted souvenir store with a window full of beadwork and stone carvings beneath a sign saying, *Indian and Eskimo Art*. Most of the pieces had three-figure price tags and a couple had four. There was a notice taped to the door saying the store was closed but would open again next year.

Set back from the road was an old church graced by a couple of maple trees, and beside it was an equally old primary school. Both looked too big for the town's needs. They'd be relics, Liam guessed, of the long-ago days when the North with all its riches looked like the place to be if you wanted to get ahead. Nowadays, apart from the lumber, it was probably only the tourists that kept the place alive.

On the road leading away from the lake there was a hardware store, a small, ugly, modern library, two bars, one of them with a police station right next door, a drug store and two cafés. Liam realized he was hungry at the same time as he realized both cafés were closed. In fact—he looked about him—everything was closed. Not only that, there was no one, not a single soul, on the street. Apart from a couple of dogs sniffing round outside the cafés he was on

31

his own. He looked at his watch: just after seven. Just after seven on a Thursday evening and the place was a ghost town.

For an irrational moment he wondered if his brain was making the whole thing up; not just this lonely northern town carved out of the wilderness but everything: Fiona, the past eight years, his so-called career, his life. Several times in the course of the day's drive he'd become aware that he wasn't concentrating: he felt dazed, he hadn't been sleeping well and had a dull, persistent headache. From time to time he'd had the sensation of things slipping, a dizziness, as if inside his head things were sliding down a steep hill. On the drive he kept telling himself it was tiredness and he told himself that again now. Go back to the house, he thought. Find something to eat and go to bed.

On his way back, just to complete the picture, he took a detour down to the lake and stood for few minutes looking out over the water, its smooth, clear surface reflecting the last light from the sky. It was uncannily quiet. Still just visible, the distant shoreline was ragged with bays and inlets. All it needed, Liam thought, was a moose coming down for a drink and he'd be standing in the middle of a travel ad. He hunched his shoulders—it was cooling down fast— and headed home.

Mrs. Orchard's house—his house—was on the last side road at the northern end of town. He'd left the lights on downstairs when he went out and now he stood in the darkness of the street, studying it. He guessed it was about the same age as the church and

32

the school, Victorian probably. It was made of wood, which made sense given the number of trees, and was substantial and well-proportioned. Property wouldn't be worth all that much this far north, but added to the money Mrs. Orchard had left him it would still be a significant windfall. At the very least it would buy him some time to think.

He'd stay for a couple of weeks, he decided now, climbing the steps of the porch. Consider it a holiday. If he was lucky the good weather might last into October. Whatever happened, though, the minute he saw the first snowflake he'd put the house up for sale and leave. He had no wish to experience a northern winter. It was bad enough down in Toronto.

He was glad he'd left the lights on. When he'd walked up to the front door this afternoon he'd had a curious feeling that it was about to open and Mrs. Orchard would be standing there, smiling a welcome, looking exactly as she had looked the last time he'd seen her, which was … what? Thirty, thirty-one years ago? Something like that.

He closed the door behind him and then paused, thinking he'd heard something, a sound so faint it was hardly more than a stirring of the air. But there was nothing. He waited, listening. Nothing. Imagination working overtime. He glanced into the living room—all was as he'd left it.

He went into the kitchen, filled the kettle and switched it on, then went around the house closing curtains—something he had never done in all his years living in cities with people walking past six feet from the door. The rooms had a stuffy smell; in the morning he'd open the windows and air the place out.

In the living room there was a television—practically an antique: he switched it on and flipped through a series of grainy channels until he got the news. He didn't care about the news, he just wanted something to dispel the silence. He turned up the volume and went back to the kitchen to look for something to eat. All the usual things were in the cupboards: flour, sugar, salt, Salada tea, instant coffee, cans of Campbell's soup, cans of tuna, a can of peaches; nothing he wanted. On the counter, though, there was a large glass jar with a tightly fitting cork stopper, half-full of cookies. He pulled out the stopper and sniffed. He remembered the smell: they were oatmeal, not his favourite as a kid—those, which she'd made every time he came, were chocolate chip—but she and Mr. Orchard had always had the oatmeal ones and the smell of them now made him smile. It was a connection with them and with the past; it made the present situation feel a little less strange.

He opened the refrigerator and studied the contents. Mrs. Orchard must have had a clear-out before going into hospital because there were no obvious perishables like milk or meat or fruit. There was a jar of salad dressing, one of marmalade, an almost empty tub of margarine, and a package of cheddar, growing mould, which he slung into the garbage bag under the sink. The bag was empty; either she'd emptied it just before she left or the woman who cleaned for her had come in some time afterwards. There were a dozen eggs—experimentally he cracked one, recoiled at the smell, cracked them all and flushed them down the sink, an unexpectedly difficult job requiring much stabbing and rattling round with a fork.

Eggs were the sort of thing you'd buy in readiness for coming home if you thought you'd only be away for a few days. He saw Mrs. Orchard in his mind's eye (the woman in the photos on the sideboard, but older), scrambling the eggs, eating them at the little kitchen table, or maybe in the other room, watching the TV, as he intended to do, relieved that her ordeal in the hospital was over. He wondered when she'd realized she wouldn't be coming home.

He made himself a cup of coffee, added two teaspoons of sugar to make up for the lack of milk, and took it plus the jar of cookies into the living room. For an hour he chain-ate slightly stale cookies and watched fuzzy images waver about on the TV. At ten o'clock he went upstairs. He identified Mrs. Orchard's room (the one that looked lived-in), left it undisturbed and chose one at the back of the house for himself. He put his suitcase on a chair and rummaged around for his toothbrush. He brushed his teeth in the cracked basin in the bathroom, and went back to his room.

The bed was made up, which was a relief; he took off his clothes, left them lying where he dropped them, and got in. He lay for a minute, suddenly aware of his own exhaustion, then switched off the bedside light, closed his eyes and instantly became prey to all the thoughts he had been fighting to keep at bay during the long drive north. The slow, relentless disintegration of his marriage, the decision to split, the months of increasingly savage disputes over the house, and the final, never-to-be forgotten evening, back at what once had been home, to decide the division of possessions.

*You take it, you always liked it more than I did.*

*It was your birthday present, I bought it for you. It's yours.*

*I don't want it. Take it or junk it.*

Books, records, ornaments—the Greek vase, souvenir of that long-anticipated, once-in-a-lifetime holiday, which had been riven from arrival to departure by quarrels and resentment. Bed linen, cutlery, the dinner service. Fiona wrapping crystal wine glasses (a wedding present from her favourite aunt) in newspaper—wrapping so fast, so hard, that the stem of one of them snapped. Her scalding tears. A marriage drawn and quartered, piled into cardboard boxes, seven of hers, four of his, in the middle of a living-room floor.


After a while he gave up trying to sleep. He switched on the bedside light, got out of bed, and searched in the zipped pocket of the suitcase for the letter from Mrs. Orchard, written eight years ago and rediscovered in the back of a drawer when he and Fiona were dividing up the wreckage. He sat on the bed, took the letter from its envelope and spread it out on his lap.

*Dear Liam,*

*You may scarcely remember me; your parents moved into the house next to ours in Guelph when you were three years old and you were still only four the last time we saw you. But for that brief spell you played a very big role in both my life and that of my husband, Charles, so I thought that I should write to you now.*

*Charles died three months ago, at the beginning of March. I would have written to you earlier but I was a little bit low after his death. He had appendicitis and needed surgery and in the course of the operation there was a problem with the anaesthetic which resulted in his death. On the chance that you do remember him, I thought you would like to know of his passing.*

*You will see that I am no longer living in Guelph but have moved to Solace, in Northern Ontario. My eldest sister lives here and she kindly invited me to come and live with her.*

*I don't know if you will receive this letter—I'm sending it to the last address Charles had for your father, which was some years ago. I simply write to you in hope, and out of gratitude for the joy you gave Charles and me.*

*My dearest wish is that you are well and enjoying your life, Liam. I think of our times together often, and they make me smile.*

*My love to you, always,*
*Elizabeth Orchard*

He folded the letter, put it back in its envelope and placed it on the bedside table. He dimly remembered both Mrs. Orchard and her husband; they'd been good to him and he'd spent a lot of time at their house. He remembered huge distress once when leaving them, presumably to do with saying goodbye when his family moved to Calgary. Though wouldn't he have been too young to know it was the last time he'd see them?

He'd reread the letter at least half a dozen times since rediscovering it, but now, sitting on a bed in Mrs. Orchard's house eight years, one broken marriage and one jettisoned career after it initially arrived, he recalled another bit of emotional freight associated with it: when it had come, he and Fiona had been in the process of sending out wedding invitations, and it had precipitated a row between them.

Both of them had recently found jobs in Toronto; good jobs—Fiona was a lawyer, Liam an accountant—earning decent money and sure to earn more. What with moving from Calgary, buying a home and getting married, there was a lot to do, so Fiona (the organized one) suggested they divide the major tasks between them. Among other things, Liam chose to deal with the purchase of the house; among other things, Fiona chose to plan the wedding.

Being the organized one, when there were tasks concerning the wedding that only Liam could do, such as the writing of invitations to his friends and family, Fiona scheduled the time when he was to do it. That night was the time.

The letter had been waiting for him on the hall table when he got home from work. His name was on the envelope but it had been sent to his father's address at the University of British Columbia with the words *please forward* printed neatly on the front. There was no sender's name or return address and he didn't recognize the handwriting—a beautiful, slanted, slightly old-fashioned script. Puzzled, Liam opened it, saw Mrs. Orchard's name at the bottom of the letter, and was instantly transported back thirty years.

He'd read it then and there, standing in the hallway. The news of Mr. Orchard's death upset him more than seemed reasonable even to him, seeing that for almost thirty years he hadn't given either of the Orchards a thought. But the letter suggested that he'd been important to them and he had a profound sense, standing there, that it had been mutual. He decided to reply immediately.

"Where's the writing paper?" he called. Fiona was in the kitchen getting supper. The deal was: she cooked, he washed the dishes.

"Top drawer, left-hand side of the desk."

He found the paper and a pen, took them into the kitchen, sat down at the small, round Formica table and began to write.

*Dear Mrs. Orchard,*

*I have just received your letter and I am very sorry to hear …*

He screwed up the page and started again.

*Dear Mrs. Orchard,*

He paused.

"You're using the wrong paper," Fiona said. She was breading pork chops, dipping the pieces in a bowl of beaten egg, then coating them in crumbs.

"What?" he said, glancing up.

"That's ordinary notepaper. The paper for the invitations is pale blue."

"This isn't a wedding invitation. I'm replying to a letter. It's just come—it's from a woman I knew when I was a kid. Her husband's died."

"Oh. That's a shame."

He went back to the letter. He wanted it to be good—he wanted it to be filled with memories of Mr. Orchard, things he could tell Mrs. Orchard that he enjoyed looking back on. The problem was, his memories were so vague they were scarcely more than an impression.

"Maybe you could do it when you finish the invitations," Fiona said. "Then you'd be able to concentrate on it."

"I want to get it off to her straight away," he said absently.

"You can still do that. But if you do the invitations first there won't be any time pressure, so it'll be easier."

"There isn't any time pressure now. This is fine."

*I remember the fun we had ...*

He screwed up the paper. Then straightened it out again—he'd use it to rough out a draft.

"I really think you should get the invitations out of the way first," Fiona said.

"I want to do this first. It's important."

The wrong thing to say; he knew it the minute the words were out of his mouth, but his frustration with the letter had morphed into general irritation.

"Oh, I see," Fiona said. "I see. *That's* important."

He closed his eyes. Here we go, he thought. Smart, funny and beautiful though she was, Fiona took offence faster than anyone he'd ever met. "You know that's not what I meant."

"I think it is what you meant."

"OK." He tossed his pen aside. "You're right. One old woman who's lost her husband isn't important compared to a bunch of wedding invitations." He pushed the chair back, got up and went to the living room. Found the pale blue paper, brought it back to the table, sat down, picked up the pen.

"What do you want me to say?"

"Whatever you like, they're your letters." Her voice no longer had an edge to it; she was always magnanimous in victory. He, on the other hand, was now thoroughly annoyed. He wasn't going to be able to write to Mrs. Orchard tonight and maybe not for several nights, because each time he set pen to paper he'd remember this conversation and be too pissed off to think straight.

"You had a form of words you were using," he said tightly.

"Yes, but that was for my friends. You might want to say something different to your friends."

"I'm sure your words will be best."

And so it went on. Not a terribly serious row. No words flung like spears across the room or furious silences lasting for days. The irony of quarrelling over wedding invitations didn't occur to him until later. But it was the first time he'd wondered—a fleeting thought, swiftly repressed—if he even liked Fiona, let alone loved her enough to spend the rest of his life with her.

The wind picked up during the night and in the morning he woke to the sound of the ancient birch tree outside the bedroom window tossing its limbs about. He went over to the window to watch; it had immensely long trailing branches of small golden leaves that were flowing back and forth across the back of the house. *Rapunzel, Rapunzel,* he thought.

In the bathroom he noticed the floor around the sink was wet. Too wet to be accounted for by him brushing his teeth last night. He squatted down, felt around the pedestal. The wood was damp and soft. He'd have to look at it at some point.

He had two oatmeal cookies and a cup of coffee for breakfast, then drove in to town to get some proper food. In the car he switched on the radio and learned that eleven Israeli athletes had been murdered at the Munich Olympics. Before the announcer had time to tell him more, the radio signal dissolved into fuzz. Liam flicked stations—more fuzz—and switched off in disgust.

The grocery store was on the basic side. It specialized in cans—canned stew, canned beans, canned peaches, caned ham—which was odd, given that the town was surrounded by farms. Maybe people bought their fruit and vegetables directly from the farmers. Maybe it was too far north to grow much in the way of fresh produce and too expensive to ship perishable things in from further south.

He and Fiona had always shopped together on Saturday mornings. Now that he didn't have to consider her, he wasn't sure what to buy. He dropped a box of Shredded Wheat into his shopping cart, added a plastic pack of cheddar (the only cheese on offer), a carton of milk and a vat of margarine. Sliced white bread (no other option), a pack of ground beef. Peanut butter. Marmalade—the jar in the fridge was almost empty. More coffee. Eggs. At the end of the first aisle he saw that there was some fresh produce after all, sitting in crates on the floor—corn on the cob, carrots, beans, onions, a box of apples, another of pears. Fiona would have bought all the vegetables so he bought only apples and pears—there was defiance in the act, which he calmly accepted as childish. As he was carrying his two paper bags out to the car he saw quart baskets of blueberries outside on a table made of upturned crates so he went back and bought one of those as well.

On the way home he made a detour down to the lake again, parking the car on the ramp down to the beach. It had looked so peaceful the previous evening; now breakers were rolling in, tossing up great plumes of spray where they met the rocks, charging up the beach, dragging at the pebbles as they withdrew. He watched them for a while, feeling and thinking nothing, then pulled himself back to the present and returned to the car.

Back home he unloaded his groceries from the trunk and dumped them on the kitchen counter. He went back to close the front door, hesitating en route because, again, he thought he heard something. Again, he decided that he'd imagined it, and so reached the door just in time to see a police car rolling into the drive.

## Four

# CLARA

She thought she'd dreamed the man but she hadn't; in the morning his car was still there. She had a sudden panic about Moses. What if the man found him? What if he didn't like cats? He might kill him! The cans of cat food, Moses's feeding bowl, the litter box— all of them were in the mud room. A can lasted two days and it was just luck that there wasn't half a can of cat food in the fridge right now. If the man hadn't noticed the cans already he soon would and he'd know Moses was there. Clara imagined him tracking Moses down. Searching. Peering behind furniture and under beds, on and on until he found him. Moses, terrified, backed into a corner, eyes blazing, back arched, mouth stretched wide in a silent scream of terror.

She would have to move his things. She'd have to sneak in while the man was out and grab them, and put them ... Where would she put them? Moses couldn't come into her house because her mother was allergic to him. The garage. She would put them in her parents' garage. She could feed him in there too.

Except she couldn't, that first morning, because the man was still in the house when the time came to set off for school. Which meant that Moses was going to be hungry all day. It brought back the panicky feeling until Clara remembered what a good hunter he was. He was forever bringing home dead birds. (Clara didn't like it but Mrs. Orchard said cats were hunters. "It's in their natures, Clara. It's part of being a cat.") Still, Moses would think she'd forgotten him, he'd think he'd been abandoned.

Worry about Moses joined worry about Rose and Mrs. Orchard, and the three worries churned inside her all day. They gave her a stomach ache and she wasn't able to concentrate on a thing Mrs. Quinn said.

Since Rose's disappearance Mrs. Quinn had been especially nice to Clara. She could be strict, and if you weren't paying attention she'd tell you off, but Clara couldn't pay attention now no matter how hard she tried, and Mrs. Quinn didn't tell her off and didn't ask her any questions in class and also didn't ask her about Rose's disappearance, all of which were good.

Clara's friends did mention it. Mostly in the playground at recess and lunchtime.

Ruth said breathlessly (she had a new skipping rope and was trying to do one hundred skips in a row), "Mommy says (breath) your sister's wild (breath) and she was asking for trouble."

Susan, head tipped curiously to one side, asked, "Why did she run away? Were your parents mean to her?"

Sharon asked, tugging at her hair, which was long and blonde and formed itself into ringlets which she

46

hated, "Was she having a baby? 'Cause she went around with boys a *lot*, didn't she?"

Jenny, Clara's best friend, whispered, "Don't worry, I'm still your friend. I'll always be your friend, no matter what anyone says," in a pleased way that made Clara not want to be friends with her anymore.

She took to staying close to the school steps during breaks, drawing pictures of Moses in the dust with a stick. Two round circles, a small one with two ears, two eyes, a nose and a mouth with three whiskers each side, on top of a large one with a tail and two feet. That was how you were supposed to draw cats. She drew the pictures and erased them with her foot again and again. That way she didn't have to look at anyone.


When she got home the man's car was still there. That didn't necessarily mean he was, though. He could have walked into town or he could have gone down to the beach; she should wait and see. Her mother wasn't in the kitchen or the living room so Clara went upstairs. The door to her parents' bedroom was closed but as she hesitated outside it her mother's voice said, "Hello, sweetheart, come in."

Clara opened the door. The curtains were drawn so the room was dark but she could make out the shape of her mother in the bed.

"I'm just having a little lie-down," her mother said. There was a smile in her voice but you could tell it was just pretend. "I'm a bit tired. But I'll get up soon and get your supper. How was school?"

"OK," Clara said.

"Good. I'll get up in a few minutes."

"Are you all right, Mommy?"

"Yes, I'm fine. You go back downstairs now. I'll get up soon."

Clara went down to the living room and took up her vigil, this time at the side window. She made sure she was mostly hidden by the edge of the curtain so that the man wouldn't see her if he looked out of Mrs. Orchard's window. It was thirteen days since Rose had left, which was almost two weeks. Last night she'd heard her mother say furiously to her father, "You know what's hardest to take? Your optimism. Your continual, everlasting *optimism*, based on *nothing*! As if we were on some sort of *picnic*!"

There was a pause and then her father said, so quietly Clara could hardly hear him, "Di, I'm just trying to get through this. Just like you."

"It is *not* just like me and don't pretend it is! You weren't the one who had the row with her! You never are, you leave all that to me so that you can play the kind, understanding father! So now you can tell yourself it's not your fault she left! You are not to blame! So don't pretend you're going through what I'm going through!"

Clara listened, everything in her clenched so hard it ached. Mom and Dad are really, really upset, she said to Rose inside her head, Rose out there in the world somewhere, beyond anywhere Clara had ever been. You have to come back, Rosie. Please come back.

*

There was no sign of anyone next door and she was just about to chance going over to remove Moses's things when the man wandered into Mrs. Orchard's living room eating a cookie. You weren't supposed to walk around when you were eating, you'd get crumbs all over the floor, you were supposed to sit down at a table until you were finished.

The man went over to the bookcase and stood looking at Mrs. Orchard's books. His back was to Clara but when he turned his head she could see his jaws moving. If Moses was in the house (though probably he wasn't, he'd probably escaped to the garden and the woods beyond) he'd be under the sofa, watching the crumbs fall, watching the man's feet walking back and forth on Mrs. Orchard's floor. Wishing, as Clara wished, that he would go. Go and stay gone. Then Mrs. Orchard would come home and Rose would come home and life would go back to normal.

Finally, having finished his cookie, the man went out. He didn't take the car, he walked down the drive to the road and then turned left and headed into town. Clara waited a few minutes in case he changed his mind, then took Mrs. Orchard's keys and crept over to the house. She couldn't help creeping, even though she knew the man wasn't there. She used the back door—the mud room door—because that was where Moses's things were and also because that meant she didn't have to go into the kitchen or hall or living room, all of them danger spots, and if she heard the man coming back she could slip out without running into him.

There was no fence between their backyards, just a row of trees, so she didn't have to go around the front of the house at all. In the mud room she gathered up Moses's bowl and the cans of cat food (there were only three left, she'd have to ask her mother to buy some more) and took them over to her own garage. She put them in the corner, where her father wouldn't run over them when he drove in. Then she went back for the litter box. She'd have to tempt Moses into the garage with a bowl of food; he didn't like strange places.

The plan worked perfectly up to the point where it went wrong. She'd forgotten about opening the cans. Mrs. Orchard's electric can opener was fastened to the wall in the kitchen and Clara was frightened to go into the kitchen. If the man had left the door between the hall and the kitchen open he'd see her as soon as he walked through the front door. She went back to her own house and got her mother's manual can opener and took it outside, but she couldn't get the sharp point to puncture the can. She tried again and again until her hand hurt and her body got so anxious it forgot how to breathe.

She went into the kitchen to ask her mother to do it but her mother was still in bed. Clara went back outside and sat down on the kitchen doorstep, still holding the can. She couldn't think what to do. But then Moses appeared and sat down beside her, which was unusual and very nice of him. He sat neatly, his tail wrapped around his feet, and watched two crows on the roof of the garage. The crows watched him back. Every now and then one of them would jump up and down and scream at him but Moses didn't even blink. It occurred to Clara that he wasn't showing as much interest in the can of cat food as he should be, given that he'd had no breakfast. Which could only mean he'd been killing things. She had to feed him regularly so he wouldn't kill things.

The two of them sat side by side, birdwatching, and Clara's breathing gradually returned to normal. Finally she steeled herself and said to Moses, "We have to go into Mrs. Orchard's kitchen and use her can opener, and we have to do it right now or he might come back." She stood up and so did Moses and they crossed the two backyards. Clara unlocked Mrs. Orchard's mud room door again and stepped inside with Moses at her heels. She listened for a moment, heart thumping, but Moses slipped past her into the kitchen, which meant the man definitely wasn't there. Clara went in on tiptoe nonetheless. She crossed the kitchen floor, held the can of cat food up to the opener so that the magnet grabbed it, and switched it on—then instantly switched it off again, her heart leaping with fright. She hadn't realized it made such a noise. She listened. No footsteps. No sound of keys in locks. Moses was winding himself around her legs, birds forgotten.

"You have to listen really hard," Clara whispered to him. "You have to tell me if he's coming. Do you understand?" Moses stopped circling her legs clockwise and started circling counter-clockwise to see if that sped things up.

51

She switched on the machine again and held her breath while it opened the can. Then she grabbed the can and the two of them fled.

*

Days went by. At home things got worse. The house seemed to be getting tighter somehow, or maybe, Clara thought, she herself was getting tighter. Sometimes it felt as if there was no air in the house. There wasn't a single minute of the day when things felt normal.

At school she sat at her desk and looked at the blackboard when Mrs. Quinn wrote on it, and listened to her when she was speaking, and didn't see or hear a word.

Then something happened. One afternoon on her way home she saw Dan Karakas up ahead, standing by the side of the road. It was a stretch of road where there weren't any houses either side, just woods, so there was no reason to be there unless you were walking home from school, which he wouldn't have been; he was Rose's age and was in her class at the high school. His father was a farmer and the family lived a long way out of town so like all the kids who lived out in the sticks, Dan took the school bus there and back. This afternoon he must have got off the bus miles before he should have.

He didn't seem to be going anywhere, though. He was just standing there, a cigarette in one hand, as if he were waiting for someone. It couldn't be Clara he was waiting for, though; older boys wouldn't be seen dead talking with younger kids, particularly girls.

She kept walking towards him. Rose liked Dan, she remembered now. Or rather, she didn't despise him. She'd said at least he wasn't a moron like all the other boys.

"Hi," he said as Clara got near.

Clara stopped in surprise because he said it as if he knew her and wanted to speak to her. She'd never even met him; she only knew who he was because Rose had pointed him out to her once, and that was from a distance. But he had quite a nice face, she decided. His hair was black and so thick it stood on end even though it was more than an inch long. He took a drag on his cigarette, dropped it and ground it into the dirt with his shoe. There were other butts scattered round him.

"Hi," she said uncertainly. Did he really want to speak to her or should she walk on?

"You're Clara, right?"

She nodded.

"I was just wondering," he said, not looking at her, scuffing at a stone with the toe of his shoe. "If you'd heard anything from Rose. Like, if she'd sent you a card or a message or something."

Clara's eyes opened wide—how did he know about Rose saying she'd send a message?

"Have you?" he said, glancing at her quickly, then back down.

"No," Clara said. Then a thought came into her mind: maybe he was a messenger! Maybe Rose was sending her a message through him.

53

"Have *you*?" she asked, suddenly breathless with hope.

Dan kicked the stone hard and it popped out of the ground and rolled onto the road. He scooped it back with his foot and kicked it into the trees. "No," he said. "I just thought you might have. You haven't heard anything at all?"

"No," Clara said. And then, because finally here was someone she could tell, she said, "She told me she'd send me a message but she hasn't."

He nodded. "Yeah. She said she'd send me one too. We worked out she should send it to Rick Steel so my parents wouldn't wonder who I was getting a letter from, and then he'd give it to me. He has a pen pal in Toronto, so his parents would think it was from him. But Rick hasn't had a letter or anything."

She stared at him, a hot, bitter feeling rising inside her. He was trying to make her think Rose loved him, which was a lie, because Rose told her everything and she'd never even mentioned him except that one time when she'd said he wasn't a moron. Rose would only send a message to someone she trusted and really, really loved, like Clara. And anyway, when would Rose have told him she was leaving? She couldn't have known she was going to have the worst-ever fight with their mother that day.

"When?" Clara said flatly.

"When what?"

"When did she tell you she was going?"

"The day she left. The evening she left. She came to the farm. She asked if I wanted to go with her. I couldn't. It's harvest. I can't leave my dad to do the harvest on his own, he couldn't manage. But I said I'd come when the crops were in. She was going to write and tell me where she was."

Inside Clara's head everything spun round. Rose had asked him to go with her? For a moment she couldn't get any words out. Then she said, "I'm going home now."

"Oh," he said, giving her a quick, puzzled look. "OK."

When she'd been walking for a minute or two she heard footsteps running and Dan caught up with her.

"Hey, Clara," he said. She kept walking, but so did he. "Hey, look, I'm sorry if I said something wrong, I only wanted to know if you'd heard from her. If she was OK."

Clara kept going.

"Look," he said, "I don't know what you're mad about, but we need to keep in touch in case one of us hears something. If you ever want to speak to me, leave a note ..." He hesitated. "Um, can you read and write yet?"

Clara stopped mid-stride and spun around. "Of course I can read and write! I'm *almost eight*!" Rose was wrong about him, he was a moron.

"Oh. OK, sorry. That's great. What I was going to say is, if you want to get in touch with me give a note to Rick Steel's sister. Her name's ... Milly or Molly or something. She's in grade seven or eight. At your school. Do you know her?"

Reluctantly, Clara nodded. Molly was one of the big girls. Clara had never talked to her but she knew which one she was.

"Good," Dan said. "And if I find out anything I'll let you know through Milly too."

"Her name's Molly! She's in grade eight!"

He kind-of smiled, which was rude because there was nothing funny about what she'd said. "OK, Molly," he said. Then he said, "Bye," and turned around and walked back the other way.

*

The only good thing about the man next door was that he went out every evening around six o'clock and stayed out for at least an hour. Unless it was raining, he went on foot. Clara guessed he went to the Hot Potato for supper because he was a man and men didn't know how to cook. There were dirty plates and bowls and teacups littering the kitchen counter when she went in to open Moses's cat food, but they would be from breakfast and lunch. They made the kitchen look messy, which in turn made Clara fidgety; she had to stop herself from dragging over a chair to kneel on and washing them and putting them away in the cupboards where they belonged. Mrs. Orchard never left anything lying around.

Clara's bedtime was seven o'clock (sometimes she could stretch it to half-past), so she had a whole hour during which she could safely go next door to play with Moses and keep him from being lonely. She still fed him in the garage, but she wasn't so worried about going into Mrs. Orchard's kitchen or living room now because the man always followed the same routine.

She and Moses had a routine, too: after Moses had eaten his supper, the two of them would go into the living room, where Moses would watch for the mouse and Clara would wander around looking at things. The four boxes were still in the middle of the floor. They were taped closed with wide brown tape so Clara couldn't look inside them. They had writing on them, though. It was messy and it took her a while to work out what it said but finally she managed. One box said *Living Room*; one said *Clothes, Typewriter*; the third said *Books, Papers*; and the last one said *Misc* or *Miso*, she wasn't sure which and she didn't know what either word meant.

Sometimes she sat in the armchair that had always been hers when she and Mrs. Orchard were having a cup of tea or a glass of lemonade. There was a little table beside it at exactly the right height to put down your drink plus a small plate with a cookie on it, but now there was no tea or lemonade and no cookie because the man had eaten them all. This particular day, which was the day after she'd met Dan Karakas, she was so anxious it was hard to sit still, and sitting there on her own, without Mrs. Orchard in the other chair, gave her an ache in her chest, so she was on the point of getting up when Moses did another very unusual thing; he abandoned the mouse, jumped onto Clara's chair, curled up in her lap and started to purr. Clara was so surprised and so pleased her mouth fell open. She'd heard him purr before—it was really loud—but she'd never felt it. It made her whole body vibrate as if she was purring too.

*

57

She knew going into the house was still risky, of course; the man could change his mind and come home at any time. But apart from listening for him, there was nothing else she could do if she was to keep her promise to Mrs. Orchard. She'd tried to get Moses to move into the garage altogether—she'd asked her mother for an old towel and arranged it on the concrete floor for him to use as a bed—but he wasn't having it. The next-best thing would have been for him to stay outside but he wasn't having that, either, and anyway it was getting too cold for him to stay out at night, even in the garage. He insisted on living exactly where he'd always lived, in Mrs. Orchard's living room.

Clara decided he was waiting for Mrs. Orchard in the same way that she was waiting for Rose. In Moses's mind abandoning the house would be abandoning Mrs. Orchard. Clara understood that perfectly. She also understood why he spent almost all his time under the sofa nowadays except when she was there. He was permanently scared. So was she. She was more afraid every day and she didn't even know what of.

*

Nine days after he moved into Mrs. Orchard's house and twenty-one days after Rose left, the man brought some empty boxes into the living room and started putting Mrs. Orchard's things into them. Things he had no right to touch, let alone move from their places. If he packed them up, that meant he was going

58

to take them out of the house without asking Mrs. Orchard. And that meant he was a thief.

Fortunately it was a Saturday, so Clara wasn't at school and saw him do it.

"Mommy," she shouted. She ran into the kitchen. "Mommy! The man is stealing Mrs. Orchard's things!"

Her mother was sitting at the kitchen table looking at this week's copy of the *Temiskaming Speaker*. Not the front page, one of the inside pages. Down near the bottom was a picture of Rose. Underneath the picture were the words, "Solace Girl Still Missing," and underneath that there was about an inch of type. The same picture had been in the *Speaker* last week, but bigger. The week before that, it had been on the front page and bigger still, with the headline "Have You Seen Rose?" and details about when she'd disappeared.

Clara's mother looked up at her and smiled bleakly. "It's already old news, you see," she said. "They've moved on to the next big thing. The price of corn."

You could tell by her mother's face that her head was so full of Rose there wasn't room for a single other thing. Clara wanted to put her arms around her, and she also wanted to scream at her. Her father had gone down to North Bay to ask people if they'd seen Rose. He went out after school every day as well as on Saturdays and Sundays, to every town in every direction. Clara wanted him to be at home; she didn't want to be alone in the house with her mother's despair. But often he didn't return until after Clara was asleep.

She went back to the living room. The man was taking the ornaments off the mantelpiece: a pair of brass candlesticks (he put the candles in the box loose, so they were sure to get broken); a glass bowl with a picture of a sled pulled by huskies somehow inside the glass; and a loon carved out of black stone. In a smaller, separate box he put an ornate clock with Roman numerals (Mrs. Orchard had told her they were Roman and showed her how to count to a hundred with them), and a wood carving (Clara's favourite thing in the house after Moses) of four old men seated around a table smoking pipes and playing cards, all of them perfect right down to the creases in their shirts and the tiny thread-like laces in their boots.

The man carefully wrapped the clock and the wood carvings (each old man came separately, complete with his chair and a handful of cards) in newspaper before putting them into their box. Then he went over to the table with Mrs. Orchard's photos on it (her photos of her husband, her most precious things!), selected three of them, and packed them carefully away too.

Everything else he just bundled up roughly. You could tell he didn't care what happened to those things. When he'd finished everything but the books he straightened up, rubbed his back with both hands, looked at his watch (it was almost six) and went out, as usual, for his supper.

A few minutes after the man left, the worst thing of all happened. It should have been the best thing: Clara's father arrived home earlier than she'd expected. When she saw his car turn into the driveway she rushed into the hall to meet him.

"Daddy!" she said, opening the door for him. "The man is stealing Mrs. Orchard's things!"

"Hello, Little," her father said. "What was that again?" He looked grey and exhausted but she didn't care.

"The man next door is stealing all of Mrs. Orchard's things! He's putting them in boxes and he's going to take them away!"

"Oh," her father said absently, putting the car keys down on the hall table. "Well, I guess it's up to him."

Clara was stunned. What did that mean? How could it be up to him?

"But they're Mrs. Orchard's things! When she gets home from the hospital she'll want them!"

Her father looked at her. After a minute, when he didn't speak, Clara drew in a very big breath and said it again—shouted, in fact. *They're Mrs. Orchard's things!*

Her father squatted down and put his hands on her arms. He said gently, "Clara, you're getting all worked up over nothing. You mustn't worry about the man next door. He's ..." her father hesitated, "he's sort of looking after the house for Mrs. Orchard. She won't mind. I promise you, she won't mind."

"She will mind! She loves her things! You don't know her like I do, I know she loves them!" Suddenly she was crying, great choking sobs, which she never did, because Rose, who loved her, so hated her crying. But Rose was gone and no one knew where, and they all pretended everything was all right instead of telling her the truth. Everybody, *everybody* lied to her, even Mrs. Orchard, who had said she'd be home

61

soon and she wasn't, and now a thief was taking all her things and no one even cared.

Her father tried to pull her to him to comfort her but she jerked herself away. "You're telling lies! You don't know her! I know her! I know she wants her things! You're telling lies! You're a liar!"

Her father stood up. He said, "That's enough now, Clara. I know you're upset, but you mustn't speak like that."

Suddenly he looked past her, and she turned and saw that her mother had come into the hall and the two of them were looking at each other over Clara's head. Her mother was looking a question and when Clara glanced back at her father she saw him give a fractional shake of his head.

"You're liars!" Clara shouted. "Liars! Liars! Liars!"

She sat on her bed and tore at a fingernail with her teeth. She bit it until there was no sticking-out bit of nail left, just raw pink skin with a tiny rim of blood.

# Five

# ELIZABETH

Mrs. Cox across the ward is wearing her favourite nightie. We bring our own nightclothes, which are taken home and laundered, when required, by our families, or by the hospital if we are on our own. Mrs. Cox's nightie is a fluffy pink creation, not quite knee-length. Mrs. Cox has positively the worst legs I have ever seen on a mortal being; fat, white, grotesquely dimpled, bulging with purple-black veins. She must have picked the nightie out of an Eaton's catalogue under the horribly mistaken impression that it would make her look like the girl modelling it. Clearly there is no full-length mirror in the house. Ignorance is bliss, I suppose.

I've always worn pyjamas. You're safe with pyjamas.

I'm having more and more difficulty getting my breath. I think it comes from lying down so much. It feels as if there's a weight on my chest, as if something very large is sitting on it. A bear, perhaps. This morning I mentioned it to the doctor when he was doing his rounds. He laughed and had a listen with his stethoscope and said he didn't think it was a bear. He didn't say what it was, though, just that another pillow might help, so Nurse Roberts brought me one. I think it does make a difference, though I'm still struggling a bit.

Nurse Roberts is looking unhappy. When she arrived this morning her eyes were red and she was very pale. After the doctor's rounds, when she was doling out the medications, I said to her, quietly so that the others wouldn't hear, "Are you all right, dear?" She smiled at me and gave a small shrug and said simply, "A man."

Martha cheered her up, though—she cheered up the whole ward, quite unintentionally. Nurse Roberts told her she needed an injection and Martha snapped, "I hate injections."

Nurse Roberts, sympathetic but firm, said, "I know, dear. Everyone does," and Martha said, "I hate them *more* than other people do. I *hate* having things stuck into me, I really *hate* it." There was a little pause and then she added, "I didn't even like sex all that much, to tell you the truth."

Nurse Roberts laughed so hard she had to sit down on the bed to catch her breath. She still gave Martha the injection, though. Martha sulked afterwards. Just like a child. Didn't say a word for a good half hour. It was very restful; I hope she has to have them more often. Three times a day would be nice.

*

She asked me my name yesterday. "Elizabeth what?" she asked. I felt a flicker of fear as I told her. She is about my age. But it's been thirty years and in any case, she's from some very remote northern community—they probably had no access to newspapers up there back then. Anyway, she showed no sign of recognizing it.

At visiting time this afternoon young Mrs. Dubois, who occupies the bed beside Mrs. Cox's, directly across the ward from mine, had a visit from her husband and two little boys. The younger one is about eighteen months, I'd say, still at the staggering stage, and his big brother must be coming up to three. Both of them dark-eyed with wonderful olive skin, like their mother. They were wearing matching sweaters, striped blue and yellow, and whizzed around the ward like fat bumblebees. Mr. Dubois works, of course, so he can only bring them in on the weekends. Very hard for his wife, seeing the boys so seldom when they're at this stage and changing every day. She's been here for three months already, poor girl. Surgery on her spine.

Their father is good with them, which is very nice to see. Their mother is not allowed to so much as raise her head so he lifts them up and sits them on the bed beside her so that she can touch their cheeks and smooth their hair and tell them how good they are, and how much she loves and misses them.

She tries not to cry but she doesn't always manage it and then of course they get upset too, and their father has to lift them down again and set them on the floor. He always brings a bag of toys with him to dole out at such moments so they recover very quickly. Almost too quickly. I fear that their mother might fear that they no longer miss her quite as much as they did.

But the whole ward loves it when they come. There's something captivating about the very young.

While they're here I can watch them with barely a flicker of pain. It's when they leave that I have trouble keeping the memories at bay, some of them so vivid. One in particular has returned to me so often I think it must have worn a groove in my brain. I am standing at the kitchen sink, washing out paint brushes. Thirty-five years old, wearing a ratty old skirt and one of your shirts with a worn-out collar. Quite possibly I am humming to myself, though my memory may be making that up. I have just finished applying the second coat of paint—a soft, warm yellow—to the walls of the small room we've decided will be the nursery.

I've stopped teaching kindergarten. I miss the children but I don't resent being required to give up work, I'm too happy to resent anything. We have been "trying" for three whole years and finally—finally!—the doctor has confirmed that I am pregnant, about four months along. The morning sickness has worn off and I am so full of energy and joy I hardly know what to do with myself. You being a cautious (and sometimes annoyingly overprotective) man are anxious that I might overdo it, so to stop you worrying I have agreed to leave the ceiling to you.

So there I am, standing at the kitchen sink on a beautiful sunny day in early spring, a soft breeze drifting in through the open window, watching the pale, warm yellow paint seeping out of the brush and swirling down the drain, happy beyond measure, happy beyond words, so happy in fact that for several moments I fail to register that something is trickling down my leg.

Our first loss. On Tuesday the second of April, 1934, shortly after three in the afternoon, we lost our first child.

I won't think about it anymore, dear one. I'll think about Liam instead.

Do you remember the day we met him? August 24th, 1940. The Blitz on London had begun the previous night. We listened to the BBC on the wireless every evening and every evening the news was worse.

I remember you sitting, leaning forward in your chair a little to be sure not to miss anything, your face tense and strained. I'm afraid I was of very little support to you at the time. I still feel guilty about that. The truth was I was too overwhelmed by my own suffering to think about anything or anyone else.

But to return to Liam: Ralph Kane had just arrived in Guelph, from Queens, I think. You may have been involved in recruiting him, I don't recall. Either you told him that the house next door to ours was up for sale or it was pure coincidence that they moved in there, I don't recall that either. I do remember you telling me that he was married and that you thought—but weren't sure—he had children. That detail stuck in my mind.

I was in bad shape at the time. Six weeks earlier I'd had my fifth miscarriage, this one at almost six months. They let me hold our child—our son—before they took him away. He struggled to live, but could not.

I watched the new family arrive from behind our living-room curtains, that's how bad it was. As if the mere sight of someone else's children might blow me in two. There was a vacant lot between our houses, so they were a hundred yards away and I couldn't make out faces, but I saw that there were three young children; two girls and a little boy. I could neither look at them nor tear my eyes away.

Courtesy demanded that we go over and welcome the newcomers to the neighbourhood, but I couldn't manage it. You went on your own when you got home from work. No doubt you said I was unwell, which was perfectly true.

But the next day you persuaded me that we must invite them around for a cup of tea or glass of lemonade on the weekend. "We have to do it, Elizabeth," you said. "They're our neighbours and Ralph is going to be a colleague, we cannot pretend they don't exist."

"What if I start crying?" I asked, tears streaming down. "What if I start crying and can't stop?" It was happening several times a day and I was powerless to prevent it.

You said that it wouldn't happen, that I would be all right. I was very angry with you for that, Charles, the angriest I had ever been. I shouted at you, said that you could not know that and it was a ridiculous thing to say. You studied your feet. Nothing in your many years of education had prepared you for dealing with a woman going out of her mind with grief. You were grieving too, I knew that, but felt your grief wasn't as great, as all-consuming, as mine. The knowledge that countless other women had gone through the same thing and had pulled themselves together and got on with things merely added the extra weight of guilt to my despair. I had always considered myself a strong and sensible woman, and yet now I was helpless. Our lost children were with me every moment of every day. I could not let them go, I could not put them down.

Nonetheless, we invited the Kanes for tea. Angrily, I made two cakes, one chocolate and one white, plus a dozen butter tarts. Then I made a batch of chocolate-chip cookies with precious chips, sent by a friend in America, that I'd been hoarding for a special occasion. You would not be able to accuse me of not trying. On the Saturday morning I made fresh lemonade. I chose my nicest dress and put my hair up and even applied a touch of lipstick. I was preparing myself as if I was on my way to the guillotine and determined to die bravely.

But the fear that I would break down the moment I saw the children grew as the day progressed, so that by the time they arrived I was convinced I wouldn't be able to speak at all. I would open my mouth and nothing would come out but a howl.

When the knock at the door came I followed you fearfully to greet our guests. They were grouped on the porch, the girls—I saw they were twins—in front, the parents behind, the little boy, who was about three, hanging back, clinging onto his mother's skirt, trying to drag her in the opposite direction. The scene was a touch chaotic: you were holding open the door to usher them in, Ralph was introducing the twins and urging them forward, Annette was trying to unlock the little boy's fist from her skirt, alternately scolding and pleading with him, and he was paying no attention to her whatsoever. He had one foot braced against her shoe and the other knee bent for maximum traction and he was hauling so hard and leaning back so far he was almost parallel to the ground. Mercifully, he wasn't yelling; he was saving his breath for the job at hand.

I was so distracted by this tug of war that I scarcely noticed Ralph and the girls, I'm not sure I even said hello to them.

Annette turned anxiously towards me—I had stepped out onto the porch—and apologized, holding onto the child's arm with one hand and still trying to prise open his fist with the other. "I'm so sorry," she said breathlessly. "I'm afraid he isn't very good with strangers. Liam, say hello to Mrs. Orchard."

Liam did not. He kept right on hauling. It seemed to me, though, that if you considered things from his point of view his behaviour was entirely understandable: just a couple of days earlier he had been uprooted from the home he knew and dumped down in one he didn't know and had not been consulted about. He didn't like it. He didn't like anything that was going on in his life and in particular he didn't like the idea of going to yet another new house and spending the afternoon with a "nice lady and gentleman" he'd never met before.

In other words, he wanted to meet me every bit as little as I had wanted, a minute previously, to meet him. In fact he looked so much like I felt that, incredibly, I almost laughed. I became aware of the most remarkable lightening of my mood.

I said, "Hello, Liam, would you like to come in and have a cookie?" I glanced quickly at his mother and she nodded, smiling weakly. I guessed that she was embarrassed by this poor showing at our first meeting. She may have heard that I'd been a kindergarten teacher and feared I would judge her incompetent, which at that stage I did not; it was clear that he was a strong-willed child and quite a handful.

My bribe was beneath Liam's dignity and he rightly paid no attention to it, though he did shoot a quick look at me as if trying to gauge the quality of cookie this horrible lady might produce.

I said, "Or there's chocolate cake. Would you like some chocolate cake, Liam?"

This time there was clear hesitation and I thought for a moment I had won, but no, he started hauling again. For a three-year-old he drove a hard bargain.

I shot my last bolt. "Would you like to have some cake and a cookie out here on the porch, Liam? You could sit on the step and you wouldn't have to talk to anyone."

He stopped hauling and stood hanging at a forty-five-degree angle from his mother's skirt, head down, thinking hard.

I knew his decision before he did. "Is that all right?" I said sotto voce to Annette. She said, "Well, if you're sure you don't mind."

So that was what happened. Liam sat on our porch steps and ate a large piece of chocolate cake and two chocolate-chip cookies more or less simultaneously. We have no photo of it but I don't need one, it is etched on my brain. It's one of the pictures I plan to take into eternity with me, my love. Liam on the steps, age three.

# Six

# LIAM

The police officer was in his late thirties, Liam guessed, a couple of years older than he was. Not tall but broad and exceedingly solid-looking, which, given the lumber camps and the bars in town, he probably needed to be. But he looked friendly enough.

"Good morning," he said, coming up the steps.

"Good morning," Liam said.

"This is just a kind of courtesy call," the officer said. "I'm Sergeant Barnes."

"Nice to meet you." A courtesy call? Did every newcomer to the area get a courtesy call from the cops? "What can I do for you?"

"Maybe I could come in for a minute. I won't keep you long."

"Sure, yeah, come in." Liam held the door open and ushered him into the living room. "Have a seat."

"You arrived yesterday?" the cop asked, lowering himself into one of the big stuffed armchairs. "That right?"

"Yes, I drove up from Toronto."

"A long drive. Afraid I missed your name."

"Oh," Liam said. "Sorry. Kane. Liam Kane."

"You're a relative of Mrs. Orchard, Mr. Kane? A nephew, maybe? We were all sorry to learn of her passing, by the way. She was a very nice woman—as was her sister, I must say. Did you know Miss Godwin?"

"No, I didn't," Liam said, feeling like a fraud. "And actually, I'm not any relation of Mrs. Orchard's either. She and her husband were neighbours of my parents when I was a kid. They lived next door to us. In Guelph, down in Southern Ontario. Her husband and my father both taught at the agriculture college there."

Sergeant Barnes nodded but said nothing.

"They didn't have any kids," Liam explained. "I guess I was sort of a substitute. I spent a lot of time at their place." The cop nodded again. Again said nothing. Liam added, "I was a bit ... surprised about her leaving me everything. Very surprised, in fact. I guess she had no one else to leave things to."

"A nice little legacy," the sergeant said at last. Still perfectly pleasant, still not satisfied about something.

"Yes."

"Wish someone would give me a surprise like that. I always seem to get the other kind." The sergeant smiled and shifted in his chair. "It all seems to have gone through pretty quick, doesn't it, Mr. Kane? You know what I mean? Normally with wills, probate takes a good while and Mrs. Orchard hasn't been deceased all that long. About a week, in fact.

"Yeah, I know." He was conscious that his pulse was picking up speed. "But, actually, the house was already mine."

74

"That's interesting," Sergeant Barnes said. "How did that come about?"

"She gave it to me before she died. A couple of weeks before. Everything else was covered by the will, but she gave me the house outright. As a gift."

"Why did she do that, d'you think? Like, what was the urgency?"

"I don't know. I guess she just wanted me to have something straight away." He'd asked the lawyer the same question and the lawyer had given the same answer.

Sergeant Barnes regarded him thoughtfully. After a minute he said, "Mr. Kane, I have no right to ask you this and you don't have to comply, but it would ease my mind if you happened to have a letter from your lawyer or something else that would confirm all this. And some photo ID would be good too. Though, like I say, you aren't under any obligation to provide it."

"The papers are upstairs," Liam said. "I'll get them."

*It would ease my mind*, he thought, going up the stairs. *You don't have to comply.* Right.

He went to the bedroom and dug out the will, his passport and the papers relating to Mrs. Orchard's gift of the house from his suitcase, took them downstairs and gave them to the police officer. Then he sat down again and pretended to relax.

The cop took his time. He got out a little black notebook and made a note of the lawyer's name and address, flicked his eyes over Liam's face as he checked the passport photo, went through the letters regarding the will and Mrs. Orchard's gift. Finally, he smiled and handed everything back. "All looks good, Mr. Kane," he said. "Thanks very much."

It seemed to Liam that the sergeant looked relieved, and he felt his own muscles start to loosen in response. He took a deep breath and surreptitiously let it out.

"Let me tell you what all this is about," the sergeant said. "Kid next door—sixteen-year-old girl—ran off a couple of weeks ago. Had a row with her mom, said she was leaving and wouldn't be back. She's done it before, apparently, but always been back within a couple of days. Whereas this time it's been coming on for two weeks. Her parents are getting pretty worried."

"Oh," Liam said. "Right. Must be ... difficult."

Sergeant Barnes nodded. "Being sixteen she's old enough to leave home if she chooses, and no one can make her come back. But two weeks without anyone seeing her or hearing from her is cause for concern."

Liam nodded. "Do you ... is there any reason to suspect ... what do you call it, foul play?"

"Nope. Nothing going on beforehand that anyone knows. I talked with her friends, the school, kids in her class, sent out photos and missing persons bulletins to towns she might have gone to, checked the police info centre ... all the usual stuff. We did a big search, everyone in town turned out including a couple of trackers from the Ojibway reserve. Got two police dogs and their handlers from North Bay. Combed the bush, barns, outhouses, you name it, everything for miles around. Found exactly nothing. Not a trace.

"Anyway, reason I'm sitting here taking up your time is that you're a stranger in town and you've moved in right next door. Plus you arrived kinda quick, like I said, and Mr. and Mrs. Jordon are a little wound up at the moment. They'll be anxious about their younger daughter too, she's seven or eight. I wanted to be able to assure them that you are who you say you are, for your sake as well as theirs. Also thought you should know what's going on next door."

Liam nodded. "Makes sense. Thanks for telling me."

There was a brief pause and then the cop said, "You planning to settle down here, Mr. Kane, or you going to sell the house?" He smiled at Liam and made a random motion with his pencil. "This is just me being nosy, not me being a cop."

"I'll be selling it but I thought I'd have a couple of weeks' holiday before putting it on the market," Liam said. "I haven't decided exactly how long I'll stay. It'll depend partly on the weather. I've just quit my job so I don't have to get back at any particular time."

"Yeah? What was the job?"

"I'm an accountant. I worked for an accountancy firm—Jarvis and Jones—in Toronto."

"Sounds like a good job."

"Good money, lousy job."

Resigning had not been a rational decision—he had no new job to go to—but he wasn't thinking straight at the time; his brain had still been clotted with the bile and vitriol of his last meeting with Fiona. Everything in his life seemed to be falling apart, he'd been bored at work for years, why not quit? He was between projects and had a lot of vacation owing to him, so he was able to leave straight away. Which gave him a lot of time to sit staring at the walls of his box-like, newly rented Toronto apartment, paralysed with inertia, wondering if he was going nuts.

Ten days after he'd left Jarvis and Jones, a letter arrived from Mrs. Orchard's lawyer in Sudbury informing him that he was now the owner of a house in Northern Ontario. Grateful but baffled, Liam phoned his father.

"An old woman's just given me a house," he said. "Mrs. Orchard. Do you remember her?"

There was a moment's pause. Then his father said, "That's very nice. Did this come out of nowhere?"

"Well, not quite. She got in touch a few years ago, when her husband died. We've been writing back and forth since then—just the odd letter. I've never met her or anything."

"Really," his father said. He sounded, Liam thought, as if he was staring into space. "Well, she was very fond of you when you were small. They were childless, so I guess ..." The sentence trailed off. "Have you told your mother?"

"No." He rarely phoned his mother and then only out of duty.

"Might be best not to," his father said. "Look"—his voice became brisk—"I have a meeting in five minutes so I have to go, but congratulations. You were due for some good news."

Liam cut in, "Why shouldn't I tell Mom?"

"Oh, there was bad feeling of some sort between them. I don't know the details. I wouldn't worry about it, just enjoy your legacy."

*

He intended to write to Mrs. Orchard that day, thanking her for her remarkable gift, but he didn't get round to it, and a couple of days passed, and then a few more, guilt growing all the time. And then a second letter from the lawyer arrived, saying that she had died, and that apart from a small sum left to the woman who came in to clean the house Liam was the sole beneficiary of her will.

Before he'd finished reading the letter he'd known he was going north; there was no sense to it, it just seemed the only thing to do. All of his belongings were still in boxes so he loaded them into the car that evening and, at four in the morning, unable to sleep, he set off. By a quarter to five he was on Highway 400; after Barrie he had the road to himself. When he reached Sudbury he went to the lawyer's offices, signed documents and picked up the keys to the house. By six in the evening, nightmarish northern roads notwithstanding, he was walking up the steps of Mrs. Orchard's porch, with Toronto, his career and his marriage behind him.

And now, not much more than twelve hours later, somewhat dazed and very short of sleep, he was sitting in a strange house, which he happened to own, trying to explain it all to a cop.

"Plus my wife and I are in the process of getting a divorce," Liam heard himself say. "So things are a bit … up in the air."

"Sounds like, what do they call it, a mid-life crisis."

"Guess so." He was trying to figure out why he'd just said what he'd just said.

"These things happen," Sergeant Barnes said. "Kinda rough, though."

"Yes."

The cop got to his feet, stuffing the little black notebook into a back pocket. "Well, thanks for your time, Mr. Kane. Hope you enjoy your holiday." He smiled. "In fact, hope you decide to stay, we need some new faces up here, we're all getting tired of each other."

It struck Liam as the police car was driving off that this was the first time he'd spoken more than two words to anyone apart from lawyers since he'd walked out of his office at Jarvis and Jones three weeks ago. In fact, if you left out work-related discussions with his colleagues, it might be a contender for the longest conversation he'd had with anyone, including his wife, in the past year.

Fiona would have said this was a perfect illustration of what she'd figured out years ago, namely that Liam had no close friends for the simple reason that he was incapable of forming relationships, just as he was incapable of love. She had made the observation many times, most recently in an eye-poppingly expensive restaurant (her choice, of course) on their eighth and final wedding anniversary. He had replied that he'd managed to stay married to her for eight years, which was an achievement in anybody's book. The conversation had ended with them agreeing to divorce. "It's nice that we can agree on something," Fiona had said. "Don't you think?"

In Mrs. Orchard's kitchen he stood with hands in his pockets, staring blankly at the still-unpacked bags of groceries on the counter. The talk with the police officer had added to the rabble of undigested thoughts and emotions churning around in his mind. Clearly the cop had been suspicious of his story, and though the lawyer's papers had seemed to satisfy him, it was possible he was still unconvinced. The more Liam thought about it the more likely that seemed, and if so, it changed things: he'd thought spending a couple of weeks up here might be relaxing, a holiday during which he could recover from the stresses of the past few months and figure out what came next. Being a suspect in a case involving a teenager's disappearance or abduction didn't fit the bill.

There was nothing to stop him from changing his plans; the sergeant hadn't told him he had to stay in town. He could pack his boxes back into the car and take off right now. The clearance of the contents and the sale of the house could be arranged from anywhere in the country; if he put his mind to it, he could be out of Solace in a couple of hours, make it as far as North Bay tonight. Then in the morning he'd have an early start and head to … where, exactly? To do what?

In the course of thinking all this, as if his brain was going in one direction and his body another, he discovered he'd unpacked the groceries, which were now standing on the counter waiting to be put away. If he was leaving he should pack them up again and take them with him.

He studied the groceries for a minute. Toss a coin, he thought vaguely. He wandered into the hallway

81

and sat on the stairs, elbows on knees, hands dangling, listening to the utter silence of the house, and suddenly, out of nowhere, was blindsided by a feeling of desolation and despair so profound it left him breathless. Afraid he was going to pass out, he bent forward, head in hands, eyes closed, breathing carefully. He didn't know what was happening. It was like being caught up in an avalanche.

After a time, the feeling began to recede. He opened his eyes, focused on the floor. Pale, honey-coloured beech, like the floor in the hallway of his parents' home in Calgary, where they'd moved after leaving Guelph. There'd been a small rug. Red and blue. It was inclined to slide about, particularly if you were running.

He saw himself, aged ten or so, not running but sitting on the stairs as he was now, listening to his sisters giggling up in their bedrooms. Saw the four of them—two older than him, two younger—streaming down the stairs past him, into the kitchen where their mother was getting supper. Heard her laughing at some story they were reporting. He remembered how empty the hall had felt, with all of them in there. Their laughter. The hollowness inside him. In his memory, this had happened many times, it was always happening. If he walked into a room where they were all chattering, they would stop. Turn to him and say hi, their faces expressionless.

There must have been a reason, it couldn't have been simply that they were girls and, as the only boy, he was naturally excluded. There had been a barrier between him and the rest of them—particularly between him and his mother; the girls, he decided now, probably took their cue from her. Mostly, his mother had seemed indifferent to him, but there had been times when he'd felt something close to hostility emanating from her, which he'd been, and still was, completely at a loss to understand. It was as if he'd unknowingly committed an unforgivable crime.

He shifted on the step. Why are you thinking about all this now? he thought. It was decades ago. It doesn't matter anymore.

Cautiously, he straightened up and pushed himself to his feet. He felt OK. The avalanche had moved on.

He decided he wasn't up to making a decision about staying or going; he needed to do something mindless, something physical. He went upstairs, into the bathroom, squatted down and felt the floorboards again. Still wet and spongy. He ran his hand around the U-bend of the waste pipe. Wet. Mystery solved. He tried tightening the joint by hand; it didn't budge. He needed a wrench. He'd seen no tools in the house or garage but there was a hardware store in town.

Exercise seemed called for and it was a nice day, hot sun, cool breeze off the lake, so he walked. In the ten minutes it took him to reach the centre of town only one car passed him, but in town there were people on the street. Mostly residents, he guessed; the tourist season was over. Some of them smiled at him and said good morning. He managed a nod in return. In Toronto—in any big city, no doubt—people focused straight ahead or on their feet and didn't so much as acknowledge your existence. He decided he preferred it that way, it was less effort.

There was an old man behind the counter in the hardware store. He had a stoop and a suspicious look. He nodded—a mere jerk of the head—at Liam, who nodded back. Another misanthrope, Liam thought; we should get on well. The store was a windowless cave, a couple of bare light bulbs suspended from the ceiling. There were tools hanging on walls, piled in bins, stacked on counters, heaped on the floor. Hooks had been screwed into beams in the ceiling; suspended from them were axes, handsaws, scythe blades—anything with a hole for a string to hang it by.

"Whatcha looking for?" the old man asked. His manner was brusque, as if he wanted to get this over with and Liam out of his store as fast as he could.

"I need a wrench," Liam said.

"What for?"

A woman walked in from the back room carrying a mug of coffee. "Here you are, Dad," she said, then nodded at Liam. "Good morning," she said, polite rather than friendly.

"Good morning," Liam said. The woman was mid-thirties. Good-looking. Nice figure.

"What for?" the old man repeated sharply. The woman put down the coffee and left. Liam watched her go.

"Pardon?" he said.

"*What do you want the wrench for!*" A near-bellow. "*What do you want to do with it!*"

Smash your head in, for a start, Liam thought. He considered walking out but decided against it, this being the only hardware in town. "The U-bend on the bathroom sink. The joint's leaking."

"OK. What you want is this." The old man shuffled down to the end of the counter and took a large wrench out of a bushel basket. Liam paid for it, skipped the thanks and left.

He walked home thinking about sex, about how unrelenting the drive was. The very last thing he wanted right now was a woman in his life and yet his body—that bit of it, anyway—couldn't help hunting, like a gun dog scenting deer.

It had been sex, of course, that first attracted him to Fiona. She had lots of other things going for her, she was beautiful and clever and witty and he appreciated all of those things, but most of all she was sexy. She was exceedingly aware of her body and liked it and was happy to share it, which made a change from other girls he'd gone out with, who were tediously worried about how they looked. Fiona was very confident about how she looked. Very sure of herself. It had turned him on.

He hadn't realized that, in the daily routine of earning a living, shopping, cooking and all the rest, with the best will in the world, you don't spend all that much time in bed. There's the rest of the day to get through. The rest of your life.

Unlocking the door of Mrs. Orchard's house (now his house), going upstairs to the bathroom with its leaky sink (now his leaky sink and hence his problem, a positively welcome one because, unlike all his other problems, it had a solution), squatting down and tightening the joint above the U-bend with his new

85

wrench, Liam decided that if he and Fiona had ever been genuinely "in love," which he doubted, it had been for a year and a half at most. Eighteen very exciting months followed by seven years of gradually increasing disillusionment and boredom, towards the end of which sex had been just about the only thing that was still any good.

And then, closer to the end, Fiona had lost interest even in that. Bitterly, Liam had turned elsewhere.

There was a knock at the front door. He straightened up, wrench in hand, and went downstairs.

"Me again," Sergeant Barnes said.

Liam felt a lurch of apprehension. "Come in," he said, opening the door wider.

"That looks kind of ominous," the cop said, nodding at the wrench. "You expecting trouble?"

"Oh," Liam said. He put the wrench down on the small table by the door. "Sorry. I've been trying to fix a leak in the U-bend upstairs."

The cop grinned. "That's a relief. For a minute there I thought things were going to get lively. Yeah, there must be a lot of stuff like that to do, old people tend not to notice things. You need to look at the roof, by the way, those shingles have had it. Anyway, I won't keep you. Just something I meant to say this morning and forgot. Don't know if you're aware it's bear hunting season. Lots of happy hunters wandering round with .30-30 Winchesters, way more dangerous than the bears. It's a good idea to give the bears some distance too, though. In other words, it's not a great time for a walk in the woods. Just thought I'd mention it."

"Thanks," said Liam, who'd had no intention of walking in the woods now or ever. He was trying to work out if this second visit had an ulterior motive; if the cop was trying to catch him doing something incriminating.

"Good luck with the repairs." The cop raised his hand in a sort-of salute and turned to go back to his car.

"Um …" Liam stopped him, "a question. You know if there's a carpenter or builder or someone like that in town? The bathroom floor's rotten where it's been leaking, might be a big job."

"Sure. Jim Peake. He can do pretty much anything. He's busy, though, so you might have to wait a bit. You'll find him at the gas station. He has a workshop round the back."

"Thanks. Another thing—the cafés in town, I saw two of them. Is there one you'd recommend?"

"Nope," Sergeant Barnes said. "But the Light Bite's closed for the winter so it's the Hot Potato or nothing. I'd recommend nothing, but suit yourself."


The waitress was a big woman, getting bigger the further south you went: a small head with a frizz of yellow hair, no neck, sloping shoulders, gigantic bosom flowing lava-like down and along the rolling foothills of her gut, God alone knew what lay below.

"What's it to be?" she said, standing over Liam. You wouldn't want to pick a fight with her, that was for sure. The place was empty but for the two of them—there was no one to come to his aid.

"Could I see the menu?"

"No menus this time of year."

"Oh. OK, what've you got?" For a moment, foolishly, he entertained the hope that Sergeant Barnes had got it wrong and out back in the kitchen there happened to be a world-class chef who'd come north to get away from it all.

"Burgers and fries or poutine."

"Nothing else?"

"No one round here wants anything else." Behind her, from the direction of the kitchen, came an anguished cry. The waitress ignored it.

"Guess I'll have a burger and fries," Liam said. "With all the trimmings." He hesitated: "D'you have trimmings?"

"Onions mustard ketchup relish."

"A slice of tomato?" Tomato was good if the burger was overcooked, which it would be.

"No tomatoes."

"I'll have everything you've got," Liam said.

"Coffee?"

"You have coffee? That's great!" He overdid it a bit and the look she gave him reminded him of a rattlesnake, though he'd never seen a rattlesnake. She rolled off with his order.

Unaccountably the conversation had cheered him up. The door opened and two men in Ontario Hydro gear walked in. They nodded at Liam and he nodded back and watched as they wedged themselves into a booth by the window. His coffee arrived, bitter but drinkable; in fact, loaded with sugar and cream it was almost good. In the empty booth opposite him there was a crumpled newspaper; he retrieved it and sat back down. It was called the *Temiskaming Speaker* and was published in New Liskeard—he'd driven through New Liskeard on his way here, a small northern town, though a metropolis compared to Solace. He looked for news about the shooting at the Munich Olympics, then realized the paper was a weekly, and also a week out of date. On the front page was a photo of the winner of a ploughing competition, and beneath it an article on a building boom in New Liskeard. Local news, farming reports, no mention of Nixon or Vietnam. It was kind of restful, Liam decided. Like being on a desert island or somewhere out in space.

The waitress reappeared with his burger and fries. Liam thanked her as profusely as he dared; he didn't want to find dead flies in his burgers from here on. When she left he peered under the top bun, under the onion rings, under the beef itself. All clear so far. He sampled a fry. Not too bad.

He read the *Speaker* while he ate. Solace didn't get a mention until the bottom of page five, where there was a small photo of a girl, her hair backcombed into a huge beehive, eyes ringed with black, staring belligerently at the camera. Underneath was the caption: "Solace Girl Still Missing."


The door was opened by the girl's father, which was a relief. Liam didn't feel up to meeting a distraught mother.

"Sorry to bother you," Liam said. "Just wanted to introduce myself. I'm Liam Kane, I'm ... next door. In Mrs. Orchard's house. Moved in this afternoon."

"Oh," the man said. "Right." He held out his hand. "John Jordon, good to meet you. Karl—Sergeant Barnes—told us you'd moved in." He paused. "He said he'd told you about ... things here." He forced a smile.

"Yeah, he did. Sorry, it must be ..."

"I'd invite you in but my wife's kind of ..."

"Yeah, no, I just wanted to introduce myself. I'll see you another time."


He closed all the curtains when he got home. If there had been shutters he'd have closed those too. Shut out the world. There was too much pain out there.

He went into the kitchen. The hamburger hadn't satisfied him. In fact, he felt as if nothing would satisfy him, ever. He looked at the groceries still scattered on the counter. It seemed like weeks since he'd bought them. He wanted something sweet; ice cream would be good, he should have bought some. The only thing on the counter that had any appeal was the blueberries. He ate them directly from the basket. They were small and piercingly sweet, entirely different from the fat, tasteless farmed variety you got further south. He ate them by the handful, spitting out twigs and the occasional leaf.

It was when he was about to leave the kitchen that he noticed the electric can opener on the wall by the fridge. There was a lid stuck to its magnet. He walked over, took the lid carefully between finger and thumb and pulled it off the magnet, turned it over and sniffed. It smelled disgusting. There was a smear of whatever the can had contained on the inside of the lid; he drew his finger across it: sticky. Drying out but not dry. It had been there a day or two at most.

He went over to the sink, opened the cupboard underneath it and looked in the garbage bag. No cans. He dropped the lid into it, stared at it for a moment more, then shrugged and went to bed.

# Seven

# CLARA

She'd been sent to her room and told to stay there until she calmed down. It took a long time. She felt like she imagined Rose must have felt after rows with their mother, so hot and furious inside she could almost set fire to things just by looking at them. She'd never understood how Rose felt before but now she did. It made her miss her more than ever.

When she'd stopped crying, when she could breathe properly again, she crept out of the bedroom and down the stairs. She could hear the low murmur of her parents talking in the kitchen; they'd think she was still in her room.

First she went to the side window in the living room to check that there was no sign of the man and there wasn't, so he must have gone for his supper early, which was good. She'd have to be quick, though, because her father might decide to come upstairs and talk to her.

She took Mrs. Orchard's key from the little bowl on the hall table, slipped out of her own house and into Mrs. Orchard's and went straight to the living room. Moses slid out from under the sofa and began wrapping himself around her ankles.

"He's a bad man and we have to do this," Clara told him. "But you have to warn me if he's coming, so pay attention."

She thought about Rose to give herself courage. Rose would not hesitate. She wouldn't care about the consequences if she was caught. Rose said no one had the right to tell anyone else what to do unless they were hurting someone else. The thief was hurting Mrs. Orchard.

"Anyway, he won't know it's us," Clara said to Moses. Her heart was beating very fast. Who knew what the man would do if he figured out it was her? But if she did nothing, Mrs. Orchard would come home and find all her things gone.

She had a sudden unsettling thought: Rose stole things sometimes. Never anything expensive or important, though, and never from a person. It was called shoplifting, which wasn't really stealing, Rose said. Once she had been caught by Mr. Haas, who owned the grocery store, slipping a Hershey's Bar into the pocket of her jacket. When Mr. Haas told her off Rose had told him to go screw himself so Mr. Haas phoned her parents, who were so furious (even their father, who was never furious) that Rose wasn't allowed to go out with her friends for three months. "Three months for a Hershey's Bar!" she'd raged, up in their room that night. "Three months for a stupid Hershey's Bar! From now on I'm going to steal from that moron every chance I get!"

But Rose would never steal a person's things, things that they loved, like the man was doing.

She started with the smaller of the two boxes. The wood carvings of the old men had been laid on top of everything else, so they came out first. She put all the pieces back on the mantelpiece exactly where they had been, each old man in his own place, the table squarely between them. It was easy to do because there were bare patches in the dust showing the little figures' positions, but she could have done it anyway, she knew precisely where they belonged. Next she took out the clock, unwrapped it and put it back in the absolute centre of the mantelpiece. Then the three photos the man had selected from Mrs. Orchard's collection. Then the rest.

"Those are her most precious things," she said to Moses when the box was empty. "Now we'll do the big box." Her anger had seeped away by now and been replaced by a fierce and righteous pride.

Moses was interested in the empty box. He stood on his hind legs and peered into it, then leapt in and started wedging himself into the corners, one after another.

"You're supposed to be listening for him!" Clara scolded. "You have to pay attention!"

In fact it wasn't the man returning she was worried about—he'd be out for a while longer. It was her father going upstairs and finding her gone. She worked as quickly as she could. When the second box was empty and everything was back in its place, she rapidly smoothed out the paper the man had used for wrapping things, folded it neatly and put it in the large box. Then she stood back and surveyed the room, hands on hips.

"Done!" she said triumphantly to Moses, who was now corner-shaped, hind legs stretched along one side of the box, front legs along another. "You're a silly cat!" Clara said, though at any other time she would have been enchanted. "But we have to go."

Her father tried to persuade her to join him and her mother for supper.

"Just this once, Little," he said. "It would be a treat for your mother and me to have you with us."

"I can't," Clara said. She was at the front window, not watching for Rose (she'd explained to Rose inside her head) but for the man's return. She would move to the side window when she saw him coming but, in the meantime, she didn't want her father to see her watching the house.

Though probably it didn't matter—her father seemed to have forgotten all about their row. That was normal for him. Anything unpleasant he forgot instantly and he expected you to forget it too. He wanted everybody to be happy, all of the time. "He's fucking exhausting," Rose said once. "I don't know how he stands himself."

"Supper's all ready and on the table," Clara's father said now, coaxingly. "Come and have it with us, Little. Just this once. Then you can go straight out and feed the cat and you'll still have plenty of time to look out of the window for a while before bed. How does that sound?"

"I can't, Daddy!"

Her father placed his hand on her head. "Clara, we know how hard this is for you, we feel the same. But it's important to carry on normally, you know. It's important for ..."

"It isn't normally!" Clara said, spinning around and facing him, shaking off his hand. "Nothing's normally! I have to stay here! You promised I could!"

"OK," her father said quietly. "OK, that's fine. You stay here."

After all her fears, when the man arrived home what happened was almost an anticlimax. He must have been thinking about something else because although he'd switched on the light he'd reached the middle of the living room before he noticed. Then he stopped dead. Clara held her breath. For a long moment he stood there, completely motionless. He was facing sideways and she couldn't see his expression. But then he turned slowly round, a full circle, inspecting the room, and she could see him properly.

She'd expected him to look angry but he didn't. He looked puzzled and almost ... scared. Which pleased her. It served him right.

The next day everything was still where it belonged. She checked before she left for school and again when she got home. Everything was as it should be.

The man must have learned his lesson. It was something good to have achieved, in this time of everything being bad. It helped loosen up her insides. She imagined telling Mrs. Orchard about it when she came home from the hospital, and Mrs. Orchard thanking her. She imagined telling Rose when Rose came home, and Rose hugging her and saying how brave she was and that she was proud of her.

But it was a very small thing. Everything else was bad and getting worse.

*

Mrs. Quinn came to talk to her parents. Clara was just getting into bed, having scrambled up a fresh selection of clothes on the floor for Rose, when she heard the knock at the front door. She had a sudden wild surge of hope—maybe it was Sergeant Barnes coming to say he had found Rose. But it wasn't.

The grown-ups went into the living room and closed the door. Clara waited a few minutes to be sure they were staying there and then slid out of the bedroom and down the stairs. She stood in the hall, her feet curled up against the cold of the floor, her ear pressed to the wall. No one ever told her the truth so it was their fault she had to eavesdrop. Rose had taught her about eavesdropping. "It's an important skill to know," she'd said.

They were talking so quietly she could only make out a few words. "Never any tears," Mrs. Quinn said. Then something about taking part. Then something about friends.

*

The thing about her friends was, they kept asking her about Rose or things related to Rose. "My mom said she saw your mom in the grocery store and she looked really awful, she said she looked *sick* with worry." Clara wished they'd just talk to her about normal things; it was as if they'd forgotten she was an ordinary girl like them.

"The police are after her, aren't they?" Ruth said, and Clara shouted, "The police are *looking for* her! *Looking for* her not *after* her, stupid! *After* her doesn't *mean* that!"


"Little," her father said the next morning, "your mother and I were wondering if you'd like to invite your friend Jenny to come and play after school."

"No, thank you," Clara said.

"No? How about ... I don't know the names of the others. Is one of them called Sharon?"

"Yes."

"How about her, then?"

"No, thank you."

"How about someone else?"

"No, thank you."

"Now that's a shame. Why not?"

"I don't like them anymore."


There was a new rule. Rules arrived in her head out of nowhere. The first had been scrambling the clothes on Rose's floor, the second was counting her footsteps to and from school, and now there was one about how she brushed her teeth. It had to be done in a certain way: five quick brushes on the top left, five on the top right, five on the bottom left, five on the bottom right, rinse out three times, hold her toothbrush under the tap while she counted to ten. If she didn't do everything in the right order Rose might not come home.

At lunchtime on Friday she was sick. The children sat at their desks while they ate—you couldn't go outside to play until you finished—so she was sitting there trying to eat her sandwich. It didn't want to go down and when she forced it to and drank some milk on top of it, it came up again.

Everyone else had already finished and gone outside, which was the only good thing. Mrs. Quinn took her to the sick room (it was so small it was more like a cupboard, but it had a bed) and sat with her for a while. "Would you like me to phone your mommy, Clara?" she asked. "Would you like to go home? Or would you just like to rest here until you feel better?"

"Can I stay here?" Clara said. She didn't want to be at home, it was too quiet there.

Mrs. Quinn patted her hand where it lay on the rough blanket. "Of course," she said. "You can lie here as long as you like." She smiled. "You're a brave girl, Clara. I know it's very tough for you at the moment, but it will get better. It's hard to imagine now, I know, but it will get better. I promise you that."

*

The door to her parents' bedroom was closed when she got home, which was normal now, but as Clara was about to go back downstairs her mother's voice said, "Rose? Is that you?" Her voice sounded confused, as if she had just woken up and didn't know where she was.

Clara opened the door. The curtains were closed but she could see her mother's shape.

Her mother sat up. "Rose?" Her voice was wild, shrill with hope.

"No, Mommy," Clara said. "It's just me."

"Oh," her mother said, very low, like a breath coming out of her. After a minute she said, "OK, sweetheart. I'll be down in a few minutes."

The man's car wasn't in the driveway so she went across to Mrs. Orchard's house. She didn't sit in the chair that had been hers in the olden days, she didn't want its memories, or any memories. She sat on the floor with her back against the wall and her legs straight out in front of her. She wanted her mother back. She wanted her more than anything in the world, even more, at this moment, than she wanted Rose. She wanted to climb into bed beside her mother and for her mother to draw her close and cuddle her, like she used to. She wanted to know that when she got home from school her mother would be in the kitchen getting supper, not in bed, and would turn from whatever she was doing and smile her old smile and say, "Hello, sweetheart, how was your day?" and be interested in the answer.

She hadn't expected Moses to climb onto her lap but he did. He wrapped himself into a ball, sank down into her and started to purr. She stroked him and tried not to think about anything, just to concentrate on the feel of his purring and the warmth and softness of him under her hands, but it didn't help and after a while she let her arms drop and simply sat, like a rag doll, up against the wall.

But then Moses did something so amazing that it helped after all. He stood up, his paws kneading little pits in her legs, put his front feet up on her shoulders, pressed his nose against hers and looked straight into her eyes from a distance of half an inch.

His eyes were absolutely huge, it was like looking at two great green moons. Clara went cross-eyed trying to focus on them. It made her laugh.

"Did I forget to stroke you, Mo?" she asked, her mouth almost touching his. She put her hands on either side of him and stroked his whole sleek little cat body, all the way down to his tail.

*

The man hadn't learned his lesson after all. Late on Friday afternoon, about half an hour before he would normally go out for his supper, he packed up Mrs. Orchard's things again. Clara was watching. When he'd finished packing he looked around the room one final time and then went out as usual.

Clara's supper was late that evening because her mother had a hard time getting out of bed, so Clara had to wait longer than she liked and it made her very fidgety. She ate as quickly as she could and then, her mouth pressed into a tight white line, she went over to Mrs. Orchard's house and began unpacking the boxes again. She wondered how many times she'd have to do this before the man learned.

Moses appeared from nowhere and watched.

"He's very, very stupid," Clara said to him. "Obviously." She finished the big box and started on the one with the precious things in it. Moses came over and sniffed at it, then stood on his hind legs and peered in, like before.

"You can't get into it now, silly cat, there are still things in it," Clara said, not crossly but quite firmly. "Please stay out of the way."

Moses looked up at her for a moment as if weighing up how serious she was and then leapt into the box.

"Moses!" Clara scolded. "Get out! You'll break things!"

In a flash he was out of the box and gone. She was surprised at his speed. "I wasn't mad at you," she called. "You just have to stay out of the boxes."

She unwrapped the last of the little carved men and took him over to the mantelpiece to put him with his friends so that they could continue their card game. Afterwards she couldn't recall what made her look around. Was there a sound? Or a draught from the door? Or was it just a feeling? Whatever it was, she turned and there was the man, standing in the doorway.

# Eight

# ELIZABETH

It seems I will not be going home. Directly after lunch this afternoon the heart specialist, Dr. Pauling, came to see me. He said that the results of the tests have come through and they show that my heart is, as he put it, not in good shape. He was so gentle in the telling that there was no mistaking what he meant. I felt very badly for him; it must be horrible, breaking news of that sort. I told him it was all right, that I had been waiting for a long time to join you, and he smiled and took my hand in both of his and said, "Good. Good."

I wanted to ask him how long I had left but found that I couldn't.

I felt very strange after he'd gone. Detached. Separated not only from my surroundings but from myself. I heard people speaking but only dimly, as if they were in another room. The nurses seemed to move in a continuous stream up and down the ward. They were out of focus. I was out of focus.

Time and the world carried on. Dinner came, and something about the ordinariness of the plate being set down in front of me seemed to break the spell. It was some nameless, tasteless meat in lumpy gravy but I ate it almost with relish. I even ate the dessert, rice pudding, which I detest. Between mouthfuls the knowledge that I was dying washed into and out of me like waves on the shore. When the plates were cleared away, I watched Mrs. Cox across the ward change from her lacy pink nightie into a lacy lilac affair (she has no modesty whatsoever) and it struck me that there was something almost graceful about that fat old body raising its arms to haul off the old and pull on the new. She looked at herself in her little hand mirror (kept at the ready on her bedside table), patted her hair and climbed back into bed looking pleased.

The final round of medicines appeared at the usual time. Martha continued being Martha.

There's a little pause each evening between the doling out of medicines and the turning out of lights during which she frequently treats me to her musings on life. She seems to be fairly coherent at that time of day.

"I'm the only one left," she announced when the medicines trolley disappeared through the swing doors. "All the others are gone. It's the worst thing, being the last one. I'd rather be dead."

I didn't feel like listening to her. I said flatly, "Well, you will be soon enough, just be patient."

That shut her up. But then, of course, I felt guilty, so after a minute I said wearily, "Who's dead, then? Your brothers and sisters?"

"Yes," she said, resentful but wanting to talk too badly to pass up an opportunity. Martha just loves talking about herself, she's her favourite topic of conversation.

"How many siblings do—did—you have?"

"Ten. Four boys, six girls."

"That's a big family," I said. "Did you all get on?"

She snorted. I am pleased to report that I have never snorted in my life.

"Oh," I said. "Did all of you fight, or just some of you?"

"The girls were the worst," she said, starting to cheer up. "Boys try to kill each other but then it's over. Girls keep on and on. Alice and Peggy. They were the worst. They could hold a grudge, those two. When they were in their teens they quarrelled about something, I forget what it was, they probably forgot too but that made no difference, they never forgave each other. Never spoke to each other again. Not a word. Never, their whole lives. Didn't go to each other's weddings, didn't even go to each other's funerals."

"Well, they couldn't," I said, quite reasonably, I thought. "Or at least one of them couldn't."

"Oh, I'm sure they had good excuses," Martha said, staring vacantly across the room. "People invent good excuses when they want to get out of something."

"Not that good," I said.

She turned her head and looked at me. "I thought you asked me to tell you about them," she said sharply. "Or did I get that wrong?"

I thought, I'm going to miss her. And then thought, what a ridiculous thing to think: I'll be dead.

So will Martha before long, by the look of things. She's extremely thin, skeletal almost, but she has a grotesquely swollen stomach as if she were nine months pregnant. They don't seem to know what it is. She doesn't talk about it, which is a mercy.

I had difficulty getting to sleep. I was frightened, my love. Why should that be? Why are we afraid of something that comes to us all and is as normal as the setting of the sun? I should welcome it—I have no faith in any deity, no belief in a "hereafter," but nonetheless I do absolutely believe that I will be with you again. A contradiction, I know—how can we be together if there is no "hereafter" to be together in? But I so strongly feel that I'm with you now, in all senses bar the physical, that I cannot conceive of it being otherwise. You, ever the scientist, would say that sounds very much like a lack of imagination combined with a serious case of wishful thinking. Nevertheless, I remain convinced. (I can imagine you smiling.)

Maybe it's a matter of tenses. Of grammar. Our love existed, it does exist, it will exist. On the great continuum of time, perhaps it is the tenses that will cease to be. What does the scientist in you think of that?

*

My mind is slipping. I hope I'm not going to be like Martha in my final days. It was terrifying. It wasn't a dream, it was different, it was full daylight and I was right here in this bed, and then I wasn't, I was back in Guelph, and Annette was shouting at me, her face hideous with rage, and Liam was holding out his arms and screaming, screaming. I was shaking so hard I could scarcely stand; I was trying to stop her, I opened my mouth to speak and nothing came out, and someone said, "It's all right, Mrs. Orchard, it's all right, you're here with us and you're fine." A nurse was holding my hand, patting it. "That's better," she said. "That's much better. Let's sit you up a little, you've slid right down the bed."

I have spent half my life trying to suppress that memory. When I was in St. Thomas's, the psychiatrist, Dr. Leander, said that whenever it or something similarly disturbing came into my mind I was to replace it, calmly but firmly, with something positive. He said we were all able to control our thoughts to some extent. At first I didn't believe him, I didn't see how it could be possible to simply push aside such anguish, but actually, with practice, it was. Some of the time, at least.

So I've been trying to do that. I've been methodically, one by one, recalling the details of the second time I saw Liam. You weren't there, it was the Monday or Tuesday after our tea party and you were at work. I'd been feeling rather flat—inevitable, I suppose, I'd been so buoyed up by meeting Liam there was bound to be a let-down afterwards. But then around ten in the morning I heard a strange slapping sound at the front door and when I went to investigate, there he was, left hand raised, palm forward, making ready to smack the door again. In his right hand he had a stick bigger than he was, that most vital of accessories for all small boys.

"Well, good morning, Liam," I said, carefully disguising my utter delight. "How are you today?"

He considered the question, thumping his stick up and down, then looked up at me and came straight to the point. "Can I have a cookie?" he asked. It was the first time I'd heard him speak, Annette had failed to get so much as a thank you out of him on Saturday. He had a slightly husky voice, unusual in one so young.

"I wondered if that might be why you were here," I said. "We'll have to ask your mommy. Where is she and where are your sisters? Are they coming too?"

He shook his head vigorously; no, they weren't, he most emphatically had not invited them.

"Does your mommy know you're here, Liam?"

He spotted something on the floor that needed killing and set about it with his stick.

"I'll tell you what," I said. "Let's take some cookies back to your house in case your mommy is wondering where you are. Can you show me the way you came?" I wanted to know if he had gone near the road, but thankfully he hadn't; instead he wove his way through the group of silver birch trees on the vacant lot between our houses.

We could hear the others before we reached them; they were in the backyard, skipping rope, Annette at one end, the girls taking turns at the other. They—the girls—were pretty enough, fair-haired, blue-eyed and slender, like their mother, but I remember thinking Liam outshone them by a mile. He was a truly beautiful child, even you remarked on it, Charles, and you seldom noticed such things. With that dark, glossy hair, pale clear skin and wonderful golden-brown eyes, it seemed to me that he was to his sisters as the sun is to the moon.

Annette looked startled when we came up. She hadn't noticed Liam was gone and was, quite rightly, horrified and ashamed. I made light of it, saying he had been nowhere near the road and how delighted I'd been to see him and what handsome children she had. Grateful that I seemed not to be judging her, she offered coffee, and I presented the cookies.

We brought two dining chairs outside and positioned them in the shade of the house—the sun was oppressively hot already—and the two of us sat with our coffee, watching the children explore the yard. There were two apple trees and the fruit, much of it ready for picking, was hanging tantalizingly low. The girls kept jumping up, trying to reach the apples, shrieking with laughter at each failed attempt. Liam was trying to whack the lowest branches with his stick. Annette called to him sharply to be careful not to hit his sisters, whereupon he wandered off and started digging holes in the flowerbed at the side of the garden.

A military airplane flew over and we both watched it.

"Ralph says Charles is from England," Annette said after a minute.

"Yes. He came over twelve years ago. They were doing research here at the agricultural college he couldn't get funding for at home and he wanted to be part of it."

"Does he have family in England?"

"Just his parents now. His brother was killed in May. At Dunkirk."

She was silent for a moment.

"Do his parents live in London?"

"Yes."

"Poor Charles."

"Yes."

The plane disappeared behind a distant hill and the sky was empty again, a vast and innocent blue.

Annette said, "Ralph tried to sign up, but they told him he'd be of more use at the college."

I nodded. "Charles was told the same."

"I think Ralph feels guilty, though. And I suspect he's afraid people will think it's just an excuse to get out of going."

Something in her tone caught my attention. I looked at her, wondering if she thought that herself and, if so, what it said about her relationship with Ralph.

"It isn't an excuse," I said firmly, because she needed to be put right. "Ralph's an expert on grain, isn't he? Like Charles. There are desperate food shortages in England and thousands—*hundreds* of thousands—of troops to feed. Both Ralph and Charles are far more use helping to increase wheat production here than in Europe with guns in their hands. Charles would be a complete liability with a gun in his hands."

Annette gave a nervous laugh but she looked relieved, and the conversation moved on. She asked about our garden—I had turned it into a vegetable patch as part of the Digging for Victory campaign and I promised to help her do the same with theirs on a smaller scale, leaving room for the children to play. We discussed the kindergarten the twins would be starting at after Labour Day; I knew the teacher—she had replaced me when I left and was very good. As we talked I followed Liam, who was now wandering aimlessly around the yard, with my eyes.

I remember a tingling in my blood, an excitement at the fact that Annette and I were getting along so well. I hadn't expected it, she struck me as an anxious and rather superficial woman and I hadn't warmed to her at first, but the conversation flowed quite easily between us and she seemed genuinely pleased that I had come over. It seemed to me that we might do this—have coffee together in a relaxed, spontaneous way—quite often. And hence I might get to see a good deal of Liam.

But then it nearly came undone. I'd been so busy congratulating myself on how well we were getting on that I failed to concentrate on what she was saying, and it took a minute for my brain to register that she'd just told me she was pregnant again.

It wasn't planned, she said, with an embarrassed laugh, and she wasn't very happy about it, especially as she feared that once again it might be twins. To be honest, she said, she found the three children a bit of a handful as it was. Not the girls, the girls were lovely, it was Liam. He was terribly difficult. She was at her wits' end with him sometimes, he exhausted her.

Liam was all of six feet away as she was saying this. He looked up when his name was mentioned but he was behind Annette's chair and she didn't see him. I saw him, though, and saw that he had heard. He wouldn't have understood everything his mother said but he got the gist of it all right. I saw him get it.

I was so angry. So *angry*. In a matter of seconds I went from a state of cheerful optimism to a white-hot mix of anger, jealously and despair. Her careless disregard for her child's feelings; her profligate fertility; the fact that she was going to bring into the world a child or children she didn't really want, while I was starving for the lack of a single one. I know it was an overreaction—I knew it even at the time—but the fact that she didn't think to check where Liam was before saying such things about him, combined with her being unaware, earlier that morning, that her three-year-old son had wandered as far as our place and could easily have gone out onto the road, seemed to me utterly disgraceful.

I gripped my cup, looking out over the yellowing end-of-summer grass of the Kanes's backyard, trying desperately to overcome, or at least disguise, my feelings, not because they were unfair to Annette but because I knew that if she were to have so much as an inkling of them, a certain small boy would never again come knocking on our door.

I was rescued by one of the twins, who in her efforts to reach a particularly tempting apple, ran headfirst into the trunk of the tree and came wailing to her mother. By the time she had been comforted

I was calm again, and we carried on with our coffee and chatted of other things.

I even managed, as I left, to casually raise the question of whether the children (I took care not to single out Liam) should be allowed to come over and visit me on their own if they wished. Annette was concerned that they would be a nuisance so I told her that we had been unable to have children of our own and that I would enjoy having them around. She expressed sympathy and said of course they could come. Between us we worked out a set of rules to ensure their safety: they were never to go near the road; I would phone her straight away if they came over and phone again when they left so that she could watch for them. They were never to have more than one cookie and the minute they became a bother I was to send them back home. Sensible rules devised by sensible women, to protect children from harm.

If I happened to be standing at the kitchen window I would see him coming (always Liam on his own, as I had known it would be), wandering through the birches, stick in hand like a pilgrim of old, pausing now and then to bash things (presumably unlike a pilgrim of old), lost in the mysterious world of childhood. While it was warm enough we sat on the porch steps, he with a glass of milk and a cookie, me with a cup of coffee. To begin with his visits were brief and to the point; he would have his cookie and, mission accomplished, he would leave. As he became more comfortable with me, though, they became longer. It was a lot like taming a wild bird: offer crumbs. Sit quietly. Don't expect too much too soon.

Sometimes we would talk. He might have a question—"Why are there bugs?"—or an observation—"My bottom is smaller than your bottom"—but quite often we didn't speak much. I did insist on please and thank you, but that aside I was perfectly content with his silence. (As I was with yours, my love. Neither of you was what you'd call loquacious. I must be drawn to quiet males.)

When it became too cold for the porch steps, we moved indoors and sat at the kitchen table. I bought a few toys—a wooden jigsaw, a couple of Dinky Toys, a colouring book and crayons, blank newsprint for drawing (he was very good at drawing) and a number of books: *Winnie the Pooh*, *Peter Rabbit*, *Ferdinand*, *Wag-tail Bess*.

Ordinary, simple, inexpensive things. Things that say, to anyone coming in the door: in this house, there is a child.

# Nine

# LIAM

"Won't be this month," Jim Peake said, drilling a neat little hole in fresh new wood. "Probably not October either, I got so damn much work lined up. Plus my partner's deserted me. Not exactly partner, unpaid labourer. Son, in other words. Off to some damn university down south, learning to be a vet. Easy job, vetting. Worst you have to do is crawl up a cow's ass, nothing you'd call work involved. Big money, easy life ..."

He straightened up and raked through a jar of screws. "All you do for your kids, three square meals a day, nice warm house, teach them a good trade, what do they do? Take off and learn to be a vet. I told him, you like animals so much, get yourself a dog, for Pete's sake! Get a *horse*! Get an *elephant*! Cheaper than a vet degree. I'm staring poverty in the face."

He was a big, tough-looking, weather-beaten guy but he was so proud of his son he couldn't even look at you for fear it would show, Liam could hear it in his voice.

"Hand me that screwdriver, will you? No, the little one. That's it."

Liam said, "The thing is, I want to sell the house as soon as I can and a rotten bathroom floor isn't going to make a good impression."

For more than a week now he'd managed not to make a decision about anything, large or small—what to do with his life, where to go from here, what to have for lunch. He'd spent a few days driving around exploring the country, which was beautiful, no denying it, mile upon wild mile of lakes and rocks and trees (he was getting used to the trees). Now and then he turned the car radio on and, cresting the granite hills, it sometimes picked up a signal and he'd hear a snatch of news: "*grand jury indicted five White House staff for violation of Federal wiretapping …*" Then it would be gone. "Washington Post *investigative reporters …*" Gone again.

Tourist-like activities aside, all he'd managed to do was some trivial repairs around the house—tightening a sagging hinge on a cupboard door, replacing a door handle (which had required another visit to the hardware store, where once again the old man's daughter came in but this time with a baby on her hip, the ultimate turn-off).

But the time had come for action. It might still feel like summer but it couldn't last much longer and the one thing he had decided for sure was that, come hell or high water, he'd be out of here before the first snowflake touched the ground.

"Why not sling a sheet of linoleum on top?" Jim Peake suggested. "Then nobody will ever know. Not until after they move in, anyway."

"Yeah, well," Liam said. The truth was, he felt an inexplicable need to fix up Mrs. Orchard's home properly, to get it into the best possible state before selling it. It wasn't to do with the money he'd get for it, though that was the reason he gave. He wasn't sure what it was to do with—maybe a kind of thank you to this woman he could hardly remember. It bothered him that he felt so little connection to her or her husband. He'd studied the framed photos in the living room and he'd recognized both of them all right, and he knew that he'd stayed with them some-times and had loved it, but those were factual memories rather than anything genuinely recalled. He could remember no details about the time he'd spent with them. What had they been like? What had *he* been like? It made him feel he wasn't really entitled to be living in Mrs. Orchard's house, inherit-ing everything.

Jim Peake said, "What have we here, an honest southerner? What's the world coming to? Did you say it was old Mrs. Orchard's place?"

Liam hadn't said but Jim Peake clearly knew. No doubt by now everybody in town knew everything there was to know. Since he'd arrived a succession of women had appeared on the front porch, young and old, all with smiles of welcome and gifts of food. Liam hadn't invited any of them in, not even the good-looking ones. He doubted there was just neigh-bourliness involved.

"That's right. Maybe you could just have a look at the floor and tell me what to do, what's required, so I could do it myself? I'd pay you for your time."

"Your problem with that place is not the bathroom floor," Jim Peake said. "Forget the bathroom floor, it's *nothing*. Your problem is the *roof*. Should'a been done ten years ago, rain seeping through all this time, I hate to think what's underneath. Find me another screw this size, OK?"

Liam rattled through the jar.

"Thing is, I got Jeff Patterson's roof to do first, providing the warm weather holds. Can't shingle a roof in cold weather, shingles won't stick, first storm they'll all be gone. Plus I'm on my own. No unpaid labour to do the dirty work, no one to curse at, it's gonna be grim. I need another screw the same. Thanks. Awful lot of donkey work, a roof. Up and down ladders carrying timber and shingles and what-not. Shingles look thin—well any shingle single"—he paused, thought a minute—"any *single shingle* is thin, but the buggers are heavy as lead. Then you discover the chimney's gonna fall down and you have to do that too, up and down ladders carrying bricks, buckets of mortar, no one to pass 'em up to. Doing it on your own's a long, long job, three/four times as long as if there was two of you. Take the other end of this, OK? Gotta flip it over."

He was working on a window frame, a big one, lying across two sawhorses. The top half still had the panes in. Liam took one end and they turned it over. It weighed a ton. He wondered how Jim Peake would have managed if he hadn't turned up.

"I promised Gord Bing I'd get it done this week," Jim Peake said, meaning the window frame. "Then forgot all about it. Would've been quicker to make a new one but he's a cheapskate so I'm just replacing the rotten bits. What's your trade then, Mister ... I forget your name, I'm lousy with names. Kane, was it?"

"Yeah. I'm an accountant. Used to be an accountant."

"But now you're not?"

"Right."

"How's that?"

"I quit."

"Sounds a cushy job, add a little number here, subtract a little number there. Why'd you quit?"

"I hated it." He saw no point in lying. He saw no point in all these questions either but people up here were astoundingly nosy.

Jim Peake gave a bark of laughter. "Hoo! Guess you don't have kids, eh?"

"Right." The decision not to have children had been Fiona's but Liam had been one hundred percent happy to go along with it. He hadn't enjoyed being a child and couldn't imagine enjoying being a father.

"So what you gonna do now?"

"Not sure."

Jim Peake shook his head, marvelling at the concept of choice. He was making long, smooth sweeps of the timber with a plane. Sweet-smelling curls of pale new wood bloomed ahead of the blade. "Trick is to keep up a nice, even pressure all the way," he said. "Second trick is not to take too much off. Actually that's the first trick. Keep checking. You can't put it back on."

He squatted down and squinted along the timber. "A liddle bit more," he said. "Want to have a go?"

"I have to get on with things," Liam said. He could see what the guy was thinking as clearly as if it were tattooed across his forehead. He needed someone to carry shingles and bricks up and down ladders and there stood Liam, jobless: a perfect match.

Jim Peake took another swipe with the planc. "Okey-doke. But basically what I'm sayin" is, even if the weather holds, I can't do your roof in the next couple of weeks, which means not until next spring, unless I have help. So, seems to me you have three options: one is you can decide to sell your house as it stands for a reduced price; two is you can go down to New Liskeard or North Bay and see if you can find a builder down there with nothing to do who's prepared to come all the way up here each day, which I extremely doubt; three is you can decide to give me a hand with the work I have now so that I'm finished in time to do your roof if it's still warm enough or your bathroom floor if it isn't. Choice is yours."

Liam nodded. "I'll give it some thought," he said. "Thanks for the advice."

"Any time," Jim Peake said cheerfully. "Advice is free."

Back at the house he wandered restlessly from room to room, mulling over his options as laid out by Jim Peake. Forget the idea of getting someone from another town to do the work, Jim was right, that wasn't going to happen. Which left him with a simple choice (his least favourite thing nowadays): sell it now, as it stood, which increasingly he didn't want to do, or go and lug shingles up and down ladders, which would probably kill him. Just decide, he thought. Jesus Christ, what's the matter with you?

The matter was his head was full of crap. Fiona had taken to visiting him at night, three a.m. was her favourite time. The hour of lost souls. She whispered bitter nothings in his ear: *Would it kill you to make an effort, Liam? Would it kill you to be pleasant to our friends for an hour or two on a Saturday night? You sit there like a lump of concrete, they must all wonder what's the matter with you.* When he replied, not bothering to stifle a yawn, that they were her friends, not his, her eyes opened wide: *Oh my God, you're right! I'm so sorry! Which of your many, many friends would you like to invite for dinner? Wait a sec while I get a pencil and paper, we'll make a list.*

He didn't need her to tell him, he knew it well enough; even as a kid at school he'd never had the gift of making friends. Casual relationships, yes, close friendships, no. It was as if there were a river, not wide but dark and deep, between himself and others, and he'd never figured out how to cross it.

His sole talent, which revealed itself only as he got older, was with women. They thought him good-looking, his one and only stroke of luck in the great lottery of life. It never translated into long-term relationships, though. Things would get to a certain point and he'd have to end it. The eight years with Fiona were the single exception and he knew for a fact it

121

had lasted that long only because neither of them could countenance it failing; Fiona because she refused to fail at anything, himself because he had believed, or had kidded himself that he believed, that it was going to work; that he'd finally managed to cross the river.

Failure, when it could no longer be denied, made Liam even more withdrawn than he'd been before. It made Fiona savage.

*You don't seem able to relate to the rest of us, Liam—I don't mean just me, I mean anybody, I mean the human race! I think you should see a shrink. I'm serious, I really do.*

Here's a truth about marriage, he thought, staring at the ceiling at three in the morning. People should be warned: think twice before you take those vows, because there is nothing, absolutely nothing, as lonely as a bad marriage.

And here's another truth, he thought to himself, standing in Mrs. Orchard's kitchen at three in the afternoon. You have gone over all this a *million fucking times*! Now shut up and get on with your life!


He went upstairs to look at the bathroom floor again. It hadn't changed. It never would, unless he did something about it. There was another wet patch by the toilet, the source of which puzzled him until he looked up at the ceiling; sure enough, wet stains from a leaky roof, just as Jim Peake predicted. Ditto in his bedroom. He went into the small bedroom beside his own and then into Mrs. Orchard's; both ceilings seemed to be OK, so at the moment the leaks were limited to one side of the house.

But looking around Mrs. Orchard's room reminded him that sooner or later he was going to have to deal with her effects. Why not now? The most urgent task was to decide what to do about the roof, so instead he would sort out Mrs. Orchard's belongings. He had no responsibilities to anyone but himself, he could do, not do, or evade doing, whatever he liked.

The cupboards and drawers in Mrs. Orchard's room were full of her clothes and it didn't feel right to touch them. He'd have to ask around, see if she'd had a friend in the town who wouldn't mind doing it. In the small bedroom at the back of the house he found her papers and documents. Thankfully, she'd been methodical, filing the papers in neatly labelled folders. He sorted the folders into two piles: those which could be disposed of immediately and those he'd have to go through with more care. It was a relief to be dealing with papers, whatever their subject. It was something he was used to, something he was good at.

As an afterthought he checked under the small single bed and found a battered suitcase. He hauled it out, squatted down and opened it. It was full of drawings. Not technical drawings or the efforts of a would-be artist—a child's drawings. A child old enough that the subjects were mostly recognizable—the top one was probably a fire engine, a bright, grainy-crayon-red against a background of enthusi-astically scribbled red and yellow fire—but young enough that staying within the lines had clearly been a challenge. The crisp, fragile remains of Scotch tape clung to the top corners; at one time it had been up on a wall. Liam turned it over. In the bottom right-hand corner, in Mrs. Orchard's precise writing, it said: *Liam. Age 4. December 1942.*

It rocked him back on his heels. There had been a whole wall of them—a wall of his pictures. Where had it been? In the kitchen? Yes, the wall opposite the fridge. Mrs. Orchard had called it "Liam's gallery." There'd been a wonderful stash of crayons and pencils and colouring books kept in a special drawer—his very own drawer, no sisters raiding it and wrecking the crayons or scribbling all over his painstaking work. When he'd finished a new drawing he'd show it to Mrs. Orchard, who would study it seriously for a minute or two and then say something like, "It's very good indeed, Liam. I like the fire engine in particular—look how fast it's going! Look at this, Charles, isn't it good? I think it should be in the gallery, don't you?" He remembered her voice, when she spoke to him there always seemed to be a smile in it. She'd take the picture over to where Mr. Orchard sat reading—he was always reading—and he would study it too and agree solemnly that it must go up on the wall.

His pride. He remembered his pride. The way it swelled up in him, made him feel a little bigger, a little taller; more sure of himself. Special.

Still squatting there on his haunches, another long-forgotten memory came. The day his family left for Calgary he'd tried to run over to Mr. and Mrs.

124

Orchard's house, and his mother had chased after him, picked him up and locked him in the car.

Late that afternoon he got some empty boxes from the grocery store and started packing up Mrs. Orchard's possessions. Not the furniture—that could be sold, either separately or with the house—but the small things, ornaments, photos, little odds and ends.

He began in the living room because that was where most of them were. The four boxes containing his own belongings were still where he'd put them the evening he arrived; he saw no point in unpacking them when he was going to be here for such a short time.

A couple of Mrs. Orchard's things he remembered. A Quebec carving—a really good one—of four old men around a table, playing cards. It had been on the mantelpiece in their house in Guelph, as it was here. It had been his favourite thing in the house. He decided to keep it. The carriage clock, also on the mantelpiece and also familiar, was a good one; he'd keep it too. He wrapped both items carefully in newspaper and put them in a smaller box along with three of the framed photographs—two of Mr. and Mrs. Orchard together and one of Mr. Orchard reading on the porch of the house in Guelph. The other things he was less careful with, they could take their chances.

When he'd packed everything but the books he called it a day and walked into town for supper at the Hot Potato. Over a week after arriving in Solace, hamburger-saturation had driven him to try the poutine, which turned out to be as leaden as he'd expected but also remarkably addictive, so now he alternated; stodge with meat one day, stodge with cheese the next. For several days he'd been trying to work up the courage to ask the rattlesnake if she'd consider doing a baked potato now and then. The skin would be roughage—he was conscious of being a little short of roughage.

He was early, which was a mistake—half a dozen teenagers were crammed into one of the booths, putting off going home as long as they could. They were eating fries and laughing: universal teenage activities. "Leader of the Pack" was playing on the jukebox, years out of date and way too loud. To Liam's surprise the rattlesnake didn't seem to mind the din. She watched over the rabble benignly.

He'd meant to bring one of Mrs. Orchard's books to read while he ate but had forgotten, so he read last week's copy of the *Temiskaming Speaker* for the third time, skipping the page with the Jordons' missing daughter on it. Nonetheless he found himself wondering if she would have been one of those teenagers a month or so back. He'd seen the little sister a couple of times, coming home from school. She looked desolate, he thought. Whatever her relationship with her big sister, it must be hell for her now.

He ordered the poutine, drank two cups of coffee, then wandered down to the lake in the dark.

It was too cloudy for moonlight but he could still make out the surface of the water. It was uncannily still, as if waiting for something cosmic to happen. Winter, Liam thought, turning up the collar of his

126

coat and wrapping his arms around himself. It's waiting for winter.

When he got home he went into the living room, switching on the light as he went. He was a couple of steps into the room before he noticed that everything had changed. Or rather, that nothing had changed; that the changes he had made had been unmade. That the past had been undone.

He stopped dead, gripped (absurdly, he later thought) by a spasm of pure, cold fear. It was as if time had slipped. He looked around the room, wondering if he was hallucinating. Or if he hadn't actually done the packing, he'd just dreamed he had done.

Then common sense returned. He, Liam Kane, had packed Mrs. Orchard's possessions into boxes that afternoon and someone as-yet unknown had unpacked them while he was out. There was nothing metaphysical about it. The question was who. And why. He looked around the room again, turning slowly, looking for clues. Nothing struck him. He went over to the mantelpiece. All of the ornaments were exactly— *exactly*—where they had been—that really was a little uncanny: the precision, revealed by the imprints in the dust. It must be someone who knew the place very well. Mrs. Orchard's cleaning woman? But surely a cleaning woman would have cleaned, she would have dusted.

Another thought struck him: whoever it was had known that he was out and that he would be out for quite a while; the crunched-up paper he'd used to wrap things in had been smoothed flat, neatly folded and placed in an empty box—you wouldn't bother with that unless you had plenty of time. Was somebody watching the place? Watching his movements? The idea made his skin prickle. Then a worse thought: Was someone still in the house?

He went through the downstairs rooms fast, checking the pantry, the mud room, the cupboard under the stairs, then went upstairs, checked all the cupboards, his heart beating fast. Nothing. No one. Everything was as he had left it. He went back downstairs. As far as he could tell nothing apart from the ornaments had been touched, far less stolen. His own four boxes were undisturbed. He checked the back door; it was locked, as the front door had been. None of the windows showed any sign of being forced. Whoever it was had a key—a distinctly uncomfortable thought.

He thought about calling Sergeant Barnes. But nothing had been stolen or damaged, so what would he say?

Suddenly the answer came: it *would* be the cleaner. She'd have a key, for a start, and of course she wouldn't have dusted, she was no longer employed to do so. He remembered his conversation with the lawyer; the cleaner had been left a small sum in Mrs. Orchard's will. She and the old lady must have been fond of each other, probably the cleaner had been coming for years. Perhaps her visit this time had been a sentimental one, she'd come to say goodbye to the place and had been upset to see it stripped bare. That was feasible. She'd put everything back so that she could see it one more time as it had been, as Mrs. Orchard had wanted it. She wouldn't care what Liam thought, in her mind he would be the intruder.

And either it was a pure coincidence that she had arrived when he was out or—much more likely, now that he thought about it—like everyone else in the town, she knew his movements down to the last split second.

*

His plan had been to pack everything up again the next day but lethargy struck again like it had in Toronto, brought on by a sudden conviction, at three a.m., that he and Fiona had made a mistake. They should have tried harder, he in particular should have tried harder. If nothing else, he could have made a genuine effort to be more sociable, more engaged.

At four a.m. he decided he'd phone her in the morning; in the morning he remembered what the last two-thirds of their marriage had been like and changed his mind. For the next three days he was incapable of thought, almost incapable of movement, and it might have gone on for weeks except that on the fourth morning, he was woken at seven o'clock by someone hammering on the door. Liam swore, hauled on his jeans and went downstairs.

"Change of plan," Jim Peake said, dispensing with the niceties. His truck was in the driveway behind Liam's car, two ladders, some sheets of plywood and an assortment of planks of wood sticking up out of the back. "You're in luck. Jeff Patterson's roof? I was

129

gonna do it next week? Turns out he's got money troubles. Unpaid tax dating back years, he's being slammed by Revenue Canada to the tune of many zeros. Means he can't afford to get his roof done, not this year anyway. Weather looks like holding so we can start yours tomorrow, bright and early. Do the roof first, soggy floor after that. Whadaya think?"

"Ah … great," Liam said. "That's great."

"OK then. We should go up have a look at it now, see what the damage is."

Liam didn't like the sound of "we" and said so but somehow ten minutes later there he was, sitting astride the ridge, doing his utmost not to look down. From up here you could see the lake, bigger than it looked from the beach; what had appeared to be the far shore was merely islands, beyond which bays and inlets stretched off into the distance, finally disappearing into the haze. Jim Peake didn't spare the scenery a glance; he was scrambling around prising up shingles and cursing at what he found underneath. "This side of the house, the whole damn thing's gotta be replaced," he said at last. "God Almighty, take a look at that."

"What exactly is the whole damn thing?"

"Shingles plus the plywood underneath. The plywood's what you nail the shingles to. It's rotten, price you pay for not doing the roof regularly. Have a look."

He lifted a shingle near Liam's perch and prodded the wood beneath it with a screwdriver. "See?"

Liam saw. The screwdriver sank in as if the plywood were a sponge.

130

"And see the way the shingle's curled up at the edges? Heat of the sun. Happens to old shingles."

"How much is all this going to cost?"

"Materials and labour. Biggest cost is labour, but with you working for free I'll knock a third off that."

"I thought you said it took three or four times as long to do a roof if you were on your own."

"Did I say that?" Jim said. "I don't recollect saying that." He grinned. "That was *skilled* labour I was talking about. You're unskilled. No offence intended."

"None taken," Liam said. "In fact that's good news, because you're saying I won't be much use so there's really no point in me being there. Which is a relief."

Jim laughed. "OK, let's settle on half. You help and you'll pay half the labour cost—that's my half, the skilled half, so it works out more than strictly half, of course. But it's a bargain. I'm serious. You shouldn't pass it up. We start tomorrow."

It looked as if things were going to get done after all, which Liam guessed was a good thing. When Mrs. Orchard's will was sorted out he'd come into quite a bit of money, but that could be many months away and his savings wouldn't last that long. He'd need to sell the house to keep himself going while he figured out what he was going to do in the long term.

The spell on the roof had snapped him out of his inertia and he spent the rest of the day doing small domestic chores, changing the sheets, cleaning the kitchen, doing laundry. Before going for supper he packed up Mrs. Orchard's bits and pieces for the second time. By six it was done and he went off to the Hot Potato.

Going down to the lake for a few minutes on his way home had become part of his routine but he skipped it this evening, which meant he arrived home a few minutes earlier than usual. He was thinking about the next day as he walked in, wondering what it would be like working for Jim, and it took him a second or two to realize that either the television had turned itself on or someone was in the living room. The thought turned him cold. Cautiously, he pushed open the living-room door.

The child from next door was taking the ornaments out of the boxes, unwrapping them and putting them back where they'd been to start with, all the while talking—loudly—to herself. "I wasn't mad at you," she said. "You just have to stay out of the boxes."

At first she didn't notice him. Then something made her look around and he saw the shock in her face, followed, unmistakably, by fear. He knew he had to say something to reassure her but couldn't think what. What exactly do you say to a little kid you've never met who's standing in the middle of your living room talking to herself while she messes up your belongings?

"Hi," he said.

# Ten

# CLARA

She couldn't move. She'd been about to put one of the little card players down where he belonged on the mantelpiece but her hand was frozen in space. The man didn't look angry, though, and after a moment her fright ebbed away, leaving her feeling very cross.

"They aren't your things!" she said fiercely, before he had time to say anything more.

The man looked startled. He said, "Um ... as a matter of fact, they are."

"They are not! They're Mrs. Orchard's!"

"They *were* Mrs. Orchard's," the man said cautiously. "But she left them to me."

Clara didn't know what he meant. She said, "What does 'left them to me' mean?"

The man thought for a minute. "It's when people decide before they die who they want to have their things after they're dead. Mrs. Orchard decided she wanted me to have her things."

It didn't make any sense. Clara said, "But she asked me to look after ..." She was about to say "Moses"

133

but caught herself in time. "She asked me to look after her things for her until she gets back. She's in the hospital but she'll be home soon, she said she wouldn't be long."

The man opened his mouth to say something and then closed it again. He jammed his hands into the pockets of his jeans and looked out of the window, frowning. Watching him, several of the things he'd said, plus the fact that it had now been a very, very long time since Mrs. Orchard went into the hospital, plus the fact that her parents had been unconcerned when she'd told them about the man packing up Mrs. Orchard's things, all came together in Clara's brain and fused into a single, terrible thought.

"Is she dead?" she asked, her throat suddenly so tight the words had trouble getting out.

The man turned from the window. He looked worried. "Yes," he said. "I'm sorry. I ... assumed you knew that."

There was a long silence while Clara tried to swallow this huge, impossible fact. There seemed no way to fit it into her mind. She knew what dead meant, she dimly remembered when Mrs. Orchard's sister died. They'd put her in a box and dug a big hole in the ground and lowered the box into it and she'd somehow ended up in heaven. It meant Clara would never see Mrs. Orchard again. They wouldn't have tea and cookies or watch Moses watch the mouse. She wouldn't be able to play with the little carved men. Or play with Mo. What would happen to Mo?

"Did she want you to have Moses too?" she asked miserably.

"Moses?" the man said.

"Yes. Her cat. I've been looking after him." Great hot tears were rolling down her cheeks, she hadn't even felt them coming.

The man looked alarmed. He said rapidly, "No, she didn't mention a cat—you can have him if you like. I haven't seen a cat, though."

"He's hiding," Clara said through a sob. "He doesn't like strangers. But I can't take him home because my mom's allergic to him."

"Oh," the man said. "Well, we'll work something out. Not now, though. You should go home now."

"Can he stay here but be mine?"

"Sure. But ..."

"Can I come here and play with him?"

The man hesitated. "I'm not sure about that. We'll think about it later, you need to go home now. In fact I'll come with you. I should have a word with your parents, tell them ... about Mrs. Orchard ..."

"They already know," Clara said, realizing abruptly that they must. She put the little card player down with his friends where he belonged. "They know she's dead. They didn't tell me, that's all. They pretended she was coming home. They lied to me."

Her father sent her upstairs to get ready for bed so she didn't hear what the man said, but after he left her father came up to her room. Clara was sitting on Rose's bed.

"I'm sorry, Little," her father said, standing in the rubble of Rose's clothes strewn about on the floor. "I

135

guess we should have told you sooner, Mommy and I. We were about to but with Rose ... not being here, we thought it would make you too sad, so we waited ..."

Clara knew he wanted her to get up and come over and wrap her arms around his legs and say it was OK, but it wasn't OK. Nothing was OK.

He came and sat down beside her and put his arm around her. She was trying to understand how Mrs. Orchard could not *be*. There had been an old woman called Mrs. Orchard and now there wasn't. How could that happen? After a while her father got up, kissed the top of her head and left. She heard him go into his bedroom and the low murmur of her parents' voices.

There was something else, a realization, unnamed but connected to what she had just found out. It was hovering in the darkness at the back of her mind. Something to do with lies; her parents' lies. Suddenly it swam forward: Rose. Rose might be dead too. Maybe her parents hadn't told her, like they hadn't told her about Mrs. Orchard. If she went and asked them now she knew what they'd say; they'd say Rose was fine, they were just a little worried about her because they didn't know where she was, which was what they'd been saying ever since the day she left. Clara had assumed it was true, she had held on to that belief through all the weeks of worry. Rose was alive because her parents said so.

She couldn't say that to herself anymore. She wouldn't know if anything they said was true ever again. The idea made her chest shrink inwards until it was a tight, hard little knot like a walnut, so tight she couldn't breathe. She bent forward, sitting on the edge of Rose's bed, trying to get her breath, but it wouldn't come, and wouldn't come and there was a roaring sound in her ears like a hurricane, and the room went dark and she fell down and down and down and everything disappeared.

Dr. Christopherson was there. He smiled and put his hand on her forehead and smoothed her hair and said, "This is a tough time for you I know, Clara. You aren't sick, you're just very upset, which is understandable. I'm going to give you some medicine which will make you feel calm, OK?"

Her parents were standing behind him. They both smiled anxiously at her when she looked at them. The doctor gave her some medicine in a glass. It tasted strange but quite sweet and she was able to swallow it.

"Well done," the doctor said when she'd finished. "We're going downstairs now to talk but I'll come back up before I leave just to check you're feeling better. See if you can go to sleep, all right?"

Her father and the doctor went out but before following them her mother sat down on the bed beside her and tucked her in like she used to when Clara was little. She drew the blankets up around Clara's shoulders and kissed her cheek. "Sleep well, sweetheart," she whispered. Her eyes had great purple smudges round them and you could hear how hard she was trying to sound cheerful. "Everything's going to be fine."

After her mother had gone the medicine started to work and things got blurred around the edges, but just before Clara slid down into sleep she saw the man next door standing in Mrs. Orchard's living room.

"Is she dead?" Clara asked him. He put his hands in his pockets and looked down at the ground and then out of the window, like he had before, and then he turned his head and looked directly at her, like he had before, and opened his mouth to tell her, but before he had a chance to say anything she was asleep.

She spent most of the weekend standing at the living-room windows. Quite often her mother and father came into the room and, to begin with, one or the other of them stood beside her, which Clara didn't like because it made it harder to concentrate on willing Rose not to be dead and to come home. But after a while they stopped doing that and just sat on the sofa or in one of the chairs and read a book or watched TV. They didn't normally do those things during the day, even on weekends, that was what evenings were for. Clara knew they came in to be with her. She wished they wouldn't.

Her mother stayed up all day now. Clara saw her taking pills, so maybe Dr. Christopherson had given them to her to make her feel better.

*

For a week or so Mrs. Quinn let her stay in the classroom for recess and lunch hour if she wanted to, which Clara always did, but then one day it was sunny and unusually warm, and Mrs. Quinn said, "You know, Clara, I think it would be good for you to go outside today. It's October, we won't be having many more lovely days like this."

Thursday was a lovely day too. Clara sat on the steps and drew Moses in the dust with a stick, like always. It had rained in the night and the sand had a crust which was pocked with tiny round dents as if the raindrops had been pebbles. The crust broke when she drew on it so Moses was ragged round the edges.

She hadn't wanted to come out but it was a good thing she did because after just a few minutes Molly Steel came over from the little clutch of trees where the older girls huddled at recess to talk and giggle about boys.

"Hi," Molly said, smiling at Clara. "Is it OK if I sit here for a minute?"

Clara nodded. She stopped drawing and put down her stick.

"You don't have to stop," Molly said. "That's a good cat drawing. Is he your cat?"

Clara hesitated, then nodded.

"What's his name?"

"Moses."

"That's a really good name. My name's Molly, and I know yours. It's Clara, right?"

Clara's heart was beating very fast. Molly was Rick's sister. Rick was a friend of Dan, the boy who thought Rose was in love with him and who said Rose was going to send him a message. Molly was supposed to tell Clara if Dan wanted to speak to her.

"My brother's a friend of Dan Karakas," Molly said. "You know Dan?"

"Is there a message?" Clara asked, not able to wait.

"I don't know, but Rick says Dan wants to speak to you. He's going to wait for you this afternoon after school. The same place as last time, he said. He wants you to be sure to go home the same way so you don't miss him. You know where it is?"

"Yes." It was on the road, not far from her house. It must be important. He wouldn't want to walk home again if it wasn't important.

The afternoon took a long time to be over. Then Mrs. Quinn kept them in late because someone had stolen someone else's ruler and she was giving them time to confess. But whoever it was didn't confess and finally Mrs. Quinn, by then very cross, had to let them all go home. Clara ran most of the way.

"Hi," Dan said when she came up. He was smoking again as if he hadn't stopped since last time. There were about a dozen butts scattered round his feet.

Clara said breathlessly, "Is there a message?"

He shook his head. "No. But I wanted to tell you something. Something real important. You can't tell anyone, understand?"

"Yes." Though she was so disappointed she found it hard to listen to what he was saying. Why was there still no message after all these weeks?

"If you told anyone it would get me into big trouble," Dan said. "I'd probably get arrested. So promise you won't tell anyone."

"I promise."

"Cross your heart."

She crossed her heart.

"OK." But then he didn't seem to know how to say it, whatever it was. He looked off into the trees for a minute and then finally back at Clara.

"You know when Rose came to see me? The night she left? She asked me to come with her? I said no, 'cause it was harvest." He stopped.

"You told me that last time."

"Yeah, I was just reminding you, Clara! I was just reminding you in case you forgot, OK? What I have to tell you is, Rose told me where she was going, see? So I could join her after harvest. She said she was going to Toronto and she was going to go to the YWCA because there was sure to be one, she said, they're in all the big cities and they're real cheap. She said she'd spend the first couple of nights there. And then after she found somewhere else to stay, somewhere with other kids, she'd go back to the Y once a week to see if there were any letters from me. But also she'd write to Rick as soon as she moved to the new place and tell him the address so I could write to her there. And join her there later."

He flicked the burnt-out cigarette butt away, shook out another—the last one in the pack—lit up, eyes narrowing against the smoke, and dragged so hard he started to cough.

Clara's mind was swarming. Rose in Toronto. A huge city. There'd be hundreds of cars going by, even more than in Sudbury where their parents had taken them one Easter for a treat. Big buildings everywhere. Lots of strangers. Nobody Rose knew.

"Other thing she said," Dan continued, "is she wasn't going to use her real name in case someone came looking for her. Police or someone. She was going to call herself Rowena Jones. I don't know why she chose that name, guess she just liked the sound of it and it had her initials. And also, so no one would recognize a picture of her if someone showed them one, she was going to cut her hair off, really short, short as mine, and stop wearing makeup."

He took a drag, blew it out through his nose, looked at the ground. Clara was trying to imagine Rose with short hair and no makeup. She couldn't do it.

"Thing is," Dan said, looking up again, "she didn't write. I'm not a great letter-writer myself, I'm not real good at that sort of stuff, but I wrote twice a week. Sunday and Wednesday. Posted it every Monday and Thursday. Getting more and more worried cause I never heard back.

"So last weekend I hitched down to Toronto. Took me the whole weekend to get there and back. I went to the YWCA and asked if they had any letters for Rowena Jones and the woman at the desk said yeah, they did. She wouldn't let me have them but she showed me the envelopes and they were from me. All my letters were there. So Rose never collected even one. I asked if she'd stayed there, told the woman the dates, and she looked it up and said yes, one night. It was the night after—twenty-four hours after—Rose left here. So she didn't make it to Toronto that first night, which she wouldn't, it's way too far, but she got there the next day."

He studied Clara's face. "I'm sorry to be telling you all this stuff, Clara. You're just a little kid and I shouldn't worry you. But I don't know what to do. See, if the cops are looking for her they need to know where she went and when, and what name she was calling herself, and that she didn't look like herself anymore. But thing is, she made me promise, cross my heart, not to tell anyone. I shouldn't even be telling you but I just don't know what to do and it's driving me crazy, and I reckoned she'd think telling you was OK."

Clara nodded. Dan looked relieved. He carried on.

"See the thing is, it's withholding information. That's a crime—withholding information from the cops. I could go to jail. Or they might even think I had something to do with her disappearing 'cause I was the last person to see her. The last person from round here anyway. But I promised her, cross my heart, I wouldn't say anything to anyone. But it's been more than five weeks now. I'm wondering should I tell them anyway, even if Rose never forgives me. Even if I go to jail for it. But jeez, jail. I mean, my parents ..."

He finished his cigarette and ground it into the dirt at his feet. He checked the empty packet, peering into it closely as if a cigarette might be hiding in there, then scrunched it up and threw it into the bushes at the side of the road, which you weren't supposed to do.

"What do you think?" he asked. "Should I break my promise?"

A promise is a promise, Rose said. Plus he'd crossed his heart, which made it impossible ever to break it no matter what. But if Rose was in trouble she might want Dan to break it so Sergeant Barnes could rescue her. But what if Sergeant Barnes put Dan in jail?

It was too big a problem, it made her feel panicky. "I don't know," Clara said around a fingernail.

"No," Dan said. "I don't either."

After that there wasn't anything to say so they both went home.

She went over to Mrs. Orchard's house (only now it was Mr. Kane's) as usual and gave Moses his supper. When he'd finished she sat down cross-legged on the floor and watched him fit himself into the corners of boxes—nowadays he was more interested in the boxes than the mouse. Up until then she'd been careful to leave before the man came home but this time she waited for him.

He stopped in the doorway when he saw her. He didn't look exactly cross but he didn't look happy to see her either. Moses had skedaddled when he heard the man's step on the porch.

The man said with a sigh, "Look, Clara—your name's Clara, not Clare, right?"

Clara nodded.

"So, Clara. I guess you've been playing with the cat?"

She didn't hear the question properly because her head was full of the thing she needed to ask him, but she nodded again.

The man nodded too. He said, "That's fine, and I know your mom and dad said it was OK for you to

144

come over, and I'm happy for you to do that when I'm not here. But I prefer to be on my own when I'm at home. It's not that you're doing anything wrong, I just prefer being alone. So you should go now, OK?"

Clara let his words drift past her ears. When they stopped, she waited a few seconds to be sure he'd finished and then said, "If you knew something and you didn't tell the police because you promised not to, but then you did tell them because it was really, really important, would they put you in jail?"

# Eleven

# ELIZABETH

Martha's in quite a state, poor soul. This morning the doctors paid her a visit. They pulled the curtains around her bed and spoke in low voices. Low voices are never a good sign. In due course they emerged and the nurses pulled back the curtains and the whole circus moved on down the ward. I waited for Martha to share the details with us but she didn't, which with hindsight wasn't a good sign either.

Eventually she said, more quietly than usual, so that only I could hear, "Do I have to have an operation if I don't want one, Elizabeth?"

I felt a little clutch of dread on her behalf. I hitched myself up on my pillows, painfully, a bit at a time, so that I could turn my head and look at her more easily. Even that small effort made me so breathless it was a while before I could reply. It feels as if life is withdrawing from my body, dear one. Minute by minute, like the tide going out.

When I had pulled myself together, I said to Martha, "No. It's your body, so it's your decision."

"Good," she said.

For a while that was it. Then: "I'm afraid they'll persuade me into it." She'd struggled up in the bed too and turned towards me. She looked frightened. She said, "If they try, Elizabeth, will you stand up for me? Will you say what you just said? That it's my body?"

I said, "Goodness, Martha, surely you can say that yourself?"

"I'm scared of them," she said simply. "They're so clever. You have an educated voice at least. You'd know what to say."

"Maybe it's just a little operation," I said. "What did they say was wrong with you?"

"They don't know. They said they needed to go inside to have a look. But I don't want them going inside me, I'm seventy-five years old, Elizabeth, I don't want people poking about inside me!"

I understood her fear and I also understood her being intimidated by the doctors. "Educated voice" or not, I feel the same. You're not in a strong position, lying here in your nightgown. It's easy to feel bullied. But you have to trust their judgement, they are the experts, after all.

"I think you should ask Nurse Roberts," I said. "You should ask her if it's a big operation—it might be quite simple and straightforward, you might change your mind."

I expected her to say she wasn't going to change her mind but she said nothing and when I looked over tears were sliding down her papery old cheeks. I felt terrible; I felt I'd been bullying her too, in a way. I said, "Oh, Martha, I'm so sorry. Of course I'll talk to them for you. The next time they come in

I'll say we want to speak to them, both of us together. We'll find out what it would involve and if you want to say no I'll say it for you, if you like."

She looked reassured, but she was raving in the night. Shouting at people. Crying. The crying is new.


I couldn't sleep myself. I lay there trying to reason away fear. To rise above it. I tried to think in universal rather than personal terms, to shrink the importance of "me" and see my life as merely part of the great flow of time. I imagined myself at home, standing outside the back door in the dead of night (that is an interesting phrase, don't you think? The "dead" of night?), looking up at the brilliance of the sky, and attempted to place my paltry seventy-two years alongside the billions of years of the lifespans of the stars.

You know when you throw a log on a bonfire how there is a fleeting rush of tiny sparks? Not the ones that soar joyously up towards the heavens but the tiny ones that spring up and die almost instantaneously? That was my life measured against the stars, my love. Gone instantaneously. Over before it began.


I'm anxious about Liam. I've been rereading his letters and the tone of the most recent ones worries me. I brought all of his letters into hospital with me—there aren't many, he just writes once or twice a year plus a card at Christmas and we only began corresponding eight years ago, after your death. I wrote to him then, breaking my promise to you that I would not try to contact him—he was twenty-eight by then and I reasoned that the promise no longer applied—because I thought he would want to know about your passing. He loved you, Charles. I was sure he would not have forgotten you.

I didn't have his address, but in clearing out your papers before coming up to Solace to live with Marjorie, I'd come across a list of the contact details of your colleagues, not just in Guelph and Toronto but in other universities across the country as well, and Ralph Kane's details were on it. He was at UBC, so I sent the letter via him. Fearing that even after all this time he might not want me to be in touch with Liam, I didn't put my name or address on the envelope, merely wrote "please forward."

To my indescribable joy, Liam not only received it, he replied, and his letter was wonderful. He said that although he didn't have many concrete memories of his early childhood, the best of them were of the times he spent with us. He said in his memory it was always warm in our house, in both senses of the word. He remembered you as very quiet and very kind, always reading but always ready to put down your book and listen to whatever childish thing he wanted to tell you. He said you taught him to count to twenty on your fingers and toes. (He is an accountant, so you evidently did a thorough job.)

At the end of the letter he said that he was getting married and that he and his soon-to-be wife, Fiona, would be delighted if I would come to the wedding. (I declined, of course, knowing that Annette and Ralph would be there.) He told me a little about

Fiona—that she was a lawyer, that they were settling in Toronto, which they liked very much, that they had bought a house, that sort of thing, painting me a picture of his life.

I cried over the letter. I could see him in the words, and it was a joy beyond description to be in touch with him after so many years, to hold in my hand the proof that whether or not she had tried to, Annette had not succeeded in poisoning his mind against me, to know that he was well and happy and had suffered no lasting harm.

I asked if he would send me some photos of the wedding and when they arrived I wept again, because the boy we loved was still there, Charles, his face longer and more angular (if anything, more beautiful), looking a little abashed, as often seems to be the case with men on their wedding days, as if they've been caught doing something embarrassing.

I have reread that first letter of his and all of those that followed many, many times, but it wasn't until a couple of days ago that I read them straight through at one go, and it was then that I noticed how much the tone has changed. For the first couple of years they remain positive and full of things he and Fiona had done or were planning to do, but gradually they become … "flatter" is the only word I can think of. Flatter and shorter—even the sentences are shorter—with fewer details about their lives. The most recent ones feel strained, as if he is struggling to find anything to say. As if there is nothing in his life worth mentioning.

Of course I could be imagining it, it could be merely that he is tired or has a great deal on his mind. But

I don't think so. I don't think he is happy. It worries me terribly. It makes me wonder if I've been deceiving myself, if I was wrong, when he first wrote, to conclude that all was well.

I would so love to help but I can't think of anything I can do apart from giving him some financial security. Money isn't the solution to anything but it can ease the way. I would dearly love to ease his way.

*

Time is behaving strangely. Sometimes an afternoon goes on for days and then a whole week will disappear altogether and I'll find it's Friday again, and we're having fish. I hate fish.

*

I keep forgetting things. Another reminder of decline, as if I needed reminding. This afternoon my lawyer came to see me. Mr. Grant. Short, round and perspiring copiously. He was wearing a dark wool suit, for goodness sake, it must have been eighty degrees in here, he looked like an overripe plum.

I'd completely forgotten that I'd sent for him. Apparently a couple of days ago I asked Nurse Roberts if she would phone his office and ask him to come to see me. I said to tell him it was urgent, that I didn't have much time left.

Anyway, he arrived, and I pulled myself together and told him I wanted to change my will and leave everything to Liam. Originally, you having no family and Marjorie having predeceased me, my estate was to be divided between a couple of distant cousins, but they live out west and I have had next to no contact with them. Far better to leave it all to Liam.

To my intense embarrassment it turned out I'd already made that change a year ago. I haven't the faintest recollection of it. Clearly my brain is now filing information in some dark cobwebby room to which I no longer have the key.

I was about to apologize to Mr. Grant for wasting his time when I remembered there was something else I wanted him to arrange. I've decided to give Liam the house. Not in my will but now, straight away. It is a good house, I can imagine him in it. He would be happy there and it would solve the problem of Moses. Probate can take so long, and what if I linger? Who's to say how long I could lie here, it could be months, which means it could be a year or more before Liam gets anything at all. I can't get over the feeling that he needs some help now.

Mr. Grant, to whom I have to say I've never taken—he was Marjorie's lawyer, that's the only reason I went to him—didn't like the idea. He said what if I recovered and wanted to go home, which made me cross; I am fighting for every breath, it must have been perfectly obvious that I will not be going home. I said sharply that if a miracle occurred I would rent an apartment here in Sudbury for the duration of my stay on this earth. Whereupon he changed tack and said patiently (patience can sound very condescending, Charles, especially from a man. You were guilty of it yourself from time to time) that someone living and working in Toronto was unlikely to have any use for a house as far north as Solace, it would be nothing but a liability. I said if that turned out to be the case Liam could sell it.

Mr. Grant said gently (and this was patronizing too), "Mrs. Orchard, I would urge you not to complicate things," and went into a long explanation of how it would complicate things. "Which is why," he concluded, "I would be so much happier if you simply left him the house in your will along with everything else."

By this time I was very tired. I said, "Mr. Grant, your happiness is not my top priority at the moment. I want Liam to have the house now. Please arrange it. I would like it done this week."

He gave up then and agreed to draw up the relevant papers and bring them back to me to sign by the end of the week. No doubt he will charge me a vast amount for his trouble but I don't care.


I thought I'd feel better once I got everything sorted out but I don't. Anxiety is running rampant through me, my love. It feels like buffaloes thundering.


I've just realized I forgot to tell him I want to be buried beside you in Mount Pleasant Cemetery in Toronto and I don't want a funeral. Nothing at all. I'm afraid the past might come out and my friends and neighbours in Solace might learn of it. I don't want to be remembered for that. I'll write to him tomorrow.

I keep thinking about the early days in Guelph. The days "before."

One morning I went over to the Kanes, with a casserole—this was early on, the October or November after they moved in. Annette was very big already (she'd been correct to think she was carrying twins) and I knew standing at the stove would be uncomfortable for her so a couple of times a week I popped over with a meal. As indeed did other women from the church Annette and Ralph went to; she didn't have a great many meals to prepare.

The girls had started kindergarten by then so Annette had Liam to herself all day. It should have been a golden time for the two of them, she should have revelled in it, instead of which she seemed more harried and distracted every time I saw her.

This particular morning I could hear her shouting and Liam crying as I approached the front door and when she opened it I saw Liam sitting on the floor surrounded by the shredded remains of a book, howling, beside himself with distress.

Annette took one look at me and burst into tears herself. "It's one of Ralph's reference books," she said, almost wringing her hands. "He's going to be so angry, I don't know what I'm going to tell him. Liam knows it's wrong, Elizabeth, he *knows* he is *not* to go into Ralph's study, it is the *one* room in the house none of the children are allowed into. He does it on purpose, I can see it in his eyes; he's taunting me, he's deliberately doing it because he *knows it's wrong*!"

I came close to despising her at that moment, Charles. I had to work hard not to say, That is perfectly normal behaviour for a three-year-old, Annette, he wants your attention, why don't you give it to him? And why don't you lock the door of the study during the day? Hide the key. Problem solved.

Instead I asked if she would like me to take Liam for the afternoon so that she could get some rest before collecting the girls.

She looked at me as if I had offered her the secret of eternal life. She said, "Oh, Elizabeth, would you? That would be ... that would be so wonderful ..."


I know that having no children myself I "don't know what it's like" and therefore have no right to judge. I am well aware of that. I also know, having had daily contact with hundreds of mothers over the years, that all mothers lose patience with their children now and then. But the fact is, Annette was always like that with Liam. I never saw her laughing with him or looking at him with love and delight. Not once.

He and I had the most perfect afternoon. We made a freight train out of small cardboard boxes strung together with bright red wool. In one boxcar we put macaroni, in another raisins, in the third half a dozen pea pods complete with peas, and in the fourth corn-flakes (which turned out to be a mistake on my part. I had a great deal of vacuuming to do at the end of the day). The fact that our train had no wheels didn't slow us down a bit, we hauled it by its string all around the house.

When we tired of that we made cookies, using the raisins. After that we curled up on the sofa and read *Wag-tail Bess,* in the course of which Liam fell asleep in my lap. I had thought I would never feel the weight of a sleeping child. It seemed to me almost miraculous.

At the end of the afternoon, when Annette came to get him, Liam dragged her into the living room to see our train, this marvellous thing that we had made together, and stood looking up at her face, jigging up and down with pride. She looked at it and said, "Oh—isn't Mrs. Orchard clever? Have you thanked her for giving you such a lovely afternoon?"

She didn't see how much he wanted her to admire this wonderful thing he had helped to make, how much he craved her praise. She couldn't see it, and it was as plain as day.


I remember thinking as the months went by that having almost destroyed me, the gods had had a change of heart and were positively pushing Liam into my arms. Annette's twins were due in January. Back then, mothers and babies were generally kept in the hospital for at least ten days, so Annette's mother had agreed to come and look after the children for the duration. But just before Christmas she slipped on the ice outside her front door and broke her hip.

Annette was thrown into panic and despair. Ralph's mother made it clear that she was not volunteering for the job. Money was short—academics were not well paid, then as now—and with two extra mouths to feed it was going to be shorter still, so hiring someone to come in and help wasn't an option.

I remember trying to work up the courage to ask you if we should offer to have Liam come to stay with us; that way Ralph would have only the girls, who were at kindergarten during the day, to make arrangements for. You hesitated, understandably—you hardly knew Liam, after all—and I suggested that we invite him for a weekend as a "trial run." I remember my utter joy when you agreed.

Do you remember the first night he spent with us? I was anxious that he might wake in the night and be distressed, so we set up the old camp cot at the foot of our bed and made it up for him. He looked very pleased with it when he climbed in. We were prepared for tears but there were none.

I sat up in bed all night, watching him, my love. Watching the rise and fall of his breath. I didn't know if what I was experiencing was agony or joy.

## Twelve

# LIAM

"For *weeks* it was like she was in mourning," Jim said. "*Weeks*! I need some more mortar. Wait there, I'll pass you the bucket."

They were rebuilding a chimney. Not Liam's chimney, his had been OK, this was Mrs. Vuillard's chimney, the mortar of which was crumbling so badly they could have dug it out from between the bricks with a spoon.

It had taken them a week of early starts and long days to do Liam's roof followed by two and a half days to do the bathroom floor, and in a masochistic kind of way he'd enjoyed both projects. It was good to be busy and though the work was physically hard it was mentally quite restful—no responsibility, no decisions, just do what you're told. When everything was finished he'd thanked Jim, paid him in full and said goodbye, assuming that was it, his little foray into the building business was over and he was a free man again. But when it came to it he found that spending days on his own doing nothing took him straight back to the bottom, emotionally speaking, like sliding down a ramp into a swamp of bitterness, regret and general self-loathing. He could have packed up then and headed south, sold the house from afar, but that would have required making a decision, so he went back to Jim and said the porch steps needed replacing and how about the same deal as before?

Now he was at the top of the ladder freezing his extremities off; last night the wind had swung round to the north and when he'd opened the curtains in the morning he was almost certain he'd seen a snow-flake drifting innocently down: his signal to leave.

"*Weeks*! Wandering around the house. Not sleeping. Picking at her meals. Three in the morning I'd get up to go to the toilet and the bed would be empty and she'd be in the living room, standing there in the dark, looking out of the window. Black as pitch out there. Oh yeah, I was bringing the bucket down, sorry."

He started down the slope of the roof with the bucket but his foot knocked against the caulking gun and it began to slide, picking up speed as it came. Liam lunged sideways to catch it, which made the ladder slide too—he grabbed at the eaves trough and caught it, but it was loose, he could feel it pulling away.

"Jesus Christ, Liam! Jesus!" Jim let go of the bucket and came scuttling down the roof like a panicking crab. He flung himself down flat at the edge of the roof and held out his hand—Liam grabbed it and with an immense effort the two of them managed to haul the ladder back to vertical.

"Jesus, that was close!" Jim said. "That's solid rock down there, what if I'd killed you? What would the ladies of Solace say, first good-looking man they've seen for years? They'd lynch me!"

"Thanks," Liam said, his heart racing.

"Nearly scared me to death," Jim said. He got to his feet and headed back up the roof.

The bucket had made its own way to the ground. Liam waited for his heartbeat to return to normal, then followed it down, filled it with mortar and brought it back up.

"You OK?" Jim asked.

"Sure. Thanks again."

"That's OK. Anything else wants to fall off the roof, let it. What was I saying? I was telling you something."

"Your wife was missing your kid." He climbed cautiously over to the groundsheet Jim had spread out on the roof, squatted down, picked up the hammer and chisel and set to work chipping the mortar off the old bricks so that they could be reused, taking care to make sure the chippings stayed on the groundsheet. According to Jim, if they got on the roof itself they were lethally slippery, and one close call was enough.

He hadn't met Jim's wife—Susan, her name was. A week ago she'd instructed Jim to invite him for supper. In one way it was tempting: the succession of neighbourly casseroles had pretty much dried up, word had got round that he was unsociable, which was true and fine by him, but the consequence was that he was getting a little tired of the Hot Potato.

Nonetheless, he'd declined Susan's invitation. He was no good at social chit-chat at the best of times and the thought of a whole evening evading kindly questions about his private life was more than he could bear. So he told Jim what he told everybody else, that he had a lot to do in the evenings, working through Mrs. Orchard's papers and effects. It was a lame excuse and Jim had looked puzzled, but he didn't push it.

"Yeah, Susan," Jim said. "She was low. I mean really, really low. I was feeling a bit the same myself, but we men are better at dealing with it. You spend your whole life—well, your kid's whole life—preparing him to stand on his own two feet, trying to make sure he gets an education so he has choices, all that stuff, putting a little money away every month no matter what so he can go to college if that's what he wants, and whadaya know, you succeed, and off he goes, and instead of rejoicing it's like the bottom's dropped out of the world. I didn't know what to do for her, it was like she was sick, she was even losing weight. Weekend before last I took her down to North Bay, little treat, thought if she could spend some money she'd feel better, she just loves spending money. She didn't buy a thing. That really got me worried, I can tell you. Where's the goddamn—oh. Thanks.

"He's our only one, see? When he arrived he just seemed enough, all by himself. You'd be amazed how full one kid can fill a house. And he's always been a good kid, y'know? Right from the start, never gave us any trouble, no reason to be glad when he's gone. So there we were, the two of us, her and me, creeping around all these empty rooms. Feels like it's all over for us. Which I guess it is, far as mother nature's concerned. We've done our job, she doesn't give a damn what happens to us now."

He paused and looked at Liam. "And then guess what?"

"What?"

"Just guess."

"I give up."

"He comes home. Sunday, late afternoon. The door opens and there he is, duffle bag over his shoulder ... how're you doing with the bricks, I'm running out."

Liam straightened up with a wince and took an armful of cleaned bricks over to Jim. Every muscle in his body still protested every time he moved but at least he was starting to have some muscles to protest. Nothing compared to Jim of course, Jim could carry an eighty-pound box of shingles up a ladder as if it was full of sawdust, while initially Liam had struggled with half a box (Jim snickering quietly in the background), but he was getting there. He was more comfortable on a roof too. He'd bought a pair of heavy-duty boots at Hudson's Bay, a waste of money considering he'd only be here for another week or two, but the grip was better and he didn't feel in danger of slipping off all the time.

"Where'd we get to this time?"

"Your kid had a duffle bag over his shoulder." He wasn't exactly waiting with bated breath to find out what happened, but it was better than thinking his own thoughts.

"Yeah, the duffle bag. Says he's back for good. Didn't like it down in Kingston. Too big. Too many people, too much noise.

"Susan and me were just standing there with our mouths open. Didn't know what to say—didn't hardly know how to feel, you know? Great to see him but ... all that dreaming and planning, all that homework ... And now this! Home again. Wasn't gone a month!"

He looked at Liam. Liam nodded, kneading his toes inside his boots to keep the blood flowing.

"Reason I'm telling you all this," Jim said, as if he ever needed a reason, "is 'cause I sort of wanted your advice."

"My *advice*?" Liam said.

"Well, maybe opinion's a better word. Or maybe not opinion either. Whatever. Thing is, see, I've never left Solace. I was born right here and I'll die right here, never been anywhere else and don't want to. You could call that a fault but that's how it is. I'm a Northerner. That's me. Susan's just the same.

"But you want more than that for your kids, you know? You want them to go out into the big wide world and see stuff and do interesting things and have a bigger life than you did. And the kids want that too, or at least the ones with a bit of get up and go. They're just dying to get out of here. But funny thing is, Cal isn't the only one to make the break and then come ricocheting back. Seems to happen a lot. Kids just can't take it, outside. And I've been wondering if that's normal or if it's something about up here. Like the North gets its hooks into them at birth and just won't let go. So here's what I wanted to ask you: I'm guessing you went to university, right?"

"Yeah."

"In your hometown?"

163

"No. I grew up in Calgary and went to U of T. Toronto."

"Was it hard to go? Like were you homesick?"


No. He hadn't been homesick.

Near the end of his final year in high school, his mother, passing him on the stairs one day, said in the offhand tone she used with him, "Oh, by the way, Liam, before I forget, your father phoned a few days ago to say he'll support you through university. Apparently you already know about this." An accusation.

Liam nodded cautiously. "Yes."

"How long have you been in touch with him, just out of curiosity?"

"A couple of years." He'd been six when his parents divorced and his father moved out to Vancouver. When Liam was sixteen, after ten years of complete absence from his life, his father had written to him saying that he was coming to Calgary for a conference and suggesting they meet for lunch. It had been an awkward meal, neither of them knowing what to say. His father had seemed apologetic more than anything else—not that he'd said so, it was just the look of him. Thinking about it later, Liam decided it was because his father had known, or at least guessed, how wretched his life had been, and still was, in that house full of females, and hadn't known what to do about it when Liam was smaller. After that they'd met up whenever his father was in town. Liam didn't exactly find their meetings fun, but he looked forward to them and was grateful for the contact, the more so because his father seemed to be grateful for it too.

Having no other topic of conversation they invariably talked about school. Liam's grades were good, particularly in math, and in due course his father encouraged him to go to university. "If you're good at math, do math," his father said. "Most people can't, so you'll never be out of a job." It had seemed a good idea. At the very least it was a ticket out.

"I see," his mother said, her mouth set in its familiar bitter line. "Have you decided where you want to go?"

"Toronto."

"You've been accepted?"

"Yes. Provided I get the marks in the finals."

"So you'll be moving out."

"Yes."

"It would have been nice to be kept informed."

She turned and continued down the stairs. She didn't ask what he would be studying, where he'd be living, what his plans were for the future. They didn't discuss the subject again. In October of that year he had packed his bags and left.


So he hadn't been homesick.

"No," he said to Jim after a moment. "But the circumstances were different."

"Like how?"

"Just ... different."

*

165

That evening he got out the drawings from his childhood that Mrs. Orchard had so carefully preserved and spread them around the spare room, looking for clues. Found nothing but the scribblings of a child. He couldn't remember ever painting or drawing after his family moved to Calgary. He had a dim memory of someone, presumably a teacher, certainly not his mother, encouraging him to draw a picture and him refusing. That part of him seemed to have shut down permanently. In fact, looking back, he wondered if the whole of him had shut down for a while. When he tried to picture himself back then, what he saw was a little kid sitting on his own.

Things improved as he got older, and high school was largely good. He'd learned how to carry on a conversation by then and got on well enough with his classmates. Some of the boys used to get together after school and mess around for a bit, laughing and talking, drinking hooch out of Coke bottles. He knew he could have joined them, they'd indicated as much, but he didn't. Still couldn't cross the river. Couldn't risk it—though exactly what it was he couldn't risk he didn't know. That they'd see through him, maybe. See that something major was missing. So he kept apart. It earned him the reputation of being standoffish, but he could live with that.

To put off going home after school he went to the public library and did his homework there. He didn't mind homework, in fact he found most of the subjects quite interesting, particularly math. He was intrigued by numbers, their profound simplicity, the way they were ruled by unalterable and immensely satisfying laws. They made sense, which was more than you could say for the rest of life.

When he was fifteen or so, girls started appearing in the library after school too, a remarkable number of them wanting help with their math homework.

"What don't you understand?" he'd ask.

"Well, anything, really." Which in some cases turned out to be the literal truth, but he did his best to help. It took him a while to realize that it wasn't his brains they were interested in, and it certainly wasn't the math, but he finally figured it out. He also figured out that sex was sometimes on offer by way of thanks, at which point life became a whole lot more interesting.

He spent as little time at home as possible, timing things so that he walked in the door just as supper was being put on the table. The girls gabbled non-stop throughout every meal. Their mother listened, smiling, interjecting the occasional question or mild reproof. Liam might as well have been invisible. He felt invisible. He tuned them out, ate his supper, said nothing, left.

Once, his mother, startling him with the unexpectedness of it, turned to him and said, "Have you *nothing* to add to the conversation, then, Liam?" Hostility in her voice.

He looked at her blankly for a moment, then said, "No."

His mother regarded him with a tight smile. "Sometimes I wonder why you bother to join us."

"For the food," he said, and got up and went to his room.

*

Once he left home, he never went back.

*

He and Jim were starting on a sizeable job the following day, putting in a new kitchen for an old couple out on the point, so when they finished the chimney they went over there to do some measuring. The house was warm and the old couple were generous with the coffee and cookies, and the thought of spending a week or two there put them both in a good frame of mind. Jim got chatting with the owners just like he got chatting with everyone, so it was late when they finished. Liam went straight to the Hot Potato rather than going home first, and had a quick wash in the men's room before eating.

He was starting to feel more at ease in the café. The waitress still treated him with contempt but the locals nodded to him and there were seldom any kids in there at suppertime during the week. He slid into his favourite booth, opened this week's issue of the *Temiskaming Speaker* (he bought his own copy now) and took his time over his burger and fries. Despite what he'd said to Jim about sorting out Mrs. Orchard's papers, he was in no hurry to get back to the empty house with its faint but unsettling links to his childhood and decisions still waiting to be made.

When he got home, though, the house wasn't empty; the little girl from next door was back, sitting cross-legged on the living-room floor. In the two weeks since their meeting and his conversation with her father, he hadn't seen her, and he'd assumed it would stay that way.

"Look, Clara," he said, and he explained, nicely, because he felt sorry for the kid and had nothing against her aside from the fact that she was in his living room, that it was fine if she came to play with the cat when he was out, he was happy for her to do that, but he liked being alone and didn't want anyone in the house when he was there. Even as he was saying it, though, he could see she wasn't listening. She was staring at him with an intensity that verged on alarming.

"So you should go home now, OK?" he finished.

The child waited a moment as if to be sure he'd finished and then said, "If you knew something and you didn't tell the police because you promised not to, but then you did tell them because it was really, really important, would they put you in jail?

Liam was so taken aback he answered off the cuff. "No," he said. "They don't send young kids to jail."

She thought about it, her large clear eyes leaving his for the first time and focusing somewhere over his left shoulder. It seemed a weirdly hypothetical question for a kid to ask and he wondered what lay behind it. Then she returned her eyes to his and asked another one and it abruptly became clear.

"What if he isn't very young?"

Alarm bells started ringing. Not a hypothetical question, then.

"How old is he?" Liam asked cautiously.

"Sixteen. Or maybe seventeen."

She knew a boy who knew something about her missing sister, there was nothing else it could be. Liam guessed it wouldn't be possible to get her to reveal his name, but if she could be kept talking more details might slip out. The hitch was, he didn't want to be the one who kept her talking. That was a job for her parents or Sergeant Barnes, or basically anyone but him. In any case, he'd be of no use, he didn't even know the answer to her question: Did Canada lock up kids of sixteen nowadays?

"I doubt it but I don't know for sure," he said. "It might depend on the circumstances. But you need to tell your parents about this right away, Clara. Now, this minute. It's really important."

"What does 'the circumstances' mean?"

There was a very firm set to that small jaw of hers. Alongside irritation he felt a reluctant twinge of admiration. Her life must be a complete mess at the moment but she had questions and she was going to get answers. Just not from him.

"Clara, this is really important. You need to talk to your parents."

"I don't talk to them anymore."

He was startled. "Why not?"

"They tell me lies."

"I'm sure that isn't true. Or if ..."

"It is true!" She scrambled to her feet, enraged. "They lie to me! When I ask them something *they say lies*!"

"All right," he said rapidly. "OK." She was on the verge of storming out and much as he wanted her gone, he knew he mustn't alienate her. But he didn't know what to do, what to say. He had no experience with kids, didn't know what they were capable of understanding at any given age, didn't know how to talk to them. The only thing he could think of was to buy time so that he could pass the problem on to someone else.

"Look," he said. "Would you like me to try to find out whether they put sixteen-year-olds in jail for ... not saying something and then saying it? I could try to find that out."

She looked at him suspiciously, her gaze flicking from his left eye to his right and back again. He found he was holding his breath.

"Yes," she said finally.

"I will, then. I'll try to let you know tomorrow afternoon when you get home from school. Or if not tomorrow, the next day. But now you have to go home."


He should tell her parents, of course. It was clearly inappropriate that he knew something relating to their children that they didn't know. But she seemed so set against them. What if it made her clam up?

He went into the hall and made a phone call. A woman answered. "Police," she said.

"I'd like to speak to Sergeant Barnes," Liam said.

"He's off duty now," the voice said crisply. "Is it an emergency?"

"Not an emergency exactly. But it's important."

"Could it wait until morning?"

He hesitated. "I guess so."

"Could I have your name, sir?"

"Kane. Liam Kane."

"Oh yes, Mr. Kane. You're Mrs. Orchard's ... you've moved into Mrs. Orchard's house?"

"Right," he said resignedly.

"All right, sir. That's fine. I'll pass on your message first thing in the morning."

Liam wandered into the kitchen and stuffed a handful of wizened, week-old blueberries into his mouth. The phone rang.

"Mr. Kane," Sergeant Barnes said cheerfully. "You rang."

Liam swallowed a mouthful of insufficiently chewed berries plus half a dozen twigs and choked into the phone.

"You all right?" the policeman asked.

Liam coughed explosively, then wiped the goo off the phone with the heel of his hand. "Sorry. Blueberries." He coughed again.

"Take your time," Sergeant Barnes said. "You have to watch the twigs, they put them in there so you'll think you've got the real thing. OK now?"

"Yeah. Sorry."

"No problem. How can I help you? Linda thought you sounded kind of concerned so she gave me a call."

"Oh. Right. Good. It's to do with the missing kid next door."

"I'm on my way," the sergeant said, abruptly all business. "I'll be ten, fifteen minutes. It's the wife's night out so I'm babysitting, gotta call her, she's just down the road. Sit tight."

Liam said quickly, "It might be better if no one saw the police car here if that's OK. Could we meet

172

somewhere?" He didn't want Clara to think he was betraying her.

"Sure. Come to the house, that'd be perfect. We live close, head into town, first road on the left, Number 8. Prowler in the drive."

Relative to Mrs. Orchard's, the house lacked charm; it was modern, two storeys, flat-fronted and uninspired. The inside was better, though; the front door opened onto a large kitchen, which in turn opened onto an even larger living room, the squareness of which was relieved by a big woodstove at one end and a comprehensive mess throughout. There were a couple of armchairs and a coffee table made out of a log grouped around the stove; Sergeant Barnes gestured at them as he ushered Liam in.

"Have a seat," he said. "I'm just making coffee."

Liam went over to the chairs, removed a sock, a newspaper, a Donald Duck comic, a squashed bag of potato chips and a pair of scissors from one of them and after a moment's hesitation put them on the floor. He sat down. Then he stood up, retrieved the scissors and put them on the coffee table—the sock suggested bare feet.

The woodstove was belting out the heat. It had a glass door so you could see the flames raging around the logs. It was a big stove but it was a big room, it would take some heating. Comfortably untidy, Liam thought. The exact opposite of his and Fiona's living room in Toronto, which had been so unrelentingly tidy you were afraid to sit down. It hadn't been a home, he thought now. Just a house. He wondered if there was a knack to turning the latter into the former; something he and Fiona had lacked. Or something they could have learned if they'd cared for the house and each other enough to try.

From a room off to the left he could hear the television. Gunshots and dramatic music—a cowboy movie. *High Noon*, in fact—he recognized the uniquely awful theme song. Grainy shadows would be galloping across the screen. Maybe if you'd grown up with crap TV reception your eye learned to fill in the gaps. Either that or, never having seen a decent image, you accepted fuzz as normal.

Sergeant Barnes put down two mugs of coffee on the small table, brought milk, sugar and a couple of spoons, lifted a pair of earmuffs, a towel and a water pistol from the second chair and dropped them on top of the others and sat down himself.

"By the way," he said. "I keep meaning to say—we can scrap the formality, my name's Karl."

"OK. Liam." It was ridiculous how pleased he was. Like a new kid at school, unexpectedly befriended by the leader of the pack. He ventured a semi-personal question: "Isn't it kind of tricky? Policing people you know?"

"Not really," Karl said. "If you've got a prison record, or if I think you should have, then I keep the 'Sergeant.' But not otherwise. If I kept it with everyone I wouldn't have any friends and the rest of the family wouldn't either, it'd be kinda lonely, all by ourselves. I keep more of a distance in the other towns, though. Don't know the people there so well."

"You cover other towns? Just you?"

"Yeah, just me. Plus Linda doing the admin. A couple of towns, plus lumber camps. Little communities. Anything anywhere. That's why I got this." He patted his paunch, though from where Liam was sitting the paunch didn't look like much.

"Too much time sitting in the prowler," Karl was saying. "All those coffee shops to sit in, listening to the gossip. All those blueberry pies—essential part of the job, you know, eating blueberry pie. How else are you going to find out what's going on?" He smiled. "Anyway. Let's have it. Start at the beginning. Don't leave anything out."

The phone rang. Karl cursed under his breath and got up. "OK," he said into the phone. "Tell them to board it up, I'll have a look in the morning."

"Sorry," he said to Liam. "Someone's chucked a brick through the window of the hardware store. Not surprising, the owner's a mean bastard, wouldn't mind having a go myself."

He thudded down into his chair again. "OK. You were about to tell me everything. Start at the beginning."

The cat was the beginning, Liam decided. "Turns out Mrs. Orchard had a cat," he said, and went on from there. When he'd told Karl everything he could think of, the policeman sat for a moment watching the flames.

"Well, you just made my day," he said at last. "Maybe my year. It might turn out to be a dead end but at least it's something. There's been *nothing* to go on. Not a single damned thing. Which means the

cops in Toronto have had nothing to go on either—
I've been liaising with them. We don't know if the
girl's there, of course, it's just where kids usually head,
it's the only place they've heard of. Think they'll pick
up a job, have some fun. Discover there aren't any
jobs, can't find anywhere to live, end up on the street.
The street isn't fun. It's a dangerous place. Especially
for young girls. And now winter's coming."

From the room next door came a tremendous vol-
ley of gunshots and a shout of glee from the kids.

"You got kids?" Karl asked.

"No."

"Well let me tell you, they come in all shapes
and sizes but they all think they know everything
and they're vulnerable as hell." He shook his head.
"Incredible stroke of luck, the little sister coming
to you."

"I can't figure it out. Why would she go to a
stranger?"

"Who knows why kids do what they do? You're
handy, being right next door. But you say she thinks
her parents lie to her?"

"Yes. She said they lied about Mrs. Orchard having
died. I went and talked to her father and told him
I'd let it slip. He was nice about it—said they weren't
going to be able to keep it from her much longer
anyway. He said they'd thought the truth would be
too much for her to handle right now."

Karl nodded thoughtfully. "You can understand
their thinking, but that could be the reason she came
to you: everyone's trying to reassure her there's nothing to worry about and she knows damn well there

is. Then you come along and accidentally tell her the truth. So she trusts you. Let me tell you something, I've been policing small towns for coming on for twenty years, and trust is everything. If people don't trust you they won't talk to you and if they don't talk to you, you're screwed. We have to make sure you don't lose her trust, no matter what."

Liam shifted uncomfortably. "Um ... I'd rather keep out of it if it's all the same to you. I wouldn't be happy with ..." He couldn't think how to put it.

"What wouldn't you be happy with?"

"C'mon, you know—a little girl coming over to the house on her own. No one there but her and me. I'm not comfortable with it. What if people saw her ... I'd rather keep out of it."

Karl studied the fire. Liam waited.

"I agree it's not a great situation," Karl said finally. "And normally I wouldn't be happy with it either. But unfortunately I can't think of an alternative so I'm afraid you're stuck with it." He smiled reassuringly. "Tell you what. Those houses overlook each other at the side, don't they? Best thing would be if you make sure her parents can always see her from their living-room window."

The way the cop casually overruled him, assumed he'd be willing to put himself in such a situation, annoyed Liam. "I don't see why I should be stuck with it. Why can't you talk to her? That would make more sense anyway."

"I'm a cop," Karl said, calmly ignoring his tone. "She's protecting this boy, whoever he is, from the likes of me. I'm the very last person she'd talk to."

177

"Well then, her parents," Liam said flatly. "They can worm it out of her."

"You told me yourself she won't talk to her parents," Karl said. "We can't decide who she'll open up to." He got up and put another log in the stove—there was a blast of heat as the door opened—then sat down again. They watched the flames licking around the new log, tasting it, then settling down to consume it. Liam chewed on resentment.

The cop glanced at him, then grimaced. "OK, fact is I've got no right to ask you to do this and you have every right to say no, being a civilian and not connected to the case. But like I said, this is the first lead we've had and I'm getting desperate. The longer she's missing the more likely it is that it'll end badly. We can't let this chance go, we *have* to find out who this boy is and what he knows."

He looked across at Liam. "Once we do, your job is over, you know. You can bar the door, change the locks. Kill the cat. Well maybe not kill the cat. So we're only talking about a couple of days. And anyway, you're selling up and leaving soon, right? So people won't have time to start thinking nasty thoughts."

It was true. Liam had temporarily forgotten that he'd be leaving soon. But the thought came to him that he'd been kidding himself earlier; that Karl's friendliness, the business about them being on first-name terms, had been nothing more than a strategy to disarm him and make him agree to do whatever it was Karl wanted him to do. Just fuck off, he told himself, sick to death of his own paranoia. It was totally irrational: Karl hadn't even known what he was going to say at that stage, hadn't known he'd need his help in any way.

Karl was studying him. "We're talking about a kid's life here, Liam. Every hour that passes the chances of finding her alive get slimmer. You just happen to be in a position to help."

To which, of course, there was no argument, whatever Karl's motives or methods of operation. Though it wasn't so much the thought of Rose, whose grainy image had stared so belligerently out at him from the newspaper, that made Liam supress his irritation and agree; it was Clara. The way she had searched his face earlier that evening, needing to trust him—to trust *somebody*—but not sure that she could. It had rung a distant, but very resonant bell.

He nodded. "OK."

"Good. Thanks."

From the TV room, right on cue, came terrible music to ride off into the sunset by. Karl heaved himself to his feet and went to stick his head around the door. "Bedtime," he said. "James—teeth. Catherine—pyjamas. Then swap places. No fooling around."

He came back and sat down. Behind him two bodies flashed past and up the stairs. Karl stood up again. "How about some ice cream?"

"Sure," Liam said.

Karl disappeared into a room beside the kitchen and reappeared with a large tub in each hand.

"Chocolate? Vanilla? Both?"

"Vanilla. Thanks."

Karl put down the tubs and disappeared again, this time through a side door that led to the garage—a blast of icy air followed him—and came back with a hammer and chisel. "This stuff is homemade," he said. "Jo at the library makes it. Part hobby, part business, you have to order it from her. Made with cream from local cows, you haven't lived till you've tasted it. But she hasn't quite figured out the texture, it sets like concrete. We kept bending spoons."

He took the top off one of the tubs and started hammering at the contents. Liam wondered what the chisel had chiselled last. Then he wondered what Fiona, germ-aware to the point of obsession, would have done if someone had handed her a bowl of ice cream hacked out of its container with a chisel straight from the garage. He thought how annoying it was that he was thinking about her.

Karl's kids appeared around the bend in the stairs. Their eyes rested on Liam for a split second, assessed him as a complete irrelevance and passed on to the ice cream.

"Hey, great!" the boy said. "Can we have some?"

"Tomorrow," their father said, chiselling. "This is Mr. Kane. Say hi and then up to bed."

"Hi," the kids said in unison.

"Hi," Liam said.

"Can we have some now?" the boy said.

"No, it's your bedtime."

"That isn't fair!" the girl said. "You're having some."

"We won't be having any tomorrow and you will. Go to bed."

"But Dad …!"

"Final time. Go to bed. Sleep tight."

They turned and slumped up the stairs.

"So what we do," the cop said, "is tomorrow ... you think she'll come over when she gets home from school?"

Liam nodded, thinking how easy this guy made life look, even when, as now, he was carrying a serious weight of worry and responsibility. How he seemed to know his place in the world and to be in all senses at home with it.

"So tomorrow you tell her that this boy will not be sent to jail for withholding information if he comes and gives it to us now."

"I take it that's true?" Liam said, steering his mind back to the subject at hand.

"Yes."

"He won't be sent somewhere that isn't called a jail but actually is a jail, like a 'young offenders' institute' or something? Because I don't want to play tricks on her. We're kind of ... using her as it is."

"Sure we're using her. I'm using you. At this stage I'd use my grandmother. But I promise nothing will happen to him for withholding information. If he's involved in a crime, of course, it's a different story."

Liam nodded, examining Karl's open admission that he was using him. With huge relief—it was pathetic how relieved he was—he decided that if the ruthlessness was honest, the offer of friendship had been too. Karl said what he meant, pure and simple.

"OK. And after I've told her, what happens?"

"Then we see if the boy contacts us."

"How long do we wait?"

"We need time for you to tell Clara and her to tell the boy, so twenty-four hours at least, which is a lot longer than I'd like. You're sure she can't be persuaded to give us his name?"

"I think she'd clam up completely. What happens if it doesn't work? If he doesn't contact you?"

"I go hunting. In fact, I'm going hunting anyway, I'll just be quiet about it."

He passed Liam a bowl containing a mountain of gouged-out hunks of ice cream and a spoon. "Dig in," he said. "Don't break your teeth."

# Thirteen

# CLARA

"But do you know for *sure*?" Clara said. Because what if Dan got arrested and put in jail for the rest of his life?

Mr. Kane had been out on his porch when she got home from school and had asked her to come in for a minute.

"Yes. I know for sure."

"How?"

He hesitated. "I asked a policeman."

Clara's heart leapt with fright.

"There's nothing to worry about," Mr. Kane said quickly. "I didn't say who the boy was. I don't know who he is, you didn't tell me, remember?"

"Was it Sergeant Barnes?"

"Yes. He said nothing bad would happen to ...whoever it is, provided he tells Sergeant Barnes everything he knows right away. But it has to be right away, Clara. It's very, very important."

That meant Rose was in terrible danger, *right now*. Maybe a man was sneaking up on her with a knife. The idea was so frightening it was a minute before she could speak. Then she said—it came out as a wail—"I can't tell him right away because he goes to high school and I have to tell someone at my school to tell her brother who's his friend who's at high school to tell him to get off the bus and meet me and that's two days."

There was a pause.

Mr. Kane said, "Sorry, could you say that again?"

She said it again.

He thought about it, looking out of the window. Watching him, seeing that it worried him, the weight of this new fear on top of weeks and weeks of the old fear was too much and suddenly everything welled up and spilled over and she was crying, properly crying, with sobs, because if Rose died now it would be because she, Clara, hadn't spoken to Dan in time.

Mr. Kane jammed his hands into the pockets of his jeans and turned away. He really hated her crying, he hated it as much as Rose did, she could tell. She tried as hard as she could to stop so he wouldn't say *You have to go home now.*

Mr. Kane turned and walked out of the room; she thought he was leaving because of her crying but then he came back with a box of Kleenex and handed it to her. She blew her nose and managed to stop sobbing.

"What if you phoned him?" Mr. Kane said abruptly. "This boy. You could phone him right now, from here, and tell him to call Sergeant Barnes."

She thought about it, the sobs subsiding to hiccups.

"I don't know his phone number."

"If you know his last name, we can look it up in the phone book—you can look it up if you don't want me to see it, I'll show you how. Do you know his last name?"

She had known it, but now the name wouldn't come.

"How about the girl at your school? Do you know her last name?"

She *knew* she knew it, but her head was aching from crying so hard and she was so terrified for Rose she couldn't think.

Mr. Kane sat down on the big chair Mrs. Orchard used to sit in, his elbows on his knees. He looked at the floor and rubbed the back of his neck. Finally he said, "Well, you're doing all you can, Clara. And when there's nothing more you can do there's no point in thinking about it anymore. Just tell the girl tomorrow."

They sat for a while and gradually the panic subsided. The floor was cold. Very quietly, so as not to remind Mr. Kane that she was still there, she got up and slid onto the other armchair, the one that was hers. For some reason Mr. Kane had moved the chairs around so that they were facing the window in Clara's house, and her chair was rammed up against one of the big cardboard boxes that had been in the middle of the room for so long.

"What's in the boxes?" she asked, forgetting about not reminding him she was there.

Mr. Kane looked up, startled. "The what? The boxes? My stuff. My things from where I lived before."

"Why did you leave where you lived before?"

He went back to studying the floor. "My wife and I decided we didn't want to be together anymore."

"Didn't you like each other?"

"We used to, but we kind of … stopped."

"Oh," Clara said. She hadn't known that could happen. She decided to think about it later. "Why don't you unpack them?"

"Because I'll be leaving soon."

When he'd arrived she'd wanted him to leave *immediately*, but now she found she didn't.

"Why?"

He shrugged. "Got to get on with life." He gave her a not-quite smile.

"Why can't you get on with life here?"

"Enough questions for one night, Clara, OK?"

"But how soon are you going to leave?"

"I don't know for sure." He bent forward and undid a shoelace, then did it up again.

Clara decided not knowing for sure meant it could be years and years, which was good. "Can we push the boxes back against the wall until you know for sure?"

It seemed to take questions a very long time to work their way through Mr. Kane's ears and into his head. Clara wondered if he had wax in his ears. She'd had it once and it made everything sound furry. She wondered if she should say it again, louder, but then he said, "I suppose so. If you like."

"It will be much neater," she explained, "and you won't need to walk round them all the time. But we have to put the empty boxes in front so that Moses can climb into them."

The man made a sound between a snort and a laugh, then looked up from his long study of the floor and smiled at her. She hadn't seen him smile before. He looked nice.

"OK," he said.

The two of them got up and pushed all the big boxes back against the wall with the smaller ones in front for Moses. The room didn't look as good as it would have without any boxes at all but it did look better. So that was one good thing that happened that day.

*

Having to wait to see Dan was like having to go to the toilet when you were in the car going somewhere far and there wasn't a toilet for miles and miles. You couldn't think about anything else. At school the next morning she sat crouched over her desk, looking at Mrs. Quinn but not hearing a word. At recess she went straight outside, her heart hammering with fear that Molly wouldn't be there, that she'd have a sore throat or an upset tummy and had stayed home. But she was there and saw Clara approaching and came to meet her.

"What do you want to see him for?" Molly asked curiously, after Clara had passed on the message. Until now she'd been really good about not asking questions.

"I promised not to tell anyone," Clara said, chewing her fingers. She didn't have any nails left and it was hard to find something to bite.

"Is it about your sister?"

Clara looked at her fearfully. What if Molly guessed and told the police that Dan knew something about Rose? What would happen then?

Molly patted Clara's shoulder. "Don't look so scared," she said kindly. "I won't tell anyone."


She couldn't eat her supper that evening and when she tried she was sick. She was still having her meals standing at the window even though it was pointless now, because Rose was in Toronto and wouldn't be coming home unless Clara saved her. The sick spattered on the window sill and onto the floor. Her mother came into the room and said, "Oh dear. It's all right, sweetheart. I'll clean it up in a minute. Would you like to lie down on the sofa for a bit? And then maybe try a plain cookie?"

Clara said no, she wanted to go and feed Moses and talk to him for a while. Her mother smoothed her hair. "All right. Moses is a good friend, isn't he?"

She fed Moses and then sat on the floor and watched him turn himself into triangles and squares and circles inside boxes until Mr. Kane stuck the key in the lock, whereupon Moses turned himself into a cat again and skedaddled.

Mr. Kane said, "Everything OK?"

She shrugged miserably.

"Did you tell the girl?"

"Yes."

"Good. That's great. So now you've done all you can."

She gave a small nod.

He waited, looking uncertain. "Did you want to tell me something? Or ask me something?"

"Can we unpack a box?"

He frowned. "Don't your parents expect you back about now?"

"I told my mom I'd be a while."

He hesitated for so long that she thought he was going to tell her to go home, but finally he nodded. "I guess so, then. Sure."

He chose the box that said "living room" and shoved it across the floor until it was in line with the side window, like the chairs but further forward. Then he got a knife from the kitchen, sliced the tape with one long, swift motion and opened the box.

It had big things in it—two table lamps with square wooden bases, a leather case containing knives, forks and spoons with fancy handles that he said were made of bone, but he didn't know whose bone. There was a wooden box with a hinged lid and little compartments inside filled with carved figures that Mr. Kane said were chessmen, though they didn't look like men at all, and that chess was a game adults played. There was a board with squares on it that went with them and he put it on the table beside Mrs. Orchard's chair and showed Clara where each of the men went. The last thing in the box was a vase, cream coloured with rust-red decorations and black figures dancing around the side. Clara liked it best.

"Can I have it when you die?" she asked, and the man gave his half-laugh and said sure.

"Can I have the little men playing cards too? It's my favourite thing."

"Is it?" Mr. Kane said. "That's interesting, it's my favourite thing too. Yes, you can have that when I die as well. Anything else?"

"No, thank you," Clara said politely. "That's enough."

They found places to put each of the things that had been in the big box except the knives and forks and spoons, which Mr. Kane took into the kitchen. The living room looked crowded, what with all Mrs. Orchard's things in there too, but Mr. Kane didn't seem to mind. He folded up the big box and Clara folded the wrapping paper and Mr. Kane put them both in the mud room.

By the time they finished it was almost bedtime, so Clara went home without being told.

She went upstairs and got into her pyjamas and brushed her teeth and then came down to say good-night to her mother, but her mother wasn't in the kitchen. "Mommy?" Clara called. No answer. Clara went into the living room to see if her mother was there and saw through the front window that she was outside talking to Mr. Kane. What were they talking about? It made Clara nervous. It went on for a long time, Mr. Kane nodding and then her mother nodding. Clara chewed her fingernails. Then they smiled and nodded once more and her mother turned and came into the house.

Clara said fearfully, "What were you saying to Mr. Kane?"

"Oh, we were just talking," her mother said. "He saw me when I took the garbage out and came over to have a word."

"Were you talking about me?"

Her mother gently brushed Clara's hair back off her face. "For a minute or two. Don't worry, sweetheart. He said you were no trouble and he didn't mind you coming in to feed Moses." Clara started to relax, but then her mother added, "But really, Clara, he could feed Moses himself, you know. There's no need for you to go over and do it anymore."

Clara stared at her in horror. If she didn't feed Moses, she wouldn't get to see either him *or* Mr. Kane. "I have to do it! I told Mrs. Orchard, so I have to! And Moses is scared of him, he's really scared. And he needs me to play with him, Mr. Kane wouldn't play with him! I have to go over!" Her voice was almost a shriek.

Her mother said, "Goodness, Clara! All right, but don't stay too long when Mr. Kane is there and don't pester him, he must want some peace and quiet at the end of the day."

So it was all right after all.

*Fourteen*

# ELIZABETH

The consultant has been to see Martha. It was just as we were finishing our breakfast and Martha had a fragment of cornflake on her lower lip. I tried to signal to her to wipe it off but she didn't see me and it was there the whole time.

Nurse Roberts told the doctors that Martha wanted me to be in on the discussion and they seemed happy enough with that. They drew the curtains around the two of us. The consultant was a large, jovial man, the mere sight of whom put Martha in such a state she couldn't say a word, so I did the talking from the start.

I asked if he could explain to us what the surgery would involve. He said cheerfully that there would be a vertical cut down the abdomen and possibly a smaller horizontal one as well. "There will be a scar," he said. "But it will fade and in any case you won't be wearing a bikini, will you, Mrs. Willis?"

Martha looked incredulous. Her eyes were wild.

I asked what it was they were looking for and he said they strongly suspected she had a "growth."

192

I asked if removing the growth, if that was what it was, would be the end of the affair and Martha would then be all right and he said, more gently now—I think Martha's wordless distress was so great that even he was becoming aware of it—that it was unlikely to be sufficient on its own; more treatment would probably be necessary. And even then, he said, they wouldn't be speaking of a "cure." It would be a question of buying time. I licked my lips—my mouth was very dry—and said, "If she didn't have the operation, what would ... how long would ..."

He nodded. "Things are getting critical, so probably not long."

"Mrs. Willis is seventy-five," I said. And he nodded again and said, "That is another consideration, of course."

We looked at each other in silence, he in his well-cut suit, me in my pyjamas, while between us on the bed, dressed in a white cotton nightie with little daisies around the collar and with a fragment of cornflake on her lower lip, lay a soul in mortal terror.


We haven't been able to discuss it. Martha was so agitated that after the consultant left, the doctor on duty gave her a sedative and she has been asleep all day. To tell the truth, I could do with a sedative myself. I feel horrible. My heart is thudding in a most erratic and frightening way.

I hope I don't die tonight. This is not the way I want to die, dear one; I want to be peaceful as I leave this life. I want to be able to feel you beside me at the end.

In the small hours I was back in Guelph. I was outside and it was night. Pitch black. I was feeling my way around the side of the house. Then I was in the kitchen, crossing the floor in my bare feet. In the doorway to the hall I stopped. The darkness was total but there was a noise, a pounding, terribly loud. I held my breath but the pounding got louder, it would waken everyone, it would waken Annette. But it was not Annette who woke, it was me.

I thought I was dying, my love. The pounding was my heart and I couldn't get my breath. It made the most terrible groaning noise in my chest when I tried to draw it, so loud it alerted one of the nurses at the night desk, and she came and lifted me onto my pillows and brought me a glass of water and helped me to drink, and I realized almost with regret that I was going to live a little longer.

Times without number I have asked myself how it could have come to that. Now, from a distance of thirty years, I see the answer clearly: little by little.

*

Annette went into labour in the middle of the night, two weeks early. I'd said that when the time came, whatever the hour, I would come and stay with the children while Ralph took Annette to hospital, so when, at three o'clock on a savagely cold January morning, there was a knock at the door, we knew what it was.

The labour was complicated. Annette hemorrhaged and lost a great deal of blood before they were able to bring things under control. Both babies (girls, to their mother's clear delight) were very small and the doctors said they and their mother would have to stay in the hospital until all three were stronger, possibly for a number of weeks. Ralph came over to see us looking anxious and apologetic: we had offered to look after his child for ten days but now he had come to ask if we would carry on looking after him for an indefinite period of time.

I told him we'd be delighted. (You weren't yet home from work.) In my case at least, it was true, I was delighted, but even if I hadn't been, what else could I have said? To your credit, when you arrived home you accepted the decision with only a faint look of surprise.

Annette and the babies were in the hospital for four weeks. Four weeks in which to all intents and purposes her small son was ours.


I cannot regret that time, my love. It would be like regretting a rainbow because of its association with rain. And the very best thing about it was watching you with Liam. I hadn't expected the two of you to develop much of a relationship; you were such a reserved, private man and you'd had very little contact with children. But Liam found a side of you I hadn't known was there, and I suspect you hadn't known about it either. For some reason—perhaps precisely because you didn't know how to speak to a child and play-acting solved the problem—from the first day he was with us you played English butler to his noble lord. Do you remember?

"Good morning, your Lordship," you would say, as Liam climbed out of bed each morning. (Your one request, when his stay was extended, was that he be moved into the "nursery." You wanted our privacy back, you said, and I could hardly protest. Liam and I decorated the room together, stencilling a row of blue elephants marching around the walls at child's-eye level—it took us three days and looked magnificent.) "I trust you slept well? Should I run your bath now?" (Liam, grinning ear to ear before he was even fully awake.)

"I'd better do it later," I'd say, *sotto voce* from the sidelines. "You'll be late for work."

"M'lady suggests later, so how about quickly getting into yesterday's togs and having breakfast right now? What do we need ... underwear, outerwear, more outerwear ... that's it. And may I suggest socks? The floors in these old castles are so cold."

Watching you attempt to help him put on his socks was a particular joy. For all your many talents, you were not a dexterous man and a four-year-old (Liam had turned four the day before his mother went into labour) doesn't have much dexterity either, especially in his feet.

"If you could point your toes, your Lordship. Um, no ... if you could point them downwards? Towards the sock? A good try but not quite. Perhaps if we ...?"

196

The mornings were rushed and of course you were at work all day, but sometimes you made it home in time to read him a bedtime story, and that is a precious thing to share with a child, watching his imagination set sail.

Not long after that you began to travel a great deal, visiting farms in Ontario and Manitoba, I think, and therefore saw far less of him, but during those four weeks the relationship between the two of you was cemented. I'm not saying you loved him in the way I did, Charles, but you were very, very fond of him. And without a doubt, he loved you.


On a Thursday morning at the beginning of March, four weeks to the day after the twins were born, they and their mother came home. Neighbours dropped in bearing tiny pink crocheted jackets, pink hats, pink socks, potato salads, hearty stews, apple pies. Annette's mother, complete with broken hip, had arrived the previous day. She installed herself on the sofa and sat there looking disapproving for three weeks.

I brought Liam over after lunch, as Annette had requested. She opened the door to us looking exhausted.

"Liam!" she said, giving him a quick hug, "Come in! Come and see your new sisters!"

(Not "I've missed you so much! It's so lovely to have you home!" Not even "Did you have a good time with Aunt Elizabeth and Uncle Charles?" Just "Come and see your new sisters." I know, I know.

She was tired and flooded with hormones and worried about the new arrivals.)

The older girls, looking like twin Madonnas, were sitting together in a big armchair holding a baby apiece. The babies were screwing up their faces and waving their fists, working up to a double-barrelled howl. Annette led Liam over to his quartet of sisters. "Aren't they sweet?" she whispered to him, touching a baby's cheek. "And aren't they tiny? You're their big brother, you know, you'll have to look after them. That's what big brothers are for!"

Liam turned away and wandered off.

"That's exactly what I thought he'd do," Annette said tiredly, watching him disappear down the hall.

"Boys are like that," her mother said sagely. "You'll know that," she said to me, "being a teacher."

"Oh—I'm sorry, I should have introduced you," Annette said. "This is Elizabeth, Mom." Her mother and I told each other how nice it was to meet each other. Annette said, "I've been telling Mom all about you, Elizabeth. We can never, ever, thank you and Charles enough. I truly don't know what we would have done without you. I do hope he wasn't too terrible."

I said he'd been extraordinarily good, that we'd both loved having him and would be delighted to have him again at any time. I said, "Don't hesitate to ask, Annette. Truly, you mustn't hesitate."

I'd been despairing at the thought of going back to an empty house but now, to my shame, I felt stirrings of hope. Annette now had five children, a husband and an invalid mother to care for. Some

198

women would have handled it without batting an eye but Annette wasn't one of them; at the best of times she was disorganized, inefficient and easily over-whelmed. And she and Liam were going to have problems, that much was clear from the moment she opened the door.

She lasted a week. The following Thursday morning there was a knock at the door and when I opened it she and Liam were on the doorstep. Both of them had clearly been crying and Annette still was. It was snowing hard and although Liam had on his coat and hat he had no mittens or boots and his shoes were full of snow. Annette wasn't even wearing a coat. I ushered them both in quickly and closed the door.

"Come in and sit down," I said. I was shocked by Annette's appearance. Her hair was uncombed, her face unwashed, she had thrown a sweater over her pyjama top and her trousers were fastened over her still-swollen belly with a diaper pin. She looked as if she hadn't slept since she'd come home, which turned out to be the case. Tears were rolling continu-ously down her cheeks as if somewhere inside her head a tap was dripping. She seemed hardly to notice and didn't bother wiping them away.

"It's just tiredness," she said. "It's just because the babies still need feeding every two hours and Liam's waking in the night too, so I'm not getting any sleep. Could you possibly have him this morning, Elizabeth? My mother … my mother finds him … if you could have him just for a couple of hours? I wouldn't ask, you've been so wonderful, but I remember you said …"

199

I said firmly that I would have him for the rest of the day and the night as well, in fact two nights, to give her a better chance of getting some sleep. At which she started to cry in earnest, this time with relief.

When she'd gone I went into the kitchen to join Liam, who was kneeling on the floor, colouring savagely, the crayon scribbling all over the page. He didn't look up when I came in.

"Your mommy's very tired," I said, squatting down beside him and smoothing his hair. He had blue shadows under his eyes and his face was hot and flushed. "It's because of the babies crying so much. She'll be better soon. But it's very, very nice to see you. We'll have a good time together, won't we?"

He looked up at me, then dropped the crayon and stood up, raising his arms, which was unusual, he was not a cuddly child. I straightened, lifting him to me. He wrapped himself around me, tilting his head back so that he could see my face and said, "I love you more than her."

I told him he mustn't say that, that his mommy loved him very much. But it tore at my heart, Charles. It tore at my heart with pity and—I hardly know how to say this—with a kind of savage joy. As if I was winning something. As if I had won.

How could I have felt such a thing, loving him as I did, wanting the best for him? How *could* I?


You and I had a quarrel that night. Perhaps quarrel isn't the right word—we had a disagreement. But it was a disagreement that shook me to my very soul.

It began with you being less pleased to have him with us again than I'd expected.

"It's just for a night or two," I said. "To give Annette a break. I didn't think you'd mind."

"I don't mind," you said. "Not for myself. But it's a shame, isn't it? He should be with his family. Getting to know the new ones. Being part of the family again."

"It's just for a couple of nights, it won't do him any harm. He'll enjoy it—you can see how much he loves coming."

You nodded, watching me. After a minute you said, "He loves coming because you give him so much time and attention, which his mother isn't able to give him right now."

"Time and attention are what he needs, Charles. And I'll tell you something; his mother never gives him much of either, she didn't even before the babies arrived. She prefers the girls. It's painful to watch sometimes."

There was something in your face I couldn't read. "What?" I said.

"He isn't our child, Elizabeth. The amount of time Annette gives to him isn't our business."

"Oh, I know it isn't!" I said hastily. "I know that. I was just mentioning it because I've noticed, that's all. But that's beside the point. The point is Annette was in tears when she brought him over. She isn't getting any sleep. She asked if I'd have him for the morning but I could see she was longing for us to take him for a night or two, so I offered. Is that all right? That's all I'm asking. I mean, I can say we'd rather not ..."

You got up, went into the kitchen, poured yourself more coffee without offering any to me—an unheard-of failure in courtesy—and sat down again. I was hoping that you would leave the subject now, but you did not.

"It isn't only Liam I'm concerned about," you said. "It's also you."

"Charles, I have never been happier in my life!"

"I know, that's what concerns me. Because this can't last and I'm worried about what happens when it's over. When the situation settles down and Liam goes home. How are you going to deal with that? If you don't keep some sort of distance ..." You stopped, studied your coffee, looked up. "I'm afraid you're starting to love him as if he were ours, Elizabeth. And to treat him as if he were ours—the other day I heard you telling him that something he was look-ing for was in his room. It isn't his room, he's just sleeping in it temporarily. It isn't appropriate to call it that. It could confuse him."

You paused. "To be honest, I'm afraid you already love him too much for your own good. And for his good too."

I listened to you with fear and horror. I saw that you might try, "for my own good", to bring an end to the miracle that had delivered Liam to me. I saw that I could lose him. Lose another child. I replied instinct-ively, furiously, knowing that I was twisting what you'd said, and not caring, stressing my superior knowledge of children, using every weapon I possessed.

"Charles, I have taught small children for *ten years* and I can tell you that there is no such thing as loving a child too much. A child *needs love* if he is to develop into a confident, emotionally secure adult. Liam is not getting love from his parents right now and *he needs to get it from somebody*! If he was hungry, would you say I shouldn't give him something to eat? Because for a small child to thrive, love matters as much as that. As much as food and drink! He *cannot do without it*!"

My voice was shaking with the need to convince you, my heart hammering, I could feel the flush spreading over my face.

You sat back in your chair, staring at me. I stared back angrily, accusingly, as if you had sent a starving child from our door.

"All right," you said at last, not taking your eyes from mine. "All right. That's fine."

I see now that you were feeling your way. My depression was still very fresh in your mind and you didn't want to upset me, to damage the fragile happiness this child had brought into my life. And you knew that things genuinely were very difficult in his family at that time, and wanted what was best for him as well as for me.

You must have decided that, for the moment at least, the only thing to do was let things take their course, and hope for the best.

# Fifteen

# LIAM

The morning after Liam had agreed to act as an unofficial deputy for Karl, Jim Peake's son came back to work with his dad. After listening to Jim talk about him pretty much non-stop for weeks, Liam was curious to see the kid, but he was just a carbon copy of his old man, tall and big-boned (though rake-thin—maybe the bulk would come later) with the same open, handsome face and pale blue eyes. Apart from age, the only noticeable difference between them was that Cal hardly said a word. Which figured, Liam decided, given that for the whole of the boy's life he'd never have been able to get one in anyway.

"Hi," Cal said, proffering an uncertain smile and a big square hand. Liam shook it and said it was nice to meet him, wondering if Jim was going to tell him to go home, the job vacancy having just been filled. But it seemed not. They were making a start on the new kitchen, which meant ripping out the old one first, and there was plenty of work for all. They'd wondered if they were going to have to set up an interim kitchen in the laundry room so Mr. and Mrs.

Baker would be able to function normally while the work was going on, but it turned out they had arranged to stay with their daughter and her family until the job was done. It meant the three men had a warm house, electric light, a kettle and a full cookie tin to themselves, which made it pretty much the dream job.

Jim talked all morning, with Cal interjecting the odd correction. "It was a cow not a horse, Dad, and it was Mr. Leaver not Mr. Schnauert and Mr. Leaver's foot wasn't actually broken, it was just bruised."

"Whatever."

After lunch—ham sandwiches, made by Susan, enough for ten men but they managed, sitting in a row on dining chairs which were lined up in the hall—Jim went off to take the old stove to the dump, leaving Liam and Cal to take up the ancient, cracked linoleum and scrape out the years of grime encrusted around the edges.

The two of them worked in silence for a couple of minutes. Liam bet himself ten bucks that Jim had instructed his son to ask his advice about university and then another ten that it was going to be the very first thing Cal said.

"Dad says I have to ask you about university," Cal said, taking a pair of pliers to one of the nails holding down the edges of the linoleum.

Liam gave himself twenty bucks. He decided to get a new pair of jeans at Hudson's Bay and spend the rest on fruit pie at the Hot Potato. It turned out that hamburgers and poutine weren't the only items on the menu after all, there were a variety of pies—apple, pumpkin, blueberry, lemon meringue, each one better than the last. Whoever was back there in the kitchen was a genius at pastry.

"Yeah?"

"Yeah. Sorry. We don't have to actually talk about it, I just had to ask you. So now we're done."

"I don't mind talking about it. What are you supposed to ask?"

"What to do, I guess. Like whether to go back or not."

"I don't think anyone can tell you that."

"I know." Cal heaved backwards on the head of a nail. "Why did they use two-inch nails, d'you think? Like, where did they think the linoleum was going to go? Are you glad you went?"

"Yeah. It was mostly good."

Cal nodded, then fell over backwards as the nail came free. "Victory!" he said. He scrambled upright and started on the next. Liam got the sense that he was broader in his viewpoint than his dad, as if somehow, despite living in the same house in the same town all his life, he'd nonetheless had more contact with the outside world. The consequence of TV, probably. Jim's generation wouldn't have grown up with TV. It must have been like living on the moon.

"I know I have to make up my own mind and all that," Cal said finally, "but let's say someone backed you up against a wall and held a gun to your head and said, 'Tell him what to do or I'm gonna blow your head off.' What would you say?"

"Under duress, then."

Cal flashed him a grin. "Yeah, under a little duress."

"I guess I'd say go."

"You would?" The boy sounded stricken. "Why?" Liam glanced at him and saw that Cal was scared of the big wide world out there. Scared of the rest of his life. Which made sense, Liam thought. It was scary all right.

"It's a new experience, and it gives you options later on. Plus you can always quit if you still don't like it in a few months' time, but you can't always go back if you think you've made a mistake a couple of years down the line."

Cal nodded unhappily. "Makes sense, I guess," he said. "Thanks."

Liam would have liked to point a gun at someone else's head and ask the same question for himself. He had no more idea of what he was going to do next than he'd had the day he'd arrived here.

They packed up at three. He decided he had enough time before Clara got home from school to go to the library and place an order for a tub of vanilla ice cream. The library was a flat, ugly, modern building, all expenses spared. Inside was just as bad, the one concession being a skylight over the reception area, the light from which drew the eye from the dark and uninviting stacks and focused it on the librarian behind her large, cluttered desk. She was fair-haired and nice-looking, though not what you'd call pretty; too thin, with a long, angular face. And not all that young, either, on closer inspection. Older than him by a couple of years.

She had a nice voice, calm and low. Voices were important. You could close your eyes but you couldn't close your ears. She was talking to an elderly woman who had discovered in her bookcase a book she'd withdrawn from the library in 1942, making it thirty years overdue. The old woman and the librarian were discussing the fine. They finally settled on nothing. "That seems fair," the old woman said, and hobbled off down the stacks.

The librarian smiled at Liam. "Hello," she said. "Would you be Mr. Kane, by any chance?"

Liam admitted that he was.

"It's good to meet you, Mr. Kane, I've heard so much about you. I'm Jo Kaslik. Have you come to join our library? We have an excellent library here."

"I ... Actually I was hoping to buy some ice cream."

The librarian inclined her head. "I'm afraid the ice cream is reserved for library members," she said gravely.

Liam said, in that case, he'd join.

"Excellent!" she said. "We always welcome new members, I'll make out a card for you. What sort of thing do you like to read? I'm guessing not fiction. History, maybe? Biography? Perhaps you'd like to choose some books while you're here. You can take out three at a time."

Liam hesitated. The librarian laughed and took pity on him. "Which flavour did you want, Mr. Kane? I do wild blueberry, chocolate and vanilla—I have some vanilla in the freezer that I could let you have straight away, if you'd like to come and collect it this evening."

"Vanilla's great," Liam said, wondering if it was only ice cream on offer. "And, yeah, I can come round tonight. Thanks."

Driving home he was struck by the thought that, increasingly, his life prior to coming north seemed to be taking on the quality of an old movie, one in which he'd been deeply engrossed while watching it but which now seemed trivial, unconvincing and profoundly lacking in either colour or plot. Solace had colour and plot in spades, maybe too much. In every way it was coming to seem more real than Toronto, with its endless malls and traffic jams and high-powered jobs.

Though maybe, if he went back to Toronto, the same would be true in reverse. Maybe when he'd been back for a couple of months he'd find that it was Solace that seemed unreal, its unremarkable streets and stores like something from a dream, its dramatic landscape fading to nothing, like a holiday photo left in the sun.

He was thinking about Clara when he turned down the road leading home—how to impress upon her the urgency of speaking to the mystery boy without scaring her to death—so he didn't notice until he was a couple of hundred yards away that there was a car in his driveway. He recognized it right away, though. It was Fiona's.

She was standing beside the open door of the car as if she'd only just arrived. She'd had her hair cut, long at the front, short at the back, the style she'd had in the early days of their relationship when he couldn't look at her without wanting her. She was still beautiful, maybe even more so.

"Hello," she said when he got out. "I thought I'd surprise you."

He'd never liked surprises. "Hi."

There was a silence. Reluctantly, Liam broke it. "Have you done the whole trip in one go?"

"No, I spent the night in North Bay."

He noted that she'd dressed carefully for the occasion: ankle boots, jeans, a roll-neck sweater beneath a padded jacket, none of which he'd seen before, all of which you could bet your life would be top of the range. There was nothing spur of the moment about this visit. He didn't know how he felt about it. Wary, mostly. But curious too.

"I just wondered how you were," she said, smiling. "I wanted to be sure you were OK."

A phone call would have done it. She had his number.

"I'm fine," Liam said. "How about you?"

"I'm fine too. In fact, I'm really well. *Really* well."

"Good." He glanced down the road in the direction of town. He didn't want Clara to see a stranger here and be put off.

Fiona gestured towards the house. "So this is it! The gift! It's quite charming, isn't it? Oldy-worldy."

"Yeah, it's nice."

She shivered suddenly, shuffling her feet, and gave a little laugh. "But it's cold up here! Much colder than at home. Can we go in? I'd love to look around."

"Um … not right now," Liam said. "I have an appointment. Someone's coming. But later maybe, if you want."

"That sounds interesting. Is it to do with selling the house, is there a buyer coming? I could pretend to be another buyer, pretend I'm in love with it, bump up the price for you." She grinned, bright-eyed.

"No," Liam said distractedly. He thought he saw Clara in the distance. "It's nothing to do with the house. Actually, I have to get ready. Sorry, but could you … there's a coffee shop in town, called the Hot Potato. I'll meet you there afterwards, if you want. I'll probably be half an hour or so."

She tipped her chin down. "It's a woman, isn't it?" she said, teasingly, knowingly. "That's so nice, Liam. I'm so happy for you. In fact one of the reasons I'm here is that I've met someone too, and I wanted to be sure you were OK with it. You know, not hurt. So this is lovely. Both of us starting new lives."

"I have to go," Liam said. "I'll see you later."


When he'd spoken to Clara he phoned the police station, badly needing to talk to Karl. It was going to take longer than they'd thought for Clara to speak to the boy who had information on Rose, and the cop wasn't going to be happy about it. But Karl was out, prowling around the country, looking for trouble. Liam left a message saying he'd be in that evening and would Karl please phone him. Then he went into town.

Fiona had chosen a booth near the back of the restaurant and sat facing the door. If it was privacy she was after she needn't have gone to so much trouble—apart from the waitress there was no one else in the place. She smiled at him when he walked in and he nodded in return. He'd kept her waiting nearly an hour but she wasn't showing any sign of being annoyed, which in Liam's experience was a first.

There was a half-empty cup of coffee in front of her. He wondered how she'd got on with the waitress.

"What can I get you?" Fiona asked as he sat down.

"Coffee would be fine," he said. "Thanks." His head was still full of Clara. Her desperate concern for her sister. Her struggle to halt the tears, followed almost immediately by a request to move his boxes. She wanted them neat. He guessed her world was low on order at the moment.

"It's terrible coffee," Fiona said, "and you'll have a very long wait. It took her about half an hour to bring me mine."

"Yeah, she takes her time."

Fiona lifted a perfectly manicured hand to signal the waitress, who became fascinated by something across the road. She stood at the window with her back to them, hands on hips, feet planted wide.

"Is this really the best place in town?" Fiona asked, not bothering to keep her voice down.

"It's the only place in town."

"I take it you don't eat out often in that case."

"Almost every night."

Fiona gaped.

The waitress turned. Her face expressed surprise and pleasure (*pleasure!*) at seeing Liam. She came over to their table. "Coffee, sir?" she asked, eyebrows politely raised.

"Thanks," Liam said. He hadn't known she could do politeness. It was for Fiona's benefit, he knew—clearly it had been hate at first sight—but that made it kind of fun.

"Piece of blueberry pie, maybe?"

"Actually, that would be nice. Thanks."

She beamed at him—it was an afternoon of firsts—rolled off and returned seconds later with coffee and pie.

When she'd gone Fiona shook her head as if to clear it. "Wow," she said. "Wow." Then she flicked her hand the way she did when she was dismissing something irritating but trivial. "Anyway, how was your meeting?"

"My meeting?" Liam said. "It was fine."

Fiona smiled. "You don't need to pretend, Liam. I'm delighted for you."

Liam forked up tender, buttery, blueberry pie.

"You're a fast worker where women are concerned," Fiona said. "But then, you always were." There was a smile in her voice but he didn't look up. "I imagine they've been standing in line; rich, *ferociously* good-looking, unattached man rolls into town ... But so long as you've found someone who's good to you, I'm thrilled."

He considered asking if she thought she'd been good to him and decided against it. Keep it civilized, find out what she wanted.

"Who's this new guy, then?" he asked politely.

Fiona looked vague. "Oh, just someone I met at a party. He's a lawyer too. Not with our firm, though.

Very nice, very good-looking." She smiled at him. "He has a great sense of humour. We laugh a lot. Which is important, isn't it?"

Liam nodded. There was no other man. It was childish to be so pleased.

"What have you been doing with yourself up here in the bush?" Fiona asked brightly. "Living a life of leisure? Enjoying the fall colours? They're magnificent, aren't they, I was noticing them on the drive up."

"I've been working."

"Really? They need accountants up here?"

"Not as an accountant, as a labourer. I've been working for a builder."

"Good grief!" Fiona said. "Whatever for?"

"It's kind of fun."

"How much does he pay you?"

"He doesn't. Can't afford to." He was about to explain about payment in kind but Fiona threw her head back and laughed.

"*Of course* he can't! Oh Liam, Liam!" The laugh was loud enough that the waitress turned her head to look.

"Why are you here, Fiona?"

It came out flat and hard and she looked sharply away. The silence extended across the room: he refused to break it. Fiona looked down, studying the skin on her coffee.

"I've been thinking about us," she said finally. "I've been wondering if we tried hard enough to make it work. I'm not sure I did and I've been feeling guilty about it." She lifted her head and met his eyes. He

214

couldn't remember the last time she'd looked at him like that, without anger or derision. In spite of himself it made something in him ache.

"We had something really good once, Liam. I've been wondering if we should give ourselves another chance. Try to get it back."

There was nothing left of the pie but crumbs. He mashed them carefully with the back of the fork; licked them off. Tried to figure it out. Self-doubt and uncertainty were his preserve, they weren't part of Fiona's makeup. As for guilt, she wouldn't know how to spell it. So what had brought about this change of mind? The odds were, he decided, that in the months since their decision to divorce she'd had a couple of relationships, and they hadn't worked out. Her law firm did a lot of entertaining and Fiona being Fiona, she'd have found it humiliating to turn up at a function without a man on her arm. Maybe she'd discovered it was harder to pick up a new man than it had once been—she was thirty-five, the same age as him—and decided he was better than no one. In other words, she wanted him back because she needed a partner and had decided he was the best available for now.

He hesitated, though. Those were the odds, yes, but he'd become more aware, over the past few weeks, of his own pessimism and paranoia, always there in the background, affecting his judgement, sabotaging his life. How do you know another person's mind? How do you even know your own? Possibly, she was telling the truth. It was a long drive from Toronto, the last eighty kilometres of it over bone-jarring roads, and she'd sat for an hour in a sleazy cafe with a belligerent waitress and hadn't walked out; on some level this meeting must be important to her.

There was another thing too, namely that he'd had the same thoughts himself: that they'd made a mistake, that they should have tried harder. She had represented hope to him once. She was the one and only person he had ever been close to.

But you had to set that against the rest. Those final years with her had all but destroyed him.

"Liam," Fiona said. "Say something."

He noticed the strain around her eyes. She looked older. She was lonely, he saw. So was he. But he'd been at least as lonely in their marriage.

"I don't know what to say," he said. "I'm going to have to think about it."

For a second she looked startled, then recovered herself. "I see. OK."

He looked at his watch. "It's after six. Would you like a burger?"

"No. Not here, anyway."

"There isn't anywhere else."

"Could we go back to your place?"

"There isn't anything to eat there."

"There must be something, surely."

"Cornflakes. Bread."

"No cheese? No eggs?"

"There might be some cheese, I'm not sure."

She studied him. "You don't want me to come to the house, do you? You're afraid—what is it you're afraid of exactly, Liam? Is this new woman tucked up in the bedroom?"

216

"No."

"What is it, then? Are you afraid I'll seduce you? That you won't be able to get rid of me once I get in the door?" She leaned towards him, elbows on the table, chin in hands, the corners of her mouth curved in a smile. "Is that it?"

That was part of it all right. Without a doubt, if they went back to the house she would try to seduce him and she just might manage it. In Liam's experience, when it came to a battle between lust and common sense, lust generally won hands down. When he woke in the morning, they'd be together again.

But the other, more important, part of it was that Clara would be back there now, feeding Moses, and for reasons he couldn't quite figure out he couldn't stand the thought of Fiona meeting Clara. Not that Fiona would be unkind, just the reverse; he knew exactly how it would go: Fiona would squat down so as to be on Clara's level—or worse, sit cross-legged on the floor beside her—and ask gentle, sympathetic questions, maybe even put an arm around her, maybe, for Christ's sake, even encourage Clara to cry so that she could comfort her, draw her close, stroke her hair. Pretending to understand what it felt like for a kid when your world disintegrated around you, when you lost someone you loved and you didn't know what had happened to them, didn't know why, didn't know what was going to happen next, and you were completely powerless to do anything about it. Fiona, understanding nothing, pretending to care. All of it an act for his benefit to show him what a lovely warm person she was, after which she would get up and walk away and never give Clara another thought.

"Liam, would you please talk to me?"

"You're welcome to come and see the house but not until after eight." Clara would be gone well before then.

"How mysterious! And you won't tell me why! This is like a detective story!"

"I'll tell you why, if you like. There's a little kid next door who was very close to Mrs. Orchard. She came in to feed the old lady's cat while she was in the hospital and she still does. She obviously misses her and playing with the cat seems to help."

"And why, exactly, does it matter if a little girl is there playing with a cat when we go into the house?" Fiona asked. "Could you explain that to me, please?"

"There's a lot going on in her life. Her sister's gone missing—she's been missing for weeks, a police search and all that. Her parents are in a bad way. I think Mrs. Orchard's house is a kind of refuge for her. A sanctuary or something. I don't want her to have to deal with anything else."

"You think my coming into the house will traumatize her."

"Not traumatize her, Fiona," he said tiredly. "But it would be something else for her to deal with."

"But you being in the house is OK?"

"I mostly keep away when I know she's going to be there."

"Goodness! Who would have thought you had such a social conscience, Liam! Who would have guessed! I'm so *impressed*!"

He said flatly, "So, would you like a burger now or some bread and maybe cheese, if there is any, after eight o'clock?"

"How would it be if we went back to your place and I waited in the car while you explained to this child—what's her name, by the way?"

"Clara."

"While you explain to Clara that, for just this one night, you'd like her to go back to her own home because you have a friend coming for supper. Just this one night."

"I don't want to do that. Sometimes she wants to talk."

"Just this *one night*, Liam, so that you and I can discuss what is arguably the most important decision of our lives."

"We can discuss it here."

"Over a greasy hamburger delivered to us after a very, *very* long wait by a giant sloth."

"Why would that matter?"

"You know what?" Fiona said, putting her hands flat, palms down, on the table. "I think we've just discussed it."

Liam nodded. "So do I."


When she'd gone he ordered a burger and fries and ate them slowly, staring fixedly at a small tear in the plastic on the back of the bench seat across from him. He heard the opening and closing of the door as people came in, the shuffling of the waitress, a laugh from across the room. The waitress filled up his coffee without being asked.

219

He sat in the café until he was sure Clara would have left, then drove home. He stood in the hall for a moment, then sat down on the stairs, elbows on knees, hands dangling. In his mind's eye he saw himself and Fiona in the café, talking, one sentence leading to the next as if they were reading from a script, as if the whole thing had been preordained: they'd said what they'd said because they were who they were and because of everything they'd said before. He couldn't even agonize over whether or not he'd made the right decision because he hadn't made a decision, he'd just responded to her words with words of his own until she walked out. If there'd been a chance for them, he'd blown it, in exactly the same way as he'd blown every chance he'd ever had. And here he was. Alone. Sitting on the stairs.

The phone rang. It would be Fiona. She'd have charmed some guy in a gas station into letting her use the phone. When Liam answered she'd say something like, "That didn't go very well, did it? Let's try again tomorrow. I'll spend the night in a motel and come back in the morning." What would he say?

The phone was still ringing. With a huge effort he stood up and answered it.

"So how'd it go?" Karl said.

"Jesus Christ, Karl!"

How could he know about it already? Someone must have seen them in the café and within ten seconds the news had ricocheted around town and shot in through the window of the police station. How did anyone get away with a crime around here? You couldn't even blow your nose without the whole town knowing.

In a careful voice, Karl said, "Everything OK, Liam?"

"Apart from this whole fucking town knowing my business, yes."

There was silence. Karl said, "You left a message for me to phone. I assumed it was about your talk with Clara."

"Oh," Liam said. It felt like another life. "Sorry. I thought you were ... forget it. I'm sorry." He closed his eyes, his brain scrambling to change lanes.

"Let's start again. How did it go?"

"It went all right," Liam said, dragging his thoughts together. "It went fine. But it's a complicated business for her to get a message to the boy."

"Complicated how?"

"She has to tell a girl at her school who has a brother at high school to tell the boy, who then has to get off the school bus someplace where he can intercept Clara on her way home from school. But she can't tell the girl until they're at school tomorrow—doesn't know her last name or phone number—so the message won't get down the line until the following day. It means two days."

There was another silence.

"Want me to run through it again?" Liam said.

"No, think I got it. But the thing is, it won't be two days, it'll be three, because after the boy's talked with Clara he's going to go home and think about it. And if he doesn't believe what she's told him he still won't come to us and we still won't know who he is."

221

"Shit," Liam said.

"Indeed."

In the background there was the sound of kids squabbling. Karl's muffled voice said, "Marge? Would you close the door?" His voice clear again, he said, "He'll get off the bus near her home because there are fewer houses out there, so less risk of being seen. I'm going to ambush them."

"What if he won't tell you anything?"

"I'll arrest him."

"You can't do that without even giving him time to think!" He'd promised Clara that nothing would happen to the boy and she had believed him.

"I can and I will, there's a kid's life at stake. I'm sorry."

Anger, present and past, rage with Fiona, with himself—with his entire life—swelled up inside him like a towering wave and exploded down the phone line. "I don't give a fuck if you're sorry! You promised me and I promised—I *promised*—a seven-year-old kid!"

There was a pause. Finally Karl said, quietly, calmly, as if talking down a dangerous guy with a large knife, "Let's think this through, OK Liam? My problem is, three days is too long and I can't see what else we can do to speed things up. But I'm open to suggestions."

Liam was too shaken by his own fury to reply.

"Maybe I'm missing something," Karl said. "Some other option."

"All I know," Liam said, struggling to speak normally, "is that you can't arrest that kid."

Karl said, "You want a sixteen-year-old girl to spend another night on the street risking rape and murder so that her seven-year-old sister, who wants her back *alive*, won't think less of you? Is that what you're saying, Liam?"

Liam slammed the phone down. For several minutes he stood still, heart pounding, breathing hard, staring at the phone. Then he called back.

"I'll find them," he said. "I'll speak to him."

"You are one difficult son of a bitch, you know that?" Karl said grimly. "Why would it make any difference if it was you?"

"Because I'm not a cop and I can't arrest him and he knows Clara trusts me." He managed not to say, *Remember your little speech about trust?*

There was a very long pause. "OK," Karl said reluctantly. "We'll try it. But let me tell you, Liam, I'm gonna be right on your tail. You won't see me but I'll be there."


Liam went into the kitchen and opened the fridge. It was all but empty. Abruptly he remembered the ice cream; he was supposed to collect it from the librarian. Jo the librarian. He decided to go—adrenalin was still charging round his bloodstream, he needed some exercise or he wouldn't sleep. He checked his watch, expecting it to be near midnight, and discovered it wasn't yet eight-thirty.

Jo had given him directions and it wasn't far—nowhere in Solace was far. The temperature being what it was, there was zero possibility of the ice cream melting on the way home so he went on foot. He walked fast, an icy moon lighting his way, his breath steaming in the freezing air, the remnants of his anger—a churning gut, a raised pulse—slowly settling, leaving him wondering where the rage had come from. He was still shaken by the violence of it. There must be something wrong with him, normal people didn't react like that.

The house was tiny, a single-storey white clapboard with a screened veranda on the front, the whole thing in pitiful need of a coat of paint.

"Come in," Jo said, ushering him in and quickly closing the door against the cold. In the light of the hallway she looked at him and said, "You look as if you could do with a coffee."

"Um ... actually," Liam said. It was only the ice cream he wanted, he definitely wasn't up to an evening of small talk, the day had been too long, too hard and too depressing.

"Through this way." She led the way into a small living-room-cum-kitchen, the sink, stove and counter along one wall, dining table and chairs in the middle of the room, a wood-burner in the corner with two squat armchairs in front of it. Everyone up here huddled in front of the fire, no prizes for guessing why. Jo indicated the armchairs. "Have a seat."

Of the two armchairs only one had a baggy, sat-in look, which meant she was on her own. Between the chairs was a side table with a reading lamp and a precarious pile of books. Many more books were stacked along the walls, which fitted, he guessed. A small, almost colourless rug lay in front of the fire.

Those things aside, the room was bare; no bookcase, no ornaments or artfully positioned lamps, no pictures on the walls. Still, it was comfortable enough, with the woodstove gently pulsing out the heat. He sat down, suddenly dizzy with fatigue. He'd have a coffee, make excuses and go home.

"You should taste the ice cream before buying it," Jo said, setting the coffee pot on the hotplate. "It's expensive because there's so much cream, so you need to be sure you like it. Plus I should warn you it tends to freeze a little hard."

He opened his mouth to say he'd had some at Karl's but she had vanished through a door into what looked to be a lean-to stuck onto the back of the house. A minute later she emerged with a large tub.

"This is my own private supply, reserved for guests. Or for me if I've had a hard day. Or if I just feel like some, which as it happens, I do."

From the drawer beside the sink she took a chisel and a hammer and attacked the ice cream. "A trick I learned from Karl. Karl Barnes, whom I believe you've met. Actually, whom I know you've met. Also Jim Peake. Between the two of them they seem to be keeping you busy."

She smiled at him. Her hair had been gathered back at the library but now it was loose; when she leaned forward it fell across her face, thick and full. She pushed it back with her wrist, a smooth, graceful gesture. Unbidden—in fact unwanted—the familiar dance of sex slid into his mind: first moves, second moves, mouth, neck, breasts and so forth. Then he thought about going home to bed and the latter won.

He couldn't remember that ever happening before—it alarmed him, he wondered if he was coming down with something serious. Or having a breakdown. Or getting old.

"Cream? Sugar?"

"Just cream. Thanks."

She handed him a mug and balanced the bowl of ice cream on the pile of books. "Don't rush. Pleasures should not be rushed." She chiselled out a bowlful for herself, put the tub away and settled down into the other armchair, her legs folded under her. The room was so small that if Liam had reached out he could have touched her. They both watched the fire. It was extremely quiet. He took a spoonful of ice cream.

When he looked back on the evening in days to come he admitted to himself that, excellent though the ice cream was, it couldn't have been the mind-altering, near-mystical experience it had seemed to be at the time; it was simply very good ice cream. But he was at a low ebb, his lowest in a long time, tired and depressed and full of self-loathing and recrimination, and the chair he was in was comfortable and the room was warm and smelled pleasantly of vanilla, and the woman beside him didn't wreck it all by talking but instead sat in silence and watched the wavering flames. He ate the ice cream slowly, letting it soften in his mouth and slide, cool and sweet, down his throat, and gradually a feeling of peace stole over him—a very rare experience in his life.

When he'd finished, he set the bowl down on the pile of books and settled back in the chair. He thought he should say something—thank her, say how good it was, say that he felt positively reborn, in fact—but he didn't want to break the spell so he remained silent. Jo was still studying the fire, her empty bowl in her lap. He could see only her profile but it seemed to him that she had something on her mind, something that required careful thought. What he required was no thought at all and, for a while, with his head resting against the back of the armchair and the smell of vanilla still hanging in the air, he managed to achieve that state.

Eventually, with the air of one who has come to a decision, the woman stood up. She took the empty bowls over to the sink and then came back and stood looking down at him, her head tipped to one side the way she had at the library, her hair sliding forward, layer upon layer.

"So?" she asked.

# Sixteen

# CLARA

Dan said, "He told the police? He told Sergeant Barnes?" He looked scared, which scared her.

"He just asked him if someone would go to jail if he didn't tell and then he did."

"Yeah, but Sergeant Barnes will know what it's about, Clara! He's not stupid, he'll know!"

"But he doesn't know who you are!" She shouldn't have asked Mr. Kane, she shouldn't! But Rose! Rose!

"But who is this guy? You don't even know him! He could be a plain-clothes detective! They could've planted him in the house next door, it being empty and all."

"He isn't! It's his house now, Mrs. Orchard gave it to him, my dad said! And he's *nice*!" She had to stop and breathe. "He said you won't go to jail if you tell Sergeant Barnes right away, but you have to tell him right away because Rose is in danger! So we have to tell him now! We have to!"

Dan flicked away a half-smoked cigarette and didn't even look where it landed, it could have started a forest fire. He shook another out of the pack, lit it, and smoked it right down to his fingers in three goes, the ash trembling on the end of it like an old grey caterpillar. He dropped it on the ground, then stood looking at it, shaking his head. Clara watched him anxiously.

"I don't know," he said. "It might be a trick."

In the distance, from the direction of home, a car was coming. Dan said a bad word and slid into the shelter of the trees.

"Is it a police car?" he asked from behind a tree.

"No," Clara said. She could see it clearly now. It was Mr. Kane's car.

"Walk on," Dan said urgently. "Like you're walking home just like always. Don't stop until it's passed us and out of sight, then come back."

She walked on but the car was coming fast and she'd only gone a few steps when it drew up beside her. Mr. Kane rolled down his window.

"Hi, Clara," he said.

"Hi."

"Have you met the boy?"

Clara didn't know what to say. She wished he'd speak more softly, Dan would be able to hear every word.

"I think that means yes," the man said after a minute. "What did he say? Is he going to see Sergeant Barnes?"

She didn't know what to say.

Mr. Kane said, "Clara, why can't you tell me what he said? This is to help Rose, remember?"

He was trying not to be cross, she could hear it in his voice. It worried her even more. "He said he didn't know what to do."

229

Mr. Kane rubbed his neck.

"How long is it since you talked to him?"

She chewed a fingernail.

"Has he started walking home?"

There was no chewable nail left so she gnawed on a finger.

Mr. Kane studied her, then sat back and looked down the road, his mouth a tight line. A car went by and disappeared into the distance. Mr. Kane leaned forward in his seat and squinted at something on the ground up ahead. Clara looked too. In the dust of the roadside there was a pale patch made up of a lot of small white things clustered together. Cigarette butts. Some very white. Not dusty or rained on.

Mr. Kane sat back again. After a minute he turned to her and said, leaning towards her and speaking more loudly than he needed to, "I'm going to get out of the car, Clara. I'm not going anywhere, I just want him to be able to see me if he's somewhere close. I'm not going to try to make him do anything, it's up to him. If you know where he is, please go and tell him that if he wants, I'll drive him to see Sergeant Barnes right now, stay with him while they talk, and then drive him home afterwards. Tell him I give him my word that he will not be in any trouble if he comes now. Tell him that."

She didn't know what to do. She turned around to go and tell Dan but stopped, because then Mr. Kane would know where he was. And anyway Dan must have heard.

Mr. Kane got out of the car, walked around to the front and leaned back against the hood with his hands

230

in his pockets. Clara stayed where she was, drawing lines in the dust with her shoes, and after a long while Dan stepped out from the woods and came and got into the car, and Mr. Kane got in too, and they drove away.

"Today is Tuesday," she told Moses that night. He was moulding his head into her cupped hands, purring so loudly that it gave her fingers pins and needles. "So by Thursday night Rose will be home. Or Friday. Maybe Friday, but not later because now the policemen know what she looks like and what her name is it will be easy to find her."

She imagined Rose, at bedtime, saying, "Come, creep in beside me," like she used to, and herself climbing in and falling asleep with Rose's arms around her and her breath on her neck and the knowledge that when she woke up in the morning Rose would be there. Then someone would tell Rose that it was Clara who saved her and Rose would wrap her arms around her and rock her back and forth, saying thank you, thank you, my brilliant little sister.

Before bed she took all of Rose's clothes out of the cupboard and dropped them on the floor and stirred them round into a huge enormous mess, by way of a welcome.

*

During the morning recess on Wednesday she didn't sit on the step, she went over to the smooth patch of concrete by the white fence where the girls who used to be her friends—Ruth and Jenny and Sharon and Susan—were playing double dutch. Sharon and Ruth were turning the ropes and Jenny and Susan were running in from each side. Susan wasn't very good at it and kept stepping on the ropes. Clara was extremely good at it, or had been. She hoped they'd ask her to have a turn. At first they didn't, they just glanced at her and smiled vaguely and kept skipping, but finally Ruth stopped turning the ropes.

"Hi," Ruth said.

"Hi."

"Do you want a turn?"

"OK."

The ropes turned and she jumped in and skipped half a dozen times but then the excitement inside her got in the way of her concentration and she made a mess of it.

"I'm out of practice," she said, standing in the middle of the dead ropes.

Sharon said, "You can have another turn later when you've remembered how."


At lunchtime Mrs. Quinn said, "You're looking better, Clara. Is there good news?"

Clara said, "Not yet, but there will be soon." And Mrs. Quinn patted her on the head and said, "That's the spirit. Good for you."

*

232

Thursday came and went. On Friday during the recess, Clara stood with the other girls and watched them skip but she didn't join in. Her head was full of fuzz and she knew she'd get muddled up. When school finished she ran almost all of the way home because Rose would be in the kitchen, waiting for her, she knew it for certain.

Saturday she spent the morning standing at the window humming, a flat toneless hum. She didn't think, just hummed.

In the afternoon she went to play with Moses. He couldn't seem to concentrate either. He'd managed to fit himself into every corner of every box so many times he was tired of it and for ages now he'd shown no interest in the mouse. Maybe the mouse wasn't there anymore, maybe he'd died, like Mrs. Orchard.

It would have helped if Mr. Kane had been there, but he wasn't, he and Mr. Peake were really busy and worked late and only had Sundays off. Also, in the evenings, although Mr. Kane went to the Hot Potato at the same time as always, sometimes he was so late getting back she had to go home to bed before seeing him. She wanted to ask him why Rose wasn't home yet. She also just plain wanted him to *be* there. He was *supposed* to *be there*.

She couldn't sit still even with Moses on her lap, so she gently edged him off and got up and wandered around opening drawers and cupboards, looking for something, she didn't know what.

High up in a cupboard in Mrs. Orchard's (Mr. Kane's) kitchen she saw a goldfish bowl. She remembered it from a long time ago; it had belonged to Miss Godwin, Mrs. Orchard's sister, before she died of being really old. Once Clara had asked Mrs. Orchard if they could get a goldfish but Mrs. Orchard said Moses would eat it in ten seconds flat so the bowl had stayed where it was.

Now Clara dragged a chair over to the counter, climbed onto it and onto the counter, and carefully lifted the bowl down. She took it into the living room and put it on the floor.

"This is a goldfish bowl," she told Moses. "Do you like it?" He came over to the bowl, stiff-legged and suspicious. It wasn't as big as it had looked in the cupboard. "It's too small," she said regretfully. "There's way too much of you."

Moses walked all the way around the bowl twice, then put his front feet up on the rim and peered into it.

"You see?" Clara asked, but he didn't believe her. He hung himself over the rim of the bowl like a tea towel and studied it upside down and inside out. "If you got all of you in you might not be able to get out," Clara warned, whereupon he did such a fast somersault she hardly saw it happen; for a minute there was chaos in the bowl as he flailed around trying to get his tail in but he managed in the end and there it was, a bowlful of cat.

Clara gave a scream of delight. "Where's your head?" she shrieked. "Mo, what have you done with your head?" There was another flurry and one enormous eye appeared up against the glass, staring at her triumphantly.

She so badly wanted to show Mr. Kane that she must have magicked him up, because there was the scrape of a key in the lock and a raging blizzard of fur in the goldfish bowl and Moses shot out of it and out of the back door just as Mr. Kane came in.

"You missed it!" Clara cried. "You just missed it, and it was the best thing he's ever done, I really wanted you to see!"

Mr. Kane said, "I'm starting to wonder if Moses exists. Are you sure you aren't making him up?"

Clara was shocked—how could he could think such a thing? But then Mr. Kane laughed and she saw that he'd been teasing her, like Rose used to do.


Sunday was better, because Mr. Kane had told her it still might take a long time for the police to find Rose, so at least she knew. On Monday she went to school as usual. She counted her footsteps both there and back but she kept losing track, which frightened her because it was bad luck. When she got home Mrs. Rand from two doors down was there. She came hurrying into the hall when Clara opened the door and said, "Oh, my dear child, come into the kitchen, your mother is there."

Clara's heart leapt—Rose!—but when she went into the kitchen her mother was sitting at the table, her face blotchy, purple-red and white. Clara stopped in the doorway. She said, "Mommy?"

Her mother got up and came to her and bent down and put her arms around her. "Sweetheart," she said, "they found a girl, they don't know if it's Rose or not, your daddy's gone down to see if it's her. So we don't know. But it could be her, she's the right age."

"Didn't she say she was her?" Clara asked, bewildered.

"No, sweetheart. No, she … she couldn't. Daddy will phone us when he's seen her but that probably won't be until tomorrow morning, it'll be very late by the time he gets there. He'll phone us and then we'll know."

Another of her mother's friends, Mrs. Turner, arrived having heard the news, and the women made tea and asked Clara if she'd like some milk and cookies, but Clara shook her head.

Her mother sat down again and held out her arms, wanting her to come and sit on her lap. Mrs. Turner said, "That's it, you go comfort your mommy." Her mother's lap would be hot and damp with all the tears still inside her and the ladies would talk and talk and keep offering Clara cookies. Clara shook her head at her mother—her mother looked really upset but she didn't care, she *wouldn't* care, she turned around and went out of the kitchen and over to Mr. Kane's house.

She sat on the floor against the wall in the living room. The floor and the wall were cold but she was so hot inside that it felt good. Moses appeared, and came over and sniffed her and then stood back as if he didn't like the smell of her being unhappy. But then he changed his mind and climbed onto her lap

236

and curled up in it. He didn't purr, though. He must have known it wasn't the right time for purring.

After a long time there was the sound of a key and Moses shot off and Mr. Kane came in. He stood in the doorway for a moment, looking at her, and then said quietly, "It's probably not her, Clara. They found the … girl … in Windsor, whereas your friend Dan told us Rose was going to Toronto. Also, this girl had long hair and Dan said Rose was going to cut hers very short, remember? So it's probably not her."

Clara nodded.

After a minute, when she didn't say anything, Mr. Kane said, "Would you like to unpack another box?"


Early on Tuesday morning, Clara's father phoned. Her mother started to cry into the phone and Clara was so terrified she went rigid, but when her mother put the phone down, she said, "It wasn't Rose, the dead girl wasn't Rose. Oh Clara, it's terrible to be so glad it's someone else's child."


The dead girl kept coming into her mind. She'd be brushing her teeth or sitting at her desk at school and suddenly she'd see the dead girl lying on the ground. She could never see her face properly, all she could see was that her eyes were closed like dead people's eyes were. Or she'd be out in the playground watching the other girls skipping and suddenly she'd realize there was a body lying over by the fence, and it would be her. It made Clara's heart thump so hard she could hardly breathe.

In her sleep she saw the dead girl walking down the road ahead of her. As Clara came up behind her, the girl turned around, her eyes still closed, and it was Rose after all. Clara woke up screaming. Her mother and father came in and her mother held her and told her it was just a dream. For a moment Clara thought she meant the whole thing was a dream. But most of it wasn't.

*

On Friday afternoon Dan was waiting for her, which was a good thing, because he knew how it felt being without Rose. She could tell from a long way back that he didn't have any news, though; it was the way he was standing, head down, blowing smoke at the ground.

"Hi," he said, when she came up, and offered her a cigarette, which was really, really silly, she wasn't even eight yet and she wasn't ever going to smoke, it smelled disgusting. She shook her head and Dan said, "Sorry. Don't know why I did that. Rose would kill me."

For a while he didn't say anything else, just smoked and looked off into the woods across the road, but finally he said, "The thing I can't understand is why it's taking them so long, it's been more'n a week. Has Mr. Kane said anything?"

"He just said it might take a long time because Toronto's really big."

"Yeah," Dan said. "I know it's big. But jeez."

238

They stood side by side for another minute or two. It was windy and very cold.

Dan turned up the collar of his coat. He said, "Guess we should go home. That wind's coming from the north, it's gonna get colder." He looked down at her and gave a funny smile and said, "When Rose gets back, don't tell her I offered you a fag, OK? She'd really, seriously, kill me. She hates me smoking anyway."

Somehow it made her feel better. It was as if Rose was standing there with them, furious with Dan in just the way she used to get furious with people back in the days before she went away.

*

In the night she felt sick. Everything hurt and her body felt hot and cold at the same time. When she got out of bed in the morning her head ached so badly she cried. Her mother came in and put a hand on her forehead and said she should go back to bed. She brought her half an aspirin in strawberry jam and a glass of hot lemon juice with honey in it.

For two days she stayed in bed, only getting up to go to the toilet. At suppertime on the second day her mother asked if she'd like to come downstairs in her dressing gown and have some soup, so she did. She managed a couple of spoonfuls of soup and a cracker, and then went back to bed.

She dreamed Rose came into the room—not the dead girl but Rose herself, alive—and sat on the bed beside her. It was such a strong dream it woke her up. It was dark out but the clock on the chest of drawers said ten past eight, so her parents wouldn't have gone to bed yet. When she stood up her head pounded in time with her heart, but after a minute it wasn't too bad. The dream was still with her, still so real it was as if Rose was beside her. Clara went and stood at the top of the stairs in her pyjamas. She could hear her parents talking in the kitchen but their voices were low and muffled so the door must be closed. Unsteadily, holding onto the banister, she went downstairs, into the front room and across to the window. There were no lights on in the room and she could see out; the sky was clear and there were millions of stars and a cold, bright moon making the road look white. There were no lights next door so Mr. Kane was out, though his car was there.

She rested her forehead against the icy glass of the window and hummed to herself, feeling the vibration in her chest. She hummed for Rose, calling her home.

After a while, from far down the road, a car's headlights appeared, their light turning the moonlit road yellow, the trees at the roadside rearing up like pale ghosts as it passed. Clara stopped humming. She waited for the car to turn into someone else's driveway but it didn't. As it got closer it slowed down, slower and slower until she thought maybe she was still asleep and she was dreaming. But then it turned into the driveway, her own driveway, the tires crunching on the gravel, the headlights blinding her so that she had to close her eyes. Then the driver switched off the engine and the headlights went out, she could tell through her closed eyelids, and she opened her eyes again.

In the moonlight she saw it was a police car. Both front doors opened and Sergeant Barnes got out of one side and Dr. Christopherson got out of the other. Clara forgot to breathe. The doctor opened the back door of the car and leaned in and half-lifted someone out: a slight figure, wrapped in a blanket.

Rose.

Their father cried, right there on the porch, right there in front of Dr. Christopherson and Sergeant Barnes. He held Rose so tightly she almost disappeared inside him and he cried into her ragged, inch-long, light-brown hair. Clara's mother stood beside them, swaying slightly, her face shining with joy. Sergeant Barnes and Dr. Christopherson stood at the edge of the porch, smiling. Clara watched Rose. She wanted to run up and hug her but she was afraid to.

When her father released her, Rose stumbled back a couple of steps. Her eyes slid over them blankly and for a moment Clara, her heart lurching, wasn't sure it was really her. It wasn't the almost no hair or the lack of makeup, though those things did make her look very un-Rose-like, it was that she looked as if she didn't know who they were. Then her mother wrapped her arms around her and kissed her and whispered, "Come inside, sweetheart, it's cold out here. Come in where it's warm."

Dr. Christopherson stepped forward and murmured to Clara's father that he'd come tomorrow and then he and Sergeant Barnes got back in the car and left. Clara's mother ushered Rose inside the house and

Clara and her father followed. They closed the door and there they were, the whole family together again like it should be. Except it wasn't.


By Monday everyone knew. At school Mrs. Quinn hugged Clara and said, "You see? What did I tell you? Everything works out for the best in the end."

Ruth said, "My brother says men will have made her do things, really awful things. He wouldn't say what but he said they're really awful."

Jenny said, "My mom says she's bound to be pregnant. Is she pregnant?"

In the nights Rose thrashed around in bed and screamed and their parents came running in. One or the other of them would sit on the bed and hold her and tell her it was just a nightmare, and Rose would stop screaming and roll over to face the wall.

Her mother said Clara should sleep in her own room for a while. "Just until Rose is better," she said.

Clara shook her head. No.

In the afternoons when she got home from school, she went up to the bedroom and sat on her bed and watched her sister. Sometimes Rose's eyes wandered over Clara's face. Once they paused, and Clara whispered, "Hello, Rosie", but Rose didn't even blink.


Dan was waiting for her at the usual place.

"Is she OK?" he asked when Clara came up.

Clara nodded uncertainly.

"What does that mean?"

"She won't say anything."

"Is she eating and drinking and stuff?"

"She ate some cookies. And she drinks water sometimes."

Dan thought. He said, "Do you think your parents would let me see her?"

"I don't know."

"Do they know about me? You know, about ... everything."

"I don't think so."

"I'm coming home with you," Dan said grimly. "I'm going to ask them if I can talk to her."

"My dad won't be home yet."

"Then I'll ask your mom."

Her mom said yes. So Dan went up to Rose's room and sat on Clara's bed and watched her sleep. He came the next day as well and the one after that. If Rose woke up he'd talk to her. She showed no sign of hearing him but he talked to her anyway.

"Jim Roust got expelled this afternoon. He set fire to a gas tap in Chemistry and Rolands kicked him out. He's a moron anyway.

"You know that hill just before you get to Cooper's Corner? The one on the bend? It was sheer ice this morning, bus couldn't get up, kept sliding down backwards, ended up in the ditch. Kind of half rolled over, but really, really slow motion, we all fell on top of each other, it was kind of funny. Nobody was hurt, we all just got out and walked."

Maybe it was good for Rose that Dan was there but it meant Clara couldn't go and sit with Rose herself, it didn't feel right with him in the room. She could go to her own room but there was nothing to do there and she didn't like any of her books anymore, the stories weren't real. She could have gone into the kitchen where her mother always was, but her mother was still pretending Rose was just tired. So she ended up either playing with Moses or back in the living room, looking out of the window at the early darkness as if she was still waiting for Rose to come home.

She needed to talk to Mr. Kane but he was never home, even though she waited so late on Wednesday night that her mother came and got her and was cross.

Finally, on Thursday night, Mr. Kane was there. Clara was so relieved she was angry. She wanted to shout at him but she was afraid he'd tell her to go home so she didn't. But then when she asked him why Rose wouldn't talk to her, he said she should ask her parents and she was so furious she shouted at him after all.

He didn't tell her to go home, though. He let her unpack the box called "misc," which turned out to mean "miscellaneous," which meant "everything else.".

On Sunday Dan didn't come to see Rose because Sunday was a family day and people didn't visit, they went to church and then stayed quietly at home, so Clara was able to have Rose all to herself. She took a colouring book and crayons upstairs and when Rose was asleep she knelt down and coloured on the floor.

After lunch Rose was sleeping very soundly and Clara saw that Mr. Kane was home, so she went

244

over to his house (it wasn't "visiting" because it was just Mr. Kane) and they unpacked the final box. There was a beautiful fur hat, which he said she could have when he died, and Mrs. Orchard's two favourite photos, which Clara put back where they belonged, and it turned out Mr. Kane was the little boy in the breakfast photo. There was a terrible moment when Mr. Kane said she could have the little card players now and take them home, and she thought it must mean that he was going to die. She was so terrified she couldn't speak, couldn't even open her mouth. But it turned out he was just giving them to her for no reason, so they were hers *and* she could still play with them at his house, which was really, really nice.

When she got home Rose was awake and she looked different. Clara sat on her bed and chewed her nails and tried to figure out what the difference was. At first Rose didn't look at her but then she did, and it seemed to Clara that for the first time since she got home, Rose actually saw her.

Clara said in a whisper, "I'm glad you're home, Rosie. I'm *really*, *really* glad you're home."

Rose didn't reply but she kept looking at her and Clara cautiously got up and crossed the room, slowly, step by step, as if Rose was a small bird that might get frightened and fly away. She stood by the bed, looking down at her, gnawing on a thumbnail.

Rose looked steadily up into her eyes. Rose's eyes still looked bruised and her face was grey-white but she definitely looked better than she had. After a moment she lifted her arm, reached up and slowly pulled Clara's hand away from her mouth.

"Stop biting your nails," she whispered.

"OK," Clara whispered back.

"Promise."

"I promise."

## Seventeen

# ELIZABETH

After lunch this afternoon I told Martha what her consultant had said. I knew she wouldn't have taken it in and I'd come to the conclusion that she would never ask me because she was frightened of the answer, which left me with the dilemma of whether or not to tell her anyway. I decided she would worry less if she knew.

"It's entirely your decision," I said when I'd told her the rest. "He will understand if you don't want to go through an operation. No one will try to make you do anything you don't want to do."

She didn't reply. After a while I looked over at her but she had turned her head away. Her abdomen was bigger every time you looked at it, I couldn't understand why she wasn't in pain. The thought left me breathless with horror—the idea of Martha in pain is completely unbearable. I don't know why her in particular. Perhaps because she seems so utterly defenceless.

I tried to think about other things. I tried to think about you, my love, but you were far away.

After a long time she said in a scraped-out voice, "Thank you for talking to him for me."

"You're welcome," I said. "If you want to discuss it I'll be happy to." Evidently she didn't, because that was it.

In the midst of all the gloom there was a very touching interlude. Mrs. Dubois, who has been flat on her back with spinal problems for more than four months, was told that she could now sit up for a little while each day and just before visiting time the nurses carefully eased her up onto a stack of pillows, so that when her husband brought the little boys in to see her, there she was, pale but serene, her dark hair spread out around her in gloriously romantic chaos, reclining on her pillows like a queen.

Mr. Dubois had clearly been briefed about the great event and as well as bringing flowers and a large box of chocolates (which, under Mrs. Dubois's instructions, he gallantly offered around the ward), he had brought in two small presents for the boys, rather inexpertly wrapped but who would care, so that they would feel involved in the celebrations. Not only that; he smuggled the packages to his wife so that she could be the one to give them to them. I wanted to kiss him. (His wife did.) Such a thoughtful thing to do. Inevitably the presents were Dinky Toys and even more inevitably both boys wanted the same one and squabbled over it. It was sad but also funny, because of its predictability. Which both parents saw, I'm glad to say.

They are excellent parents. Watching them I thanked the gods I don't believe in for putting them on this earth and also for putting them on this ward on this day. New beginnings, to set against the sadness of life.

Martha appeared to be watching the goings-on but I don't think she truly saw them. Shortly after the children left, she said, "There's something I want to ask you, Elizabeth. Another favour."

I got the feeling she'd been hanging onto the question, realizing that I was enjoying the children and not wanting to spoil it. It was unlike her to be so considerate but I think it was the case.

"That's fine," I said. "Go ahead."

"Will you stay with me? At the end, will you stay with me?"

I turned my head and looked at her. "Martha, I can't promise that. I don't have long either, we don't know who'll go first."

"I know, but if you can, will you stay with me? Until I'm gone?"

"Yes. If I can, I'll stay with you. I'll be right here."


Later, remarkably, considering the slew of emotions washing around inside me, I managed to have an almost-nap, not quite asleep, not quite awake, just floating between the two. It was very peaceful. When I heard my name being called I wasn't sure if it was real or part of a dream.

"Yes?" I said tentatively, still wondering.

"Are you there?"

249

Which woke me up. "Yes, Martha, I'm here." To tell you the truth I was a little peeved; it had been a very pleasant nap.

"Did you want something?" I asked, trying to disguise my irritation.

She didn't answer.

"Martha? Did you want something?" I turned my head and saw she'd fallen asleep, her mouth hanging open in a most undignified way. Given that she'd woken me I thought the least she could do was stay awake long enough to ask her question.

"Martha?"

My heart gave a lurch. I struggled upright on the pillows. "Martha! Oh! Nurse! Please, Nurse!"

The nurses came running, but someone was wailing, a terrible sound, a long, high keening, like a lost soul. I realized it was me.


She should not have gone so soon. One of the nurses told me later that they'd expected her to have some time left. Perhaps she wanted to go. Perhaps she was so terrified of dying that she willed herself dead. If so, I envy her. I would dearly love to have that power.


In the night I was cold. Cold and hollow with grief. For Martha, and for you, my love. You died so long before your time, you had years and years left to you, not a thing wrong with you but appendicitis. It was an accident—something to do with the anaesthetic. I expected them to wheel you back to the ward, smiling groggily, and instead a doctor and a nurse came through the swinging doors looking shaken. I didn't understand what they told me. It was beyond understanding.

I fear descending into grief again. I do not want to die in such a state.

To distract myself I've written a final letter to Liam along with a covering note to my solicitor asking him to forward it in the event of my death. I asked a nurse for a large envelope into which I've put the letter, the note and the two framed photos I brought into hospital with me (the one of you in Charleston and the one of you serving breakfast to Liam). I used up the last of my stamps on the envelope, which was satisfying in a small way.

The return address gave me pause. I debated writing "The Hereafter" but decided against it. Then I found I couldn't remember the solicitor's address. I have it with me but I'm too tired to look it up.

For the moment I haven't sealed the envelope, so I can still take out the photos and look at them whenever I want to. Which continues to be many times a day.

*

I have stopped trying to erase the past, my love. I see now that it is part of the story, and the story is me. Denying it is denying that I am who I am.

*

The evening of our quarrel, when you expressed your fear that I was coming to love Liam too much, was a turning point for me. For me and for us. Our relationship was not the same for a long time after that.

I doubt that you were really aware of it. That isn't a criticism; you had a great deal on your mind and when you weren't travelling around the country you were working very long hours. Sometimes you managed a Sunday off and there were evenings when you would suddenly appear, but that aside you weren't around very much.

My feelings about your absence were complicated: I missed you, of course, but I could hardly resent it—in Europe men were being killed or wounded in action every day and at least I knew you were safe. And then there was the undeniable fact that your absence worked to my advantage where Liam was concerned. He and I spent far more time together than you knew.

But to return to our quarrel: the fault with your arguments that night was that they were rational, while I, at the time, was not. You pointed out that the situation in the Kane family was a temporary one, that eventually Annette would sort herself out and we would see much less of Liam. But the future was irrelevant to me then, dear one, or rather, I had created my own picture of it, a future in which, by one impossible circumstance or another, Liam was ours. Annette and Roger had died, perhaps, and Annette's mother had taken the girls but she didn't want Liam, so we adopted him. Or, Annette saw the strength of the bond between us and realized that it would be in both Liam's and her family's best interests if he were brought up by us.

Of course I knew these ideas were nonsense. Harmless pipe dreams, I thought. But you contributed to the fantasies, Charles, quite unknowingly, by being such a magnificent surrogate father when you were home. It is hard to resist a child whose face lights up like the sun when he sees you, and you were not proof against it. Do you remember Sundays? You must remember the breakfasts at least. Rationing hadn't yet come into force and you could still get bacon, eggs and on occasion even sausages. We would have what you called a "full English breakfast," cooked and served by you, immensely dignified in a dark suit with an apron wrapped round your middle and a starched tea towel hanging, just so, over your arm. The perfect Jeeves. Liam absolutely adored it. So did I.

Even on those days, though, I was careful not to let my gaze linger on him too long in case you were watching. Careful not to let the extent of my joy in him show. When he wasn't with us I took care not to speak of him too much and when I did I kept my tone light. You would ask about my day and I would say something like, "Let me see: this morning I bottled strawberries for Jam for Britain, and then this afternoon Annette brought Liam over and we did some baking. I let him colour the margarine, it's his favourite thing." (Do you remember the margarine? It came in a plastic bag with a little button of lurid orange food colouring inside, which we had to massage into the fat to make it look like butter. As I recall you disapproved of it strongly.)

Anyway, when I finished describing our day you would smile, and say, "Sounds fun," and I would see the relief in your face. Relief that I was calm and happy, that there was nothing to worry about after all.

Often Liam was with me most of the week. He had taken to ignoring his mother when she spoke to him and it drove Annette nearly frantic—in fact by then almost anything he did made her frantic. She would phone me in a state, Liam screaming and the babies howling in the background, and ask if I could have him, and the answer was always yes.

Sometimes he would be very subdued when he arrived, not speaking, not looking at me. I'd take him into the living room and we'd sit together on the sofa for a while. He didn't want a story at such times; I think he couldn't concentrate. Sometimes he would climb onto my lap, though not very often. He wanted to be close, though. He would examine my wedding ring, turning it round and round on my finger, or trace the ribbing on the cuff of my sweater with his finger, up and down, again and again.

When he was ready he would look up at me. I'd say quietly, "Shall we get up?" and he'd nod and slide down from the sofa and pad off to the kitchen to get out his colouring books or the blank newsprint I gave him for drawing—drawing was invariably what he wanted to do when he'd been upset, and strangely, he did some very good ones then.

You made a point of admiring them when you got home, Charles. You'd ask him questions about them, which pleased him so much he'd be unable to get the words out; he'd be stammering with the urgency of explaining them to you, his eyes fixed on your face. You would nod gravely at the explanations, and praise some particular virtue of the work. "That's exactly what an airplane at full throttle looks like," you'd say. "You've got it to a T."

On a wet Wednesday in July, during which Liam and I had drawn, coloured and cut out twelve cardboard birds and stuck them on the door of the refrigerator—a whole flock swooping up from bottom left to top right—Liam refused to go home. Annette came to collect him at suppertime, thanked me effusively, as always, failed to notice, as always, the marvellous things Liam was trying to show her, and said to him, "I hope you've been a good boy. Come and put your shoes on, it's time for supper."

Liam didn't move. He'd been pointing at a particularly splendid bird he had coloured; his finger was still touching it.

"Come on now," Annette said impatiently.

He shook his head, watching her carefully.

"Liam, put your shoes on, please."

He said—not defiantly, just stating it as a matter of fact, "I don't want you to be my mommy anymore. I want Aunt Elizabeth to be my mommy."

Annette and I stared at each other, then at him.

Annette said, "Don't be silly, Liam. Put your shoes on."

"I want to live here now," he said. "I want Aunt Elizabeth to be my mommy and Uncle Charles to be my daddy. I like them better than you."

I said rapidly—too rapidly—"Liam, you're being silly. Put your shoes on and go home with your mommy. We'll have some more fun tomorrow."

That was the moment at which all was lost, Charles. If I had smiled reassuringly at Annette and said in what you called my "headmistressy" voice, "Don't worry, it's perfectly normal, I've lost track of the number of kindergarten children who have told their mothers they're going home with me. He'll have forgotten all about it an hour from now." If I had said that, none of what followed would have happened and our lives would have taken a different course. But instead, out of guilt for my secret longings, I spoke too quickly and it made Annette pause. She looked at me for a moment, frowning, not understanding, and to my horror I felt myself flush. A second later, a matching flush spread across her cheeks and down her neck.

She said in a whisper, "What have you been saying to him, Elizabeth?"

"Nothing! Goodness, Annette, what a question! Liam, please stop being silly. It's time to go home."

He said, "I'm going to my room now," and turned and walked out of the kitchen and down the hall. Annette followed him. I followed Annette. He went into his room and over to his bookcase, pulled out *Ferdinand*, his current favourite, sat down on his bed and started turning the pages, studiously ignoring us.

Annette had stopped in the doorway and was looking around the room. She had seen it numerous times before and never noticed it, but she was noticing it now; the elephants marching grandly around the walls, the bookshelves crammed with children's books, the low table with a car park painted on the top and Liam's Dinky Toys parked in their places, the small, dark-blue rug with golden animals woven into it that I had bought at an auction to raise money for the war effort a few weeks earlier.

She took it all in, this time. Then she turned and looked at me wonderingly. "I can't believe it," she said. "You planned it. You planned the whole thing, didn't you? Right from the beginning."

"Annette—"

"You tempted him over here, first with cookies and then all this. You made him love you instead of me"—she held up her hand to stop me speaking—"you turned him against me so that he'd be horrible at home and disrupt our family, spoil our time together. And then you'd gloat about how good he was with you, as if it was my fault, as if I was a terrible mother ..."

By this time I was trembling. "Annette! That is *not true*! That is a terrible thing to say! Really terrible!"

She took a step into the room and Liam, still sitting on the bed but watching us now, shouted, "This is *my* room! Aunt Elizabeth said so! You can't come in!"

Annette crossed the room, seized his wrist, pulled him roughly off the bed, his book dropping to the floor, his mouth falling open, eyes wide with shock. I stepped forward but she pushed me aside, dragging Liam, screaming now, out into the hall. I tried to get around her, to stop her and make her listen, but she turned on me, absolutely beside herself with fury.

"You could go to jail for this!" she shouted over Liam's screams. "You can go to jail for stealing someone else's child! It's kidnapping, you can be …"

"Annette, stop! You're imagining something that didn't happen! Stop! You're not well!"

"I'm not well? *I'm* not well? You are *crazy*! Don't you come near him, ever again. Don't come near our house. Don't put a single foot on our property *ever again* or I will *call the police*!"


You were not home that night, Charles. You were somewhere in Manitoba and were due to return the following night. I had no way of getting hold of you.

For several hours I was incapable of thought of any kind. I was sick several times. I tried to lie down but could not. I walked round and round. Eventually, about nine o'clock, I thought, I must speak to Ralph, explain things to Ralph. He will be home by now.

I went over to their house. I stood at the front door for a long time, my legs shaking so hard I had to hold onto the door frame, before I worked up the courage to knock. If Annette had opened the door I don't know what I would have done, but it was Ralph.

I said in a whisper, "I have to speak to you. I have to."

He nodded, his expression grim. "Yes. But not now …" He spoke quietly but she heard him anyway and came running from the living room. Her face and neck were blotched purple-red, her eyes grotesquely swollen with crying. She flew at me when she saw me; if Ralph hadn't caught hold of her I think she would have attacked me. I turned and ran.

I was not in my right mind, Charles. I saw only that unless I did something I would never see Liam again, which could not be borne.

I waited until midnight, sitting on the bed, my heart thudding, then got my purse, the car keys, a blanket from Liam's bed, some cookies in a brown paper bag, a Thermos of water, and took them out to the car. Through the trees on the lot between our houses I could see that there was a light on in a bedroom at the back of the house. Not Liam's room, I knew where that was, he had shown me several times, it would be the babies, needing to be fed. I waited, breathless and trembling, pacing back and forth.

It was half an hour before the light went out. Wait ten minutes, I thought. Fifteen, to be sure.

Ten minutes later the light came on again. They weren't settling. I waited. The light went out. I waited. Ten minutes. Twenty.

No sound, I must make no sound. I took off my shoes and put them in the car. In my bare feet I made my way through the trees. It was so dark that I had to feel my way around the house to the back door, the bricks rough under my hands. My fear had been that the door would be locked but it wasn't and I let myself in and stole across the kitchen to the hallway. In the doorway I stopped, listening. Holding my breath. Nothing. But at any moment the babies might waken again. I crept through the hall, up the stairs, along to Liam's room. He slept the way only small children can, so soundly that once, out of curiosity, you had picked him up by his ankles and swung him gently back and forth like a pendulum while he slept peacefully on, but nonetheless as I gathered him up I was afraid he would be woken by the pounding of my heart. I retraced my steps with him in my arms, terrified at every moment. Once we were outside, I half-ran to the car.

I laid him carefully on the front bench seat of the car, tucked his blanket around him, got in beside him, put the key in the ignition and turned it. The noise of the engine was horrifying; I looked around in panic but no lights came on, no one grabbed the handle of the car door and wrenched it open. I let out my breath, slid the car into gear and drove out of the driveway.

At the road I turned left, for no reason. I had no plan about where we should go. I simply drove, Liam on the seat beside me.

Sometime after dawn I pulled over to the side of the road to empty my bladder. We were out in the country—I had no idea where—and there was no traffic so I simply squatted down beside the car. I got back in, expecting the sound of the closing door to wake Liam but he slept on. I was hungry. I took a cookie out of the bag and ate it, watching him sleep. His quiet, unknowing dreams. I tried to think what I was going to do, where we should go, but no thoughts came. Still hungry, I rustled around inside the bag of cookies, searching for broken bits so that I could give the whole ones to Liam, and as I straightened up there was a tap on the window beside me. I started violently, dropping the bag. A man was standing at the window. A policeman. Behind him was a police car. I hadn't heard it drive up.

The policeman opened the door and leaned in to look at Liam, then looked at me.

"Mrs. Orchard?" His tone neutral. His face without expression.

I couldn't speak, but after a moment I nodded, and he nodded back and reached in and took the key out of the ignition.

"How about you and the little boy come and get into my car?" he said.


A lot of what happened afterwards passed me by, dear one. You suffered far more than me. There are no words to say how much I regret that.

There was a scandal, of course. In Guelph it pushed the war off the front pages. You never mentioned it, either during your visits or after I came back home, but I knew anyway because someone anonymously sent me the newspapers. From them I learned that Annette and the children had fled to Calgary, where Annette's parents lived, to escape the attention. Ralph followed them as soon as he could. To begin with you stayed on in Guelph, though eventually it all became too much and you transferred to U of T. I clung to the thought (and cling to it still) that the war and the nature of your work meant that it didn't matter terribly where you were based, so I didn't actually destroy your career.

But in any case, you were not concerned about such things. You were concerned about me.

I was charged with abduction, a less serious offence than kidnapping—Annette must have been furious. I was indifferent. Since the moment of my arrest I had been engulfed by an all-consuming terror that Liam would suffer for what I had done, that Annette would take out her rage and bitterness on him. I desperately, desperately needed to know that he was all right. Had I realized then that I would never find that out—that not knowing was to be my true punishment—I can't imagine how I would have endured it.

So the judge's decision mattered less than nothing to me. It mattered to you, though; you were incandescent. I'd never seen you in such a state and I watched you with a kind of wonder. As far as you were concerned it was blindingly obvious that I'd acted in a moment of madness and would have returned Liam to his parents as soon as I came to my senses, so the case should be dismissed.

I remember the discussion with our defence counsel, an older man, quiet and polite, very experienced. I remember him listening closely as you made your case, nodding sympathetically, and then pausing for a moment before saying, gently, that the court would not agree. They would deem there was nothing wrong with my senses and that I was well aware that what I was doing was illegal—why else would I have waited until the dead of night (that phrase again) to take Liam? Likewise, he said, a plea of insanity would be unlikely to succeed: depression is not insanity, it does not render you incapable of telling right from wrong. He advised me to plead guilty and hope that the

262

judge would take into account the circumstances and my state of mind at the time. In the end, that is what we did.

My clearest memory of the trial is of watching you, rather than the judge, when the sentence was read out: a year in the fearsome-sounding Andrew Mercer Ontario Reformatory for Females in Toronto. I saw your body jolt with shock, Charles, and realized for the first time what I had done to you. I saw you, the most reasonable, rational of men, struggling for control. You'd been so sure that the judge, being an intelligent man, would look at the mitigating factors—my mental state, my lack of a plan, my hitherto blameless character, my remorse—and give me a suspended sentence. In fact he did take those things into account—the maximum sentence for abduction was seven years, so he was lenient. But I think you feared I was not mentally strong enough by that stage to survive a year in prison.

You were right to fear it. I had led a quiet, comfortable, sheltered life up until then; I was totally unprepared for the shock of having my freedom, my privacy, my independence, my reputation, my home, my *husband*, my *heart and soul*, torn from me. By many standards I did not suffer much, I was not beaten or abused. Nonetheless, by the time my sentence was up my condition was such that our doctor referred me directly to St. Thomas's psychiatric hospital in Kingston.

I remember my terror. I remember being sick in the car on our way there. Which was ironic, because St. Thomas's was to be my salvation. When we arrived,

I didn't know how I was going to get through the next ten minutes, far less the rest of my life. It was an absolute revelation to me that there were people who knew what to do about such things; people with the skill and knowledge to pick up the pieces of a shattered mind and reassemble them; make them whole.

Still, without your steadfastness, Charles, without your visits, your letters, your constant, unceasing love and support, they would not have been able to help me. No one could have helped me, because I would not have wanted to survive.

*

There's a new occupant in Martha's bed. Expensive hairdo, meticulous makeup. She looks dissatisfied; clearly her life hasn't lived up to expectations. I fervently hope she doesn't want to tell me about it. Mind you, her husband came in with her when she arrived and if I were married to him I'd look dissatisfied too. Arrogance is so unattractive it amounts to a disfigurement.

I kept the pleasantries to a minimum. In any case it is such a struggle to get my breath now I couldn't carry on a conversation if I wanted to. Instead I've been watching sunlight track its way across the opposite wall. The unstoppable passage of time.

I've been thinking about Charleston. Do you remember? You took me there for a celebratory holiday at the end of the war—the first "foreign holiday" we'd ever had. I'd been anxious about being so far from the hospital—I'd only been home a year and still needed to know I could go back if things got bad— but you promised we would fly home immediately if I felt the need.

The hotel we stayed in was small and a little down-at-heel but right in the heart of the old part of town and built around a courtyard full of flowers, with a fountain in the middle and tables and chairs in shady alcoves here and there. Neither of us had ever imagined such beauty. There were hummingbirds, do you remember? Flitting from flower to flower, glowing like jewels in the sun. We spent a week there. Glorious.

Nurse Roberts, whizzing past just now, paused and came over to me and said, "How are you, Mrs. Orchard dear? You're looking rather distant today."

I said, on the contrary, you were very close, which wasn't what I meant to say but that's what came out. Or possibly nothing came out. She smiled and patted my hand and whizzed off.

But you *are* very close, my love. I can feel your presence beside me.

When they'd cleared up after lunch I asked a nurse to take away some of my pillows and help me turn onto my side. My right side, I said. "Our" side. She was concerned I might have trouble breathing but I said if I did I'd call her. I get very stiff, lying on my back all the time. It feels lovely to curl up, though it is indeed hard to breathe. I have to take tiny little breaths, like sips.

From this position I can see more of the floor and I noticed the most remarkable thing. Under Mrs. Cox's bed (she of the short frilly nighties and terrible legs) there were two pairs of fluffy slippers, one pink and one lilac. Matching the nighties, in other words. I didn't know such things existed. Think what I've been missing all this time, with my sensible pyjamas and warm socks. Think of the delights I deprived you of!


Do you remember my blue-and-white pinstriped pyjamas? My favourite pyjamas of all time. The bottoms had lovely deep pockets and when we settled ourselves to sleep, my body curled warm and safe within yours, your hand would wander down my side until it found the pocket and then it would slide in for the night.

I can still feel it there, my love. It is there now, this minute. Cupping my hip.

# Eighteen

# LIAM

The prowler pulled up as he was walking home from work. He'd spent the day installing appliances in another new kitchen with Jim and Cal—now that outdoor work was no longer possible, everyone seemed to be getting their kitchens done.

"Want a lift?" Karl said, rolling down the window. "I was going to phone you later."

He'd called Liam when Rose had been found and a couple of days later to say she was home, but they hadn't spoken in the ten days since then.

"I don't think I've thanked you properly for your help," he said, as Liam climbed in. "Sorry it's been so long. There was trouble out at one of the lumber camps, and then there was a string of arson attacks over in Thurston, and then Margie got flu. I've been kind of pushed for time."

"You thanked me three times on the phone the night you brought her home," Liam said, tossing his jacket on the back seat.

"I did?"

"It was quite late and you sounded …" he glanced at Karl and grinned, "happy."

"Yeah, well, I was happy!" Karl said defensively. "Very!"

"I don't blame you. What sort of state is she in now?"

"Not great. Did I tell you the details of what happened?"

Liam shook his head.

"They found her and a couple of other girls in a derelict property on the outskirts of an area called … is there somewhere called Cabbagetown? Rough area?"

"Yes. It's on its way up, but there are still some bad patches."

"Why 'Cabbagetown'? Just out of interest."

"It was a very poor area. People used to grow cabbages in their front yards. So they say."

Karl nodded. "Anyway. It was an organized gang, the police knew of its existence but not who or where. Turns out this was one of three houses across the city. They found five girls in this one, including Rose. Tied up, raped regularly by shits who like them young. The Toronto cops reckon she was probably picked up within a day or two of arriving. Grabbed off the street, hustled into a car. It was her cropped head that was the key to finding her, by the way. That one detail. People remembered seeing her.

"Two of the men were in the house when the police broke down the door, so they're pretty happy—the cops, I mean. They took the girls straight to hospital. Phoned me about Rose, I phoned Doc Christopherson, he phoned the hospital and spoke to the doctors, they said she could come home. He's keeping an eye on her. That's the story so far.

"So it isn't a hundred percent happy ending. Never is in these cases, I'm afraid, psychological damage if nothing else. My guess is it's going to be stressful in that family for quite a while. But at least they've got her back."

Liam thought of Clara, her overwhelming joy at the idea of her sister coming home, and then the reality of it. More distress, more bewilderment.

"On to more pleasant subjects," Karl said, after a pause. "I hear you got yourself some ice cream."

"Yes. Got some a while ago." Hoping he'd kept his tone casual but not so casual as to arouse suspicion.

"What did you make of Jo?"

"She seems nice."

Karl turned the car into Liam's drive and switched off the engine. Liam felt his gaze and busied himself patting pockets here and there as if searching for his house keys.

"She is," Karl said. "She's very nice. Came up here from North Bay a few years ago. Something you should know, though. She's had a tough time. Married twice, first one beat her up, put her in the hospital for six weeks, second one took everything she had and lit off. I mean everything, not just her money. Stripped the house. Took the light bulbs. So men aren't high on her list of favourite things. I'm just telling you in case you have any ideas in that direction, save you wasting your time."

"I don't have any ideas in any direction," Liam said, opening the door and getting out. "But thanks. And thanks for the lift."

He stood in the living room pondering. He'd seen Jo half a dozen times in the two weeks since that first night. He'd been aware of her caution and if anything, it had reassured him, wary as he also was of getting involved. Now that he knew the reason for it, though, he wondered if it was OK to carry on. He decided it was. It had been her choice, after all, she'd seduced him, not the other way round. Which meant they were both after the same thing: human contact, the comfort of another body against your own, sex. Without complications.

That night Jo said, "I imagine you know all about me by now. My marriages in particular."

"Actually, I've only just heard about your marriages."

They were in bed, lying on their backs, wearing nothing under the covers but a light sheen of sweat. Jo turned her head to look at him. "Just out of interest, did you overhear it, or did someone tell you?"

Liam hesitated, then said, "Karl told me. He gave me a lift home from work today."

Jo frowned. "Karl isn't normally a gossip."

"He wasn't gossiping, he was warning me off."

"Oh," Jo said. After a moment she added, "Do you think he knows?"

"I don't think so. I think he was just … trying to protect you."

"That sounds like Karl. Sometimes he takes his job too seriously. What did you say?"

"I thanked him for the lift."

Jo laughed.

Liam said, "This business of everybody in town knowing everything before it happens, how does it work? Are there bugs in every room in Solace?"

"Probably. Is it getting you down?"

"From time to time. Not seriously."

"Look on the bright side: if we already know everything, we don't need to tell each other about it."

Liam nodded. "That's a plus, all right."

After a while, both of them gazing at the ceiling, Jo said, "The harder thing is managing not to think about it."

"Especially at three in the morning."

"Especially at three in the morning."

Under the covers she touched the back of his hand with her own. Which started things up again.

Later, she said, "I understand you're a big fan of Mr. Li's pies."

"Mr. Lee?"

"The chef at the Hot Potato. It's spelled 'L-i.' He's Chinese."

"He's *Chinese*? No kidding?"

"No kidding."

"Why doesn't he cook Chinese food?"

"Gloria won't let him."

"Who's Gloria?"

"Your waitress. Who also happens to be the owner of the Hot Potato. And also the Light Bite across the road."

"Her name's *Gloria*? Her parents named her *Gloria*? As in *glorious*?"

"So it seems."

Liam laughed. He thought about the chef, who'd maybe come all the way up here with dreams of setting up the first Chinese restaurant in the North. "It's a shame she won't let him cook Chinese food. Why not?"

"She says no one up here likes that sort of thing."

"How does she know?" Liam asked. "How do *they* know?"

"True. But at least we have the pies."


For the sake of discretion he'd changed his routine a little, had an extra coffee after supper at the Hot Potato and extended his evening inspection of the lake so as not to set out for Jo's place until there was no one about. There were no streetlights on the side roads so the chances of him being seen were small. For the sake of not setting up expectations, on her side or his own, he still didn't allow himself to go every night.

For her part, Jo made no move to step things up and never asked when or if he would come again. They were very careful, both of them, to keep a distance.

Though, inevitably, they did get to know a little about each other. He learned, for instance, that she'd been born and brought up here in Solace, that she had a brother who lived in Halifax, that when she finished high school she'd hitchhiked to New York and spent a year working in a deli before the North finally called her home. Initially she'd settled in North Bay and worked in the library there. Got married, got divorced. When her parents became ill she came back to Solace to look after them. After their death, she got a job at the library in Solace. Got married, got divorced.

"Do you think you'll always want to live up here?" Liam asked, steering clear of the marriages and divorces.

She turned on her side to face him. "I'm trying not to look ahead or set rules for myself. In the same way that I'm trying not to look back."

"Sounds smart."

"The theory's good," she said.

*

Because of spending the evenings with Jo he hadn't seen as much of Clara lately. He told himself it was for the best. In the weeks before Rose was found Clara had spent quite a bit of time in the house while he was there, which had worried him. He spoke to her mother, stressing that he didn't mind, merely wanted to check with her. He said he got the feeling that the house and Mrs. Orchard's belongings reassured Clara somehow. The familiarity, maybe. He told her about Clara's interest in the boxes, and Mrs. Jordon smiled.

273

Liam added awkwardly, "She's always in the living room. I've said she mustn't go anywhere else in the house."

She met his eyes for a moment and he saw the weight of dread and anxiety she was carrying for her other child. The depth of her exhaustion.

"Thank you," she said. "Karl Barnes has ... spoken to us." She gave him another faint smile. "Clara seems to have adopted you, Mr. Kane. It's very good of you to allow it."

"It's Liam."

She nodded. "I'm Diane."


He'd been enormously relieved, but still, he remained concerned that Clara was beginning to depend on him; it was going to make it hard on her when he left. Which had to be soon. It was now the last week in October and when the sun went down the temperature dropped off a cliff.

So it was probably a good thing, he told himself, that he was seeing less of the kid.

*

"Where's Cal?" Liam asked. It was Monday, the appliances were in and working, water came out of the taps, all they had to do was give the place a couple of coats of paint and clear up the mess.

Jim squatted down and opened the sides of the tool box with a double clang. "Gone."

"Gone?" Liam stared down at the back of Jim's head, a bald patch coming along nicely. Jim didn't look up. "What, you mean gone back south? Back to university?"

"Yup."

"Just like that?"

"Yup."

"When did he go?"

"This morning."

If he'd known the kid was actually going to act on his advice he'd have taken the bullet to the head instead. Now it was his fault—the boy's whole future, his whole life from here on was going to be his fault, and Jim wasn't talking to him. It should have been a relief, a little silence for once, but it wasn't.

"Susan says come for supper tomorrow night," Jim said morosely, still raking round in the bottom of the box. "And you damn well better come, place is like a morgue." He looked up, slit-eyed. "No dumb excuses."


On his way home Liam diverted to the lake and stood for a while watching the waves roll in, his shoulders hunched against the cold. The sky and lake washed into each other, gunmetal grey. Along the edges of the shore there was a gritty rim of ice. Overhead a long V of geese flew over, honking mournfully, heading south. You should go too, he told himself. You really should go.

Far overhead a bird was hanging in the air; an eagle or maybe an osprey. Cal had said one of them had crooked wings but Liam couldn't remember which. He'd have to look it up: in one of Jo's piles of books there was a magnificently illustrated book of birds.

As he watched, the bird suddenly hurtled down towards the lake, dropping at tremendous speed, legs swinging forward, talons opening at the last minute, raking deep into the water and then out again in one swooping movement, a large, furious fish struggling in its claws. Liam watched transfixed. The fish was so heavy and fought with such ferocity that the bird had difficulty taking off, it kept being dragged back down into the waves. Finally, wings pounding, spray flying, it managed to get airborne, the fish slung beneath it like an outsized bomb, and headed off towards the far shore.

\*

On Thursday it ended.

"Would you like some French toast?" Jo asked.

"Sounds great."

"With a side order of vanilla ice cream?"

"Even better!"

They got out of bed and dressed rapidly—the bedroom was on the north side of the house and the insulation was a joke. In the kitchen Liam built up the fire and chiselled some ice cream while Jo whipped up the eggs and made the French toast. When it was done they took their plates over to the armchairs and sat in front of the fire, listening to the wind prowling around the house. He'd get some caulking tomorrow and see what he could do to stuff up the gaps.

"This is really good maple syrup."

"It's my own. The real thing."

"Seriously?"

"My parents had five acres of woods and when I sold the house after they died, I kept the woods. There are a couple of dozen sugar maples. I tap a few every year."

"No kidding? How do you go about it?"

"You drill a hole, bang in a tap and hang a pail under it to catch the sap. That's it. The hard bit—well, not hard, just long—is boiling it down, it takes forty litres of sap to make one litre of syrup. Takes days. When you have enough you bottle it and sell it to tourists for a ridiculous amount of money. This is last season's. You tap in early spring, when the days start getting warmer but the nights are still cold. That's when the sap starts to rise."

"Well, it's worth the effort. So … ice cream, maple syrup … what else do you do?"

"Maple syrup and ice cream are my only skills."

"They're great skills. And it's two more than I have."

She tipped her head. "Surely there's something you can do."

He thought about it. "I can add and subtract. Does that count as a skill?"

"Adding plus subtracting counts as two skills."

He laughed and wiped up the last of the ice cream and syrup with the last of the toast. Jo had finished hers and was curled up in her chair, watching the fire. The stove looked as if it were filled with molten gold. Liam got to his feet and went over to the books piled against the wall. The stacks reminded him of

277

his boxes. Clara would want to tidy them up: she'd make a single row of books running around the walls like a baseboard, right-way up, spines out, arranged by height, or maybe colour.

He found the book on birds and took it back to his chair, but he didn't open it. Instead he watched the flames flickering across Jo's face, wondering why he hadn't realized before that she was beautiful.

After a minute he said, "I've noticed something about this ice cream. Something you should know."

She looked at him with a frown of concern. "What?"

"I reckon it's an aphrodisiac."

"Do you?" she said, smiling. "Have some more."

Afterwards she hauled up the blankets around their necks with a swift movement of one bare arm and shoulder and hitched herself up against him for warmth. "I need to get another blanket," she said. "I keep forgetting to buy one."

That was the moment—not when he saw that she was beautiful, not as they were making love, but afterwards, in the simple luxurious fact of her body against his own—that he realized he was falling in love with her—was already in love—and even as he had the thought—instantly, *instantly*, as if it had been waiting in the wings all this time—the past came roaring in, led by Fiona, archangel of failure and despair. *You're not capable of love, Liam. You're not capable of trusting anyone, of caring about anyone, of giving yourself to anyone. That's love, and you're not capable of it, and you never will be.*

He tried to shut her out, but could not. He tried to think of anything he had ever done, anyone he had ever truly loved, to prove her wrong, and failed. He thought about what Karl had said regarding Jo's treatment by men, and the fact that she was risking everything again with him. You'll just fuck it up, he thought, a chasm opening within him. Next week or next month or next year you'll fuck it up and walk out. She's too nice to do that to.

After a while he said, "There's something I should tell you."

"Oh?"

"I'm going to have to leave soon. I need to earn some money and there are no jobs up here." This was untrue. That very morning Jim had offered to pay him a wage, small but liveable, which he suspected was Susan's doing. He'd liked her, the evening with them had been nice. But it was the best excuse he could come up with.

She turned her head and met his eyes. "Oh," she said, after a minute. "OK. Thank you for telling me."

He steeled himself. "Would you like me to stop coming?"

"Maybe that would be best."


In the night, sick with what felt like grief, he thought, You need to get out of here now. Straight away. Get into the car and drive, doesn't matter where. Tell Jim tomorrow morning, then throw everything in the car and go.

But in the morning he remembered Clara; he couldn't just vanish without telling her. A couple of days, then; tell her and give her a couple of days to get used to the idea.

He went to work, saying nothing to Jim—there would be questions, which he couldn't face right now. When they finished for the day he went home and waited for Clara.

"How are things?" he said, when she came in. She wasn't looking good.

"She won't say anything. She just lies on her bed. Why won't she talk to me?"

"Clara," he said, gently, because she looked hollowed out with worry. "You need to start asking your parents these questions. You need to talk to them. They're the ones who ..."

"*They say she's tired but she'll be better soon! That's all they ever say!*" She was furious and on the verge of tears. He couldn't tell her today.

She wanted to unpack a box so that was what they did. It meant he was going backwards, unpacking instead of packing, but so be it.

On Sunday they unpacked the last box. At the top was a fur hat, Russian-style, an outrageous thing Fiona had bought for him one Christmas saying it made him look like Omar Sharif; he couldn't think why he hadn't thrown it out. Beside it was a large bulky envelope bearing his name and the old Toronto address. He remembered it—it had arrived just as he was about to load the boxes into the car before setting off for Solace; he was in a hurry to get away and had stuck it in a box to open later and promptly forgotten about it.

Clara put on the hat. It came down over her eyes and she pushed it up and looked at him. He forced a smile. "It looks great."

"Can I go up and see in the mirror in the bathroom?"

She was supposed to stay in the living room, but as he was going to be leaving in a couple of days he guessed it no longer mattered. "Sure."

When she'd gone he opened the envelope. Inside was a second envelope and a letter from Mrs. Orchard's lawyer saying that she had asked him to forward the enclosed parcel. The parcel contained another letter and two framed photographs. Liam read the letter first.

*Dear Liam,*

*I am writing this in the hospital, and will ask someone here to post it for me.*

*Enclosed are two photos that I brought into the hospital with me and have had beside me all this time. I thought you might like to have them. One is of Charles when he and I went on holiday to South Carolina many years ago. The other is a photograph I took of you and Charles when you were staying with us one weekend. At the time (this was when you were about four and your mother was very busy with your younger sisters) you stayed with us quite often and when your visit happened to coincide with a weekend when Charles was home, he would play a game with you at breakfast which we all enjoyed enormously.*

*Charles was from England (extremely well-brought up!) and would cook what he called "a full English breakfast" for us—bacon and eggs and so forth—which he would then serve very formally (I even had to starch white linen napkins), pretending that you were a noble lord and he was your butler. It was very funny and we all loved it. I hope you enjoy the photo and such memories as you have of Charles.*

*At the risk of embarrassing you, Liam, I want you to know that your presence in our lives was a source of delight and joy to both Charles and me. You gave us more pleasure than you can possibly imagine. I have always prayed that what you took from your time with us, what you remember above all else, is how greatly you were loved.*

*All my best wishes for your future,*
*Elizabeth Orchard*
*PS Your letters over the past few years have meant a great deal to me, Liam. Thank you for writing, and for allowing me once more into your life.*

Liam drew a breath and stood for a moment, his throat tight, then put the letter down and picked up the photo Mrs. Orchard had referred to. There he was, very small, wearing a red sweater and an enormous grin. Beside him stood Mr. Orchard in a dark suit, white shirt and bow tie, a napkin folded precisely over his arm, a silver platter resting on it. He was bending slightly from the waist, respectful but not obsequious, and saying—three decades on Liam could still hear his voice—*"A sausage, sir, along with the bacon? Yes? Just the one? Or shall I make it two? Two it is. Now the scrambled eggs: the eggs are fresh this morning, sir, the maid collected them first thing. A spoonful? Like this? A little more? Indeed, sir, it would be a shame to pass it up. Would you like a little less sausage, perhaps, to balance a little more egg—I could remove this one and hold it in reserve …? Leave this sausage but remove the other one? Of course, sir. Very good. I'll set it aside for you, no one will take it."*

He remembered the warmth when he was in that house. The feeling of being special, being loved. He'd never wanted to go home at the end of his visits. He wondered if his mother had known and decided she must have. Clara was no good at hiding her feelings and she was much older than he'd been then. It explained a lot.

Clara's footsteps sounded on the stairs and he hurriedly pushed it all to the back of his mind.

She came into the room, one hand holding up the hat at the front so that she could see where she was going. She was grinning. He was amazed at her resilience, the way she bounced back, given the smallest opportunity.

"It suits you," he said, which despite its size and hers, it did; she looked positively pretty.

"Can I have it when you die?"

"Yes, you can have it when I die. I have something to show you. Do you know this photograph?"

Clara looked at it, then abruptly pushed off her hat, letting it fall to the floor, and seized the photo from him. "Yes! It was one of Mrs. Orchard's *favourites!* She took it into hospital with her—oh, that's her other favourite, that's Mr. Orchard! Where did you find them?"

"In the box. Mrs. Orchard sent them to me from the hospital. Do you know who the boy is?"

"I don't know his name but he lived next door to Mrs. and Mr. Orchard. He wasn't their little boy but they really, really loved him."

"It's me," Liam said. "When I was a kid."

Clara looked at him, open-mouthed.

"I was about four when this was taken."

He could see her grappling with the idea, then saw it start to become real to her, a smile spreading slowly, lighting her face.

"Is that why Mrs. Orchard gave you her house? Because you were him?"

"I guess so."

He hadn't been going to tell her about leaving today but he should do it now, it was a good time, while she was seeing that things change, people grow up, things move on.

She'd taken the photos over to the sideboard where the others were displayed. "I'll show you where they go," she said in the tone of one-who-knows. "This one goes here"—setting the photo down with extreme precision—"and this one goes beside it like this." She stood back, examined them, stepped forward and adjusted one minutely, turned and looked at him, delighted, wanting him to be delighted too.

"They look great," he said. "Really good. And actually, that reminds me—there's something I've been meaning to ask you. I wondered if you'd like to have the card players now. Take them home with you."

It was as if he had hit her. He'd thought she'd be thrilled, that she'd rush over to the mantelpiece and get the little men down, and then he'd explain, and she'd be OK with it, the card players would have sugared the pill. Instead she stood where she was, rigid, staring at him, light and colour draining from her face.

"What's the matter?" Liam said, alarmed.

It took her a minute to answer. "Are you going to die?"

He almost laughed but there was fear in her eyes and he checked himself. For a moment he was touched that the idea upset her so much. But it's just because of what she's been through, he thought. She doesn't want more change, that's all. She's worried about the cat.

"No, no, I'm not going to die. Not for years and years anyway."

"Are you sick? Do you have to go to the hospital?"

"No, I'm not sick. I'm fine, there's nothing to worry about."

Her eyes searched his face as if she was trying to read his mind—which she certainly would if she could, he thought; forget such niceties as not opening other people's mail, she'd slice open his brain and examine every cell and synapse without a qualm.

She still looked doubtful. She said, "Can the little men be mine but I keep them here? So I can play

285

with them when I come over to see Moses and you? Because they belong here. Like the photographs."

He stared at her. Had she guessed what he was going to say and this was a ploy to make it harder for him to say it, and therefore harder for him to leave? Was a kid her age capable of such deviousness? Another question came to him: the business of unpacking the boxes—could that have been part of the same plan? Oh come on, he thought, she's not even eight yet! But in his mind's eye he could see her barring the door, hammering planks across the windows so he couldn't get out. There's never going to be a good time, he thought. Just tell her. Get it over with.

"Sure," he said. "You can keep them here."


He wandered around the house when she'd gone, unable to stay still, incredulous with himself. What the *fuck* is the matter with you? he thought. He went into the kitchen, opened the fridge, stared into it and closed it again. You should have gone weeks ago, he thought. You've left it too long and now you're a fixture in her life. The Keeper of the Fucking Cat. So are you going to stay here for ever just to give a cat a home? For Christ's sake, what's the worst thing that can happen? Supposing whoever buys the house gets rid of the cat. She'll get over it, her parents will get her a dog or a budgie or something, she'll forget all about it in a couple of months. Kids get over things. I got over things. More or less.

He went to the freezer and got out Jo's ice cream, chipped himself a bowlful and ate it standing at the sink. When he'd finished he ran the bowl under the tap, watching the pale liquid dilute and stream away. He stood for a long time letting the clear, cold water stream off the bowl and curl down the drain while thoughts careered around in his mind, all jumbled up in there, no sense in any of it until finally, one thought separated itself from the others and stood out on its own, undeniable: stop kidding yourself; this isn't just about a kid and a cat.

He left the bowl in the sink, went into the hall, pulled on his boots, scarf, parka, gloves and hat and went out into the night.

It was viciously cold and blowing a gale, snow driving into his face. He battled his way down to the lake, thinking to give himself just a little bit more time to mull things over, just to be certain, but the wind was so strong and so cold he couldn't face into it, and his mind was made up anyway, had probably been made up for days without letting him know, so he turned and let the wind push him into town. He went up Main Street, turned left down the first side road, turned right down the next, and in due course ended up at Jo's door.

She opened the door and stood silhouetted against the light.

"I'm having trouble leaving," he said. "I can't seem to ... do it."

"Can't you?" Jo said gravely, clutching her sweater around her. "Would you like to come in and talk about it?"

*

The snow on the porch steps was three inches deep when he got home, the wind whipping it into drifts at the sides. His head was full to the brim with Jo but nonetheless the minute he stepped in the door he had the sense of something having changed. He stood in the hall, listening: there was nothing but the wind. Cautiously, he pushed open the living-room door and turned on the light.

In the dead centre of the room sat a smoke-grey cat, tail wrapped around feet, gazing at him.

"Hello, Moses," Liam said. "It's good to meet you."

# Acknowledgements

The town of Solace exists only in my imagination, but the setting is very real: the vast and beautiful area of lakes and rocks and forests known as the Canadian Shield, in Northern Ontario. Locating the story there was an act of self-indulgence on my part; it is the landscape I think of when I think of home, and writing about it allows me to revisit it in my mind.

I am hugely indebted to the following people for the kind of information you cannot find in books or online: Bill Koehler, of Manitoulin Island, Ontario, for the low-down on life as a police officer in Northern Ontario "way back then"; Ben J. M. Rogers for his wonderfully clear and comprehensive answers to my questions about the Canadian criminal process in 1942; Maury Schlifer and Anthony Ferrelli for details about the challenges of building in the North. Who knew that a bundle of roof shingles weighs eighty pounds, or that shingles won't stick if you lay them when it's cold? Details matter.

On the subject of details, I have taken a liberty with wild blueberries: I have Liam buy a basket of them in September. There wouldn't be any that late in the year, as Northerners will know, but I wanted him to choke on a handful of them; nothing else would do.

I am grateful to *The Temiskaming Speaker*, once again, for providing an invaluable picture of what was going on in the area at the time, and to Sharon at the Haileybury Public Library for many pages of photocopying.

Heartfelt thanks, as always, to my brilliant agent, Felicity Rubinstein of Lutyens and Rubinstein, and to my wonderful editors, Poppy Hampson in the UK and Lynn Henry in Canada, for their skill, sensitivity and care. And my gratitude, as ever, to Alison Samuel, for her continued support and encouragement.

I would like to thank my family on both sides of the Atlantic, in particular my sons, Nick and Nathaniel, and my brothers, George and Bill, not only for their meticulous reading and advice but also, in Bill's case, for always finding exactly the right person for me to talk to.

Above all, my thanks to my husband, Richard, and my sister, Eleanor, who have been involved with all of the books from the very beginning. I couldn't have done it without them.

Mary Lawson, 2020

© Nathaniel Mobbs

MARY LAWSON was born and brought up in a small farming community in Ontario. She is the author of three previous bestselling novels: *Crow Lake, The Other Side of the Bridge*, and *Road Ends. Crow Lake* was a *New York Times* bestseller and was chosen as a Book of the Year by *The New York Times* and *The Washington Post*, among others. *The Other Side of the Bridge* was longlisted for the Man Booker Prize. *Road Ends* was a finalist for the Folio Prize. Lawson lives in England but returns to Canada frequently.

www.marylawson.ca